Four Sworn

There's a wild child trapped inside her, and they're hell-bent on unleashing it...

As the pretty daughter of the town whore, Shanna Davies has always tried hard to toe the line. But she just can't help it. Her boyfriend, Bo Crenshaw, has lured her untamed spirit out to play once too often. It's time to get the hell out of Dodge and make a new start where no one knows her past. After she fulfills one last, wicked fantasy.

Shanna is Bo's first everything. First kiss, first sexual playmate, first love. Yet he's never managed to convince her that he accepts her—good girl and bad—just as she is. So, she wants a memorable send off? No problem. He'll give her one that'll make her think twice about leaving.

On the appointed night, Shanna expects nerves. Yet once she crosses the threshold, the prospect of surrendering to a night of unrestrained passion with Bo *and* the three Kinzie brothers makes her mouth water—and her courage dry up.

But she asked for it, and now she's not about to blink first in this game of sexual chicken...

Warning: Four lusty cowboys prove a little domination goes a long way in breaking a stubborn woman to saddle. Lots of spanking, binding, flogging, and double-dipping can keep a girl on her toes, her back, her belly, her knees...

Breaking Leather

One for remembrance...one for healing...and one to seal her heart forever.

Chrissi Page has tried to find one man who heats her bed the way the Kinzie brothers did one shameful night years ago. She's failed miserably, leaving her with no choice but to bank that inner fire—and keep a lid on her inner bad girl.

She'd been weak, unable to choose between three men who appealed to her in different ways. And when they'd confronted her as a tease, anger had boiled over into a passion so wild, she's still trying to live it down.

Since that night, Ezra, Cade and Joshua have individually sown their wild oats with pretty much the entire available female population of Two Mule, Texas. Yet nothing erases the attraction they still feel for Chrissi. And when she ends up stranded on the road near their ranch, it's their last chance to turn their mutual obsession into an unusual proposition.

One weekend, three on one. If she can't stand the heat, they'll let her go on with her life. And try to find a way to live with the hole she'll leave behind in theirs.

Warning: A girl who thinks she can't have it all, and three brothers who set out to prove otherwise. One on one, two on one, and three on one; bondage in the wild; a bit of riding crop action. And a pickup truck load of emotion.

A Four-Gone Conclusion

One devilish night...or a chance at heaven?

Sam Logan's foster sons have a bad rep in Two Mule, Texas. Most of it earned. When it becomes clear they don't plan on giving up scootin' after every pretty pair of boots in town anytime soon, he issues the one thing he knows they can't resist: a challenge. Find a wife.

The oldest, Johnny, is actually grateful. He's had his eye on Mean Ellie Harker for a long time, and Sam's challenge is the kick in the pants he needed to ask her out. Except before he can make his move, his brothers kidnap her right out from under his nose. Now, instead of being one question away from victory, he has to compete for the woman of his dreams.

Ellie thought she'd be a dried up old spinster before Johnny finally untangled his tongue long enough to ask for a date. But instead of teaching him better uses for that tongue, his brothers have whisked her away to the ranch. At first she's furious...then intrigued when she starts to wonder what it might be like to have not just one sexy cowboy dedicated to her pleasure, but four...

Warning: Four handsome cowboys. Four choices. Will it be a single sordid night or a chance at heaven as she savors every luscious inch of the Logan brothers?

Two Wild for Teacher

It's double the trouble when two ornery cowboys come courtin', Texas-style...

Sam Logan's hell-raising twin sons have a bad rep in Two Mule, Texas. All of it earned. When it becomes clear those two troublemakers won't settle down without another nudge—make that a boot to their butts—Sam reissues his challenge. Find a wife.

There's only one woman who's ever held Mace and Jason Logan's attention for more than one night. Molly Pritchet, their former teacher. She's been too worried about a pesky morals clause to let them close, but they're older now and ready to prove to her that some rules are meant to be broken.

Molly thought her path was clear: always a teacher, never a mother or a wife. Until she finds those two Logan "boys" in her backyard, all grown up and digging around in her business. More accurately, starting her koi pond for her without asking. Well, it's about time someone taught the Logan twins some manners.

A little mud, a lot of yearnings she thought she'd suppressed, and Molly realizes she's the one being schooled in the art of indulging in forbidden desires.

Warning: Two hot-as-sin twins romance their former high school teacher. Things are bound to get down and dirty quick as two bad boys tag team to sweep one curvy, sexy woman off her feet.

Look for these titles by *Delilah Devlin*

Now Available:

Texas Surrender

Delilah Devlin

Samhain Publishing, Ltd.
11821 Mason Montgomery Road, 4B
Cincinnati, OH 45249
www.samhainpublishing.com

Texas Surrender
Print ISBN: 978-1-61921-523-8
Four Sworn Copyright © 2013 by Delilah Devlin
Breaking Leather Copyright © 2013 by Delilah Devlin
A Four-Gone Conclusion Copyright © 2013 by Delilah Devlin
Two Wild for Teacher Copyright © 2013 by Delilah Devlin

Editing by Lindsey Faber
Cover by Angela Waters

Four Sworn, ISBN 978-1-60928-213-4
First Samhain Publishing, Ltd. electronic publication: September 2010
Breaking Leather, ISBN 978-1-60928-259-2
First Samhain Publishing, Ltd. electronic publication: November 2010
A Four-Gone Conclusion, ISBN 978-1-60928-693-4
First Samhain Publishing, Ltd. electronic publication: September 2011
Two Wild for Teacher, ISBN 978-1-61921-183-4
First Samhain Publishing, Ltd. electronic publication: May 2012
First Samhain Publishing, Ltd. print publication: December 2013

Contents

Four Sworn

Dedication

To anyone who loves a tall, dark Texan, willing to go the extra mile for his girl...

Chapter One

"Dance with me, cowboy."

Bo Crenshaw didn't know what surprised him more. Her wanting to dance—or her asking him. She always cringed over her inability to master a simple two-step, and she usually avoided him like the plague in public.

But he wasn't arguing. It was Friday night after a long week of wrangling cattle. He wanted to replace the musky smell in his nostrils with something a whole lot sweeter. Giving his drinking buddy a shrug, he let Shanna Davies tug his hand and lead him onto the dance floor, pretending a reluctance he didn't feel.

Not that dancing with Shanna wasn't pleasurable—if a little painful. She danced the same way she lived—a little too fast and completely out of synch with everyone around her.

She wrapped her arms around his neck, but her head was tilted as she peeked around his shoulder. "Let's go this way." She bumped his knees, and they scooted backward toward her destination.

He pulled in her hips to slide a knee between her lethal knobs and circled so he had a view of what had caught her attention. Eyeing one particular trio of dancers at the far edge of the parquet floor, he thought he knew what had Shanna so intensely curious.

"Get me closer," she hissed.

"What're you doin'?" he asked, his tone dry.

"Tryin' to see."

"See what?"

"*Them*. Oops." She ducked her head and stared at his chest. "He knows I'm watchin'."

"Who?" he asked, pretending confusion.

"Justin Cruz."

Bo leaned closer to whisper in her ear and bury his nose in her fragrant hair, feeling sure she'd allow it—seeing as how she was trying to pretend she wasn't there to spy. "How do you know he knows?"

"He winked at me." She lifted her head and gave him a glare.

Bo suppressed a grin. "You're really curious about them."

She slid her hand down to twist his nipple through his shirt, and he winced.

"Don't make fun of me." She blew out a deep breath, frustration turning down the corners of her mouth. "Most exciting thing to happen around these parts, a real *ménage à trois*, and I can't get close enough to see."

"See what?"

She shrugged. "I'd like to see how they all dance together like that. For starters."

Bo chuckled, and then hissed when she twisted his nipple again. He'd be bruised. Worth it, though. He'd missed holding her close.

"Oh hell, they're leaving. You wanna get outta here?" she whispered.

Bo grunted and pulled her tall, slender body closer, rubbing his belly against hers. "You want to see if they do it in the parking lot, or are you horny? Thought you said we weren't gonna do that anymore—use each other." He ground out the last because the way she'd described their last sexual rendezvous still stuck in his craw.

Shanna grimaced in dismay but her brown eyes glittered with humor. "Did I make it sound that way? I'm sorry," she said, her tone anything but apologetic. "It's not that the sex isn't great, but..."

He couldn't help his impatient snort. "I know. You're blowin' this town as soon as you have the cash." Bo turned around on the floor again, fighting her for the lead and winning. He danced them into the darkest corner of the dance floor. "Hell, see what you did now?" he grumbled, pushing her hand down to the front of his blue jeans.

She cupped his erection, running her palm up and down his length, and then tossed back her dark honey-colored curls. Her laughter was low and dirty. "Guess since it's my fault, I should do something about it, shouldn't I?"

"Promises, promises," he muttered, acting like he wasn't so excited his head and heart were pounding faster and heavier than the band. "You bring a purse?"

"Do I ever?"

"Then let's go."

He dropped his arms and resisted the urge to snag her hand inside his. They walked out of the bar and into the gravel parking lot, making a beeline for his truck—but not before she'd darted a glance around the rows for the threesome's vehicle.

When her shoulders sagged, Bo opened the cab door. "Hop up."

As he climbed in behind the steering wheel, she raked a hand through her hair. "We don't have to go far."

"You in a hurry?" He turned the key and the engine rumbled to life, growling like he wanted to. He was pretty sure Shanna was right there with him by the way she clenched together her thighs.

"Don't be a shit," she said, punching his arm.

He let a grin slide across his face. "Sweetheart, I know just the place."

Bo gave Shanna a quick kiss then slid all the way inside her, sighing as her moist heat enveloped him. It had been far too long since the last time she'd succumbed to her natural urges and begged him for a quick "dick-fix".

Her legs wrapped around his hips and hugged him so hard he had to thrust a couple of times to remind her to give him a little room to move.

As he got down to work, his cock rocking inside her lava-hot little channel, he blessed his Boy Scout training for his foresight to stuff a thick blanket behind the seat of his truck. It gave him just enough padding beneath his knees to keep him comfortable and to shield Shanna's back from the cooling metal.

"This workin' for ya?" He tried to sound nonchalant when what he really wanted to do was let out a whoop it felt so good.

She gave him a coy look from beneath her lashes. "You needin' a little praise?"

She lifted her head and scooped his mouth with hers, fluttering her tongue over his bottom lip until he growled and consumed her like a bear dipping into a honey jar. She giggled into his mouth, and he pulled back, making a face. Moonlight shone so bright he could see the gleeful humor digging dimples deep into her cheeks.

He frowned. "Do you know what it does to a man when he's balls-deep and the girl starts laughin'?"

Which only made Shanna laugh harder. "Since you're not wiltin' beneath the disrespect, I'm not gonna feel sorry for you."

Bo gave a rumbling groan and tunneled deeper into her slick heat, every inch of his dick surrounded by her gently rippling channel. They grew silent, their bodies straining together.

Then, "You don't think what they're doin' is dirty, do ya?" she asked, her tone far too conversational, considering how much effort he was exuding.

He knew how her mind worked and what had precipitated this hot little interlude, but he still couldn't resist the urge to tease. "Who?" he asked, stroking deeper and cupping her butt with his palms as he powered into her.

"Dani and her two fellas."

"Long as they aren't hurtin' anyone else, I say let 'em be."

"I'm envious as hell," she groaned.

"Woman," he growled. "How the hell can you hold a thought?"

"I'm a girl. My brains don't flee south at the first sign of pussy."

Bo's bark of laughter ended in another groan. "Hush. Talk in a minute."

"A little overconfident, aren't you?" she quipped, but she was gasping now too.

Holding her against him, he rolled.

Shanna tossed back her wavy hair and gave him a look that bespoke challenge and arousal. A heady mix as she drove her slender body downward then ground against the crinkly curls at the base of his cock. Up again, she went, moonlight gleaming on the sweat coating her small breasts.

When he'd been a teenager, he'd ogled the women in his daddy's *Playboys*, but he'd been hooked on Shanna's little "fried eggs" since the first time she'd bared them in a dare. They'd still been middle school virgins.

"Now, don't you tease me," a thirteen-year-old Shanna had whispered, when he'd double-dared her into it, her hands shielding her chest after she'd let him pull her shirt up.

"Scout's honor, I won't," he'd said, so hard and excited he'd have spent himself in his jeans if she'd so much as rubbed against him.

Even now, when her hands cupped her little breasts and her eyelids slid closed, he thought her breasts were just about perfect.

"Ever think about..." She bit her lip and ground down on his cock again, a little faster and harder, and he knew she was still thinking about the trio everyone in Two Mule, Texas couldn't stop talking about.

"Ever think about what?"

Her gaze went skyward. "About doing it with another guy?"

His derisive snort brought her attention back. He gave her a scowl.

She snickered. "I didn't mean it that way. I mean doing a girl with another guy."

"Why stop at just two?" he asked, liking the conversation because he'd never seen her so hot, and moisture was seeping faster as she thought about her wicked little fantasy.

"Lord, Bo," she moaned, swirling her hips, screwing him sweetly. "You shouldn't say things like that. My legs are shakin'."

"Need me to take over?" he murmured.

"Would you? I know you've had a hard day at the ranch, but..."

"Honey, I'm never too tired for this. Not when it's you."

He could have kicked himself for that last bit. In all the years they'd snuck away to play, he'd never let her see how much she meant to him, sensing she'd shy away like a nervous filly, and he couldn't have that. If all they ever had was this, this strange, sexy friendship, then he'd savor every minute.

He rolled with her again, his hands slipping beneath her ass to cup her close. "Now, do you think we might concentrate for just a second or two? And yeah, I'm bein' overconfident again."

She grinned and slid her hands down his belly, past where their bodies joined and cupped his balls.

"Take that hand away, baby. I'm ready to come."

"Ready to go all Terminator on my pussy?"

He gave her a sexy roll of his hips, circling inside her. "I'm not out to demolish. I just want what's mine."

Her hands tugged his balls gently. "Think this pussy's yours?"

"Is someone else's dick divin' deep inside you?"

"Gawddamn, cowboy, I love it when you talk dirty."

"You're the one with the potty mouth," he said, giving her an openmouthed kiss. He pulled back because she was massaging his balls, and he was quickly getting lost in the sensations building inside him. "Shanna?"

"Yeah, stud?"

"Take that hand away so I can fuck you raw."

"Tell me more," she said, giving his sac another gentle pull then slipping her hand from between them. "Whatcha gonna do to me?"

He gritted his teeth. "Can't think. Wanna go wild on your ass and hammer until you're flyin' apart—so wet and hot and close that you can't do anything more than squeal and bleat like a pink little pig."

She wrinkled her nose. "'Cowboy, you tryin' to spoil the mood? That's so not sexy."

"It is from up here," he said dropping his voice to a purr. "I like your piggy squeals."

"I'm gonna kick your ass."

"Not until after I fuck your pussy raw." He thrust harder, cramming his swelling cock through tissue so hot and wet he thought he'd lose his mind.

Her eyes widened, and her fingernails dug into his ass. "Bo?"

"Yeah, baby?"

"Now! Do it now!" Her back arched off the truck bed, and her head dug into the blanket.

He withdrew all the way, re-centered his cock, and slammed home, not stopping until he felt the end of her channel and bounced against her cervix. He knew what that was because he'd been as avid a sex-ed student as she'd been. They'd both peeled off their clothes to explore and name of every part in high school—and they'd both gotten As.

With her eyes squeezing shut, and her moan tightening to that sexy-as-hell little squeal, he let loose, hammering her over and over until the pressure in his balls released. He shouted, come spurting deep inside her. Then chest heaving, he landed on top of her.

Her hands stroked over his back, gliding in his sweat.

"That would be just plain greedy, don't you think?" she said softly

This time, it took a second for him to recall the thread of conversation they'd dropped somewhere between the heavy thrusting. "If it's not hurtin' anyone..."

"I wouldn't want it to be a permanent thing," she said, her voice sounding dreamy. "I don't think I could be as strong as Dani."

"You think she has to be strong to have two men?"

"She has to be strong to put up with havin' everyone talkin' about her business. You should hear how the old biddies at the beauty shop skewer Dani Cruz. Even at church. Sanctimonious bitches."

Bo dragged in a deep breath and came up on his elbows so he could watch her face. "You're really curious about it, aren't you?"

Her gaze slid away from his to where she curled a finger in the hair above his ears. "It's just a fantasy. Gets me hot."

His lips twitched. "I couldn't tell. What if I told you there might be a way to satisfy that itch without anyone ever knowin'?"

She gave his hair a tiny yank and stared up at him. "I'd say you're a horrible tease, and now I'm completely horny again just thinkin' about the possibility. You did it on purpose, didn't you? Just 'cause I said we shouldn't have sex again."

He reached up to pull her fingers away from his head and kept them cupped inside his hand. "I'm not teasing. I have a solution. Guess it just depends on if you've got the guts."

She bit her bottom lip. "No one would ever know?"

"Just those there. And the guys I'm thinkin' of don't gossip."

She grunted. "How do you know?"

Gotcha, babe. "Ever hear of Chrissi Page gettin' naked and fuckin' three guys under the bleachers during halftime at the homecoming game?"

"No." Her eyes widened. "Prissy Chrissi? Really?"

He nodded.

Her eyes widened. "Were you one of those boys?"

"And if I was?" He'd been there but hadn't been one of the three havin' a go, but she didn't need to know that.

A frown dug a line between her brows. "I never would have put you with her. You said she wasn't your type."

Bo bit the tip of her nose, embarrassed now to admit his part. "She wasn't when she thought she was too good for anyone around here."

"How'd you ever talk her into it?"

He hadn't, but he gave her a wicked waggle of his eyebrows. "Now, I've already said too much."

"You're just tryin' to get me hot enough for another round," she muttered.

"And if I am?"

"Just remember, I ain't marryin' you, Bo."

"Did I ask?"

"No, but people see us together too often, they'll start makin' plans. And I already have plans."

Bo ground his hips against hers, dragging his slackening cock around and around her pussy. "No one will know about us," he said softly. "No one will start sendin' out wedding invitations. And I really can give you one hot-as-hell night. You game?"

Her teeth bit into her lush bottom lip as she studied his expression. "Who's your posse?"

He lifted his eyebrows, telling her silently that she ought to already know.

"You talkin' about the boys at the Triple X?" She stared. "Holy cow."

He could tell from the hitch in her breathing that the idea appealed.

"But why would they go for it, with me, I mean? I'm not...like Chrissi."

"Don't you dare say you aren't pretty enough."

"I'm okay, but they're..." She blew out a breath between pursed lips. "Let's just say there's not a woman in Two Mule, except maybe Dani Cruz, who hasn't thought about tryin' to lasso one of 'em. How you gonna ask them?"

"Leave it up to me."

Shanna swallowed hard. "Why would you do this for me?"

He gave her a one-sided smile, aching inside to tell her the truth, but settled for, "What're best friends for?"

Shanna reached up and kissed him then dropped her head back.

Bo was so handsome it broke her heart to look at him. Brown hair, green eyes, a lean, muscled frame were only the start of what she liked about him. His sharp-edged face, square jaw and the way he looked right into her eyes when he talked to her, never failed to make her melt.

He was the best friend she'd ever had. Knew every one of her dirty little secrets, but he'd never judged her. Never looked down on her. And she knew he'd be more than willing to take on all her problems on a permanent basis because he thought he was in love with her.

But she couldn't do it to him. He deserved better than getting smeared with the likes of Camilla Davies' daughter. Which was why she'd never let him park his truck outside the tidy little house her grandma had left to her when she moved to the retirement home.

"Blood will out." Or so Gran had always said, shaking her head mournfully whenever Shanna colored outside the lines.

And hadn't the old woman been right, after all? Just look at what she'd asked Bo to do for her.

A coyote howled in the distance, bringing her back. The ridges in the truck bed were digging into her spine, but she didn't want to be the first to push away. She wiggled her butt to realign with the ridges.

Bo lifted his head from her shoulder. "I'm crushin' you."

"No you aren't," she said, but she lowered her legs from his waist and let him slide to the side of her body. Shanna stuck an arm under her head and gazed at the stars glittering against the dark sky. "This was a great idea," she said softly. "You always know the perfect place."

Bo rolled to his back. "It's the middle of the football field. Better hope we don't get caught. There won't be any hidin' the tire tracks in the grass." Bo laughed. "At least it's better than the high school janitor's closet."

She shoved her elbow in his side. "No one found us."

"We both smelled like bleach after we spilled the supply shelf."

"Good thing we were naked then because our clothes didn't get ruined."

Smiling, Bo rubbed a lazy hand across his belly. "Have to say I was surprised you sought me out tonight."

"Just needed a partner to get out on the dance floor."

"That's not what I meant. I've hardly seen you around town. Gran said you've been job-hunting, interviewing in Austin and Houston. You didn't tell me. Thought you were avoidin' me."

"I've been lookin' for a job. Not that I have tons of options. Shoulda finished college when I had the chance."

"You hated school. Only reason you went to SMU in the first place was to get away from Two Mule. That why you've been job-huntin' so far from home?"

"Yeah. Thought it was about time to start the rest of my life. I can't stay here forever."

He stayed silent so long, she wondered if he'd fallen asleep. She glanced over at him, only to discover his head was propped on his arm while he studied her face.

"Don't look at me like that," she said, pushing out her bottom lip.

His eyebrows rose. "Like what?"

"I don't know. Like you think I'm a coward."

His eyebrows dropped. "I don't think that at all."

Shanna scowled. "I'm not like you. I don't come from a good family. Everywhere I go in Two Mule, someone whispers behind my back. They all wonder when I'll prove I'm just like my mom."

"Your mom wasn't a bad person. I liked her."

"Men liked her because most of 'em knew her in the biblical sense."

"That's an exaggeration."

She wrinkled her nose. "She was a whore, Bo, with a string of sugar daddies."

Bo nodded, his expression thoughtful. "She had some issues, but she wasn't a bad person. And you aren't her."

"People won't let me be someone other than Camilla Davies' daughter. And look at me. Look at what I want. What does that say about me?"

He rolled to his side and settled his head on his hand. "It just means you're sexually curious. So am I. Does that make me a whore? Bet I've had more lovers than you."

Shanna met his gaze, hyper-aware of his broad chest and missing his weight pinning her to the truck bed. She wished she could cuddle against him and draw on his inner core of strength. "Why haven't you settled down? You could find yourself a good woman."

His fingertip traced the length of her nose then tapped the end. "Because there's only one you," he said, smiling softly.

She hoped that wasn't true. She loved him. She knew he cared about her. But he shouldn't be *in* love with her.

She sat up and rubbed her arms. "I'm gettin' a little cold."

"Coward. You brought the subject up."

"I'm not afraid of the 'M' word. But I'm a realist. I really, really can't think of having a relationship until I'm far away from here."

His large hand cupped her thigh. "So you want me to arrange the ultimate farewell party?"

She shot him a quick glance, worried about what he thought of her now. "Am I being wicked?"

"Oh yeah." He pushed up on his arms, then leaned over and kissed her cheek. "But I like your wicked, dirty little mind."

Her lips twitched and stretched into a smile, and she was glad that the darkness hid the heat creeping into her cheeks.

Bo kissed her then backed away, keeping that talented mouth of his an inch from hers. "I'll get you what you want, sweetheart. My gift to you. Think of it as a goin'-away present."

Chapter Two

Bo rehearsed the request a dozen times, pacing in front of the Kinzie porch. He'd come early enough to catch them before they headed into town to hit the saloon, getting a rash of shit from his foreman because the old man had guessed his distraction had something to do with a girl.

Fuck. How did you ask friends to help you blow your girl's mind without looking like a fool?

"Do you think he knows we're out here?" came an overloud whisper.

Bo turned, shooting a glance over his shoulder. The three Kinzie brothers were lined up on the other side of the rail, eyeing him. Josh grinned. Cade's expression was wary, his eyes narrowed. And Ezra? Well, Bo never could get a bead on what Ezra thought because the man's expression never strayed from neutral.

He chose to address Cade's wary glance first. "I'm not here to borrow your tractor again."

"Weren't gettin' it even if you did. Got it stuck to the axle last time."

Josh leaned his butt against the rail. "Only thing ever gets you so worked up is Shanna Davies."

Bo snorted and narrowed his eyes. Josh wasn't a mind reader. He'd been drinking with Bo Saturday night when Shanna had approached him.

Josh grinned. "Well, that got a reaction. Better come in and get a beer while we get cleaned up."

Bo blew out a deep breath, glad for the reprive, and climbed the porch steps.

Inside the house, Josh headed down the hall toward the bedrooms, Cade on his heels.

However, Ezra pulled the tab of the beer he already held and settled onto a settee in the family room, not caring that his clothes were sweat-stained and covered in dust. "So what's botherin' you? You finally tell Shanna you're in love with her?"

Bo winced. How was it everyone else knew and Shanna still didn't have a clue? "I uh, have a request. Something Shanna wants."

Ezra's gaze narrowed as he studied his face. "Better blurt it out now before the other two get back."

Bo knew he was right. At least Ezra could give him a quick read. If he didn't think that his brothers would go for it, then he wouldn't have to take a lifetime of teasing from the other two. "I'd like to give Shanna something special. A Chrissi-at-halftime special."

Ezra grew still. "She knows about that?"

"She does now. Don't worry. She's not a gossip."

"As I recall, you weren't all that into sharing. You played lookout while we got busy. You hardly got a kiss in."

"This is Shanna we're talkin' about. I'd do anything for her. And she has it in her mind that she'd like a ménage."

"Sure she can handle it afterwards?"

Bo knew exactly what he meant. After that football game, Chrissi gave them all the cold shoulder, too embarrassed to meet their gazes.

"Shanna's plannin' to leave town. Been job-huntin'. She doesn't figure she'll have to see any of you again."

Ezra took a long pull of his beer then relaxed against the back of the sofa. "Does she figure on seein' you again, Bo?" he asked, his narrow gaze pinning him.

"She's leaving me too."

Ezra glanced away. "Sorry about that."

"Don't be. She's never led me on. It's my own damn fault I didn't believe her."

The pad of bare feet sounded from the hallway. Josh and Cade trailed inside, their glances going to Ezra.

"He wants us to do Shanna," Ezra said, his tone dead even.

"Is that right?" Cade asked, his eyebrows rising.

"Yeah," Bo said, his face growing hot. "She wants to experiment. It's a favorite fantasy kind of thing."

"She ask for us?" Josh said, his eyebrows meeting the blond hair falling over his forehead.

"I made the suggestion," Bo said, his tone gruff. "If you decide you're not interested, I trust you won't say a word to her."

"We don't gossip," Ezra said. "There's been enough of that around your girl."

Bo nodded his appreciation.

"Anything we should know about her?" Cade, the middle brother, asked.

Bo eyed each brother, knowing by their curious expressions that they'd agreed to the request. He let out a deep breath. "She doesn't like people mentionin' her mama. And she's self-conscious about her breasts. They're small. And I don't want her hurt or scared. So no rough stuff."

The two younger brothers looked to Ezra. Ezra's narrowed gaze fell on Bo again. "We decide what happens."

Bo's shoulders stiffened. "And if I don't like it?"

"We aren't gonna give a shit about what you want. This'll be all about her. We swear we won't do anything to harm or frighten her—too much."

Bo nodded again, slowly this time. "I'm curious. You fellas haven't shared since Chrissi, so why would you be willin' now?"

Ezra shrugged, then his face broke into an uncharacteristic smile. "It's good practice."

"For what?"

"For the day we bring a wife among us."

Bo's cheeks got hotter. He'd always known the brothers were a little crazy, but he hadn't known the depth of their kink.

He couldn't imagine wanting to share a woman he loved on a permanent basis. If he ever had the privilege of marrying Shanna, she'd have to settle for just one man in her bed.

Friday night, Shanna couldn't get any closer to Bo unless she crawled inside him. She'd climbed into the cab of his pickup and slid all the way over the bench seat, lifted his arm and snuggled against his side. She was hot and cold and scared all at the same time.

Ever since he'd told her the Kinzies had agreed to share her, she'd second-guessed herself a million times. She'd even called Bo twice to tell him she wanted to cancel, that it was all a joke, but he hadn't believed her either time. And here she was, pulling in front of the Kinzie ranch house, and her stomach was so taut she thought she might throw up.

The trip from her place in town to the ranch took only fifteen minutes, but she'd held her breath most of the way and felt winded.

"It's gonna be okay," Bo said, pulling her close and kissing her temple. He raised his arm over her head, put the truck into park and killed the engine. Then he turned back to her, his moss-colored eyes crinkling at the corners with his strained smile. "You don't like something, all you have to do is say so. If you want to change your mind, just head for the door. I won't judge you."

Shanna gripped one of his hands and squeezed it, glad of the darkening shadows that hopefully hid the blush heating her face. "I can't believe this is gonna happen, and that you're okay with it."

His eyebrows lifted up and down in a quick, wicked waggle. "Why wouldn't I be? You want it. I want you happy."

"That's what friends do, huh?" she said, lifting her chin in challenge. "Find a group of men willing to gangbang their girlfriend?"

His sigh seemed to come all the way from his toes. "It's not gonna be like that, Shanna. I swear, it's not gonna feel dirty."

"How do you know? Are you a girl?"

His chin firmed. "You wannna leave? We can head to Shooters. I'm okay with that. We can drink ourselves shitfaced. I'll see you home and tuck you in safe—and alone."

Shanna glanced away, staring blindly at the sprawling white ranch house. "I've dreamed about this every night since you said they'd do it, you know. I dream that tomorrow I'm walking through Two Mule, but I'm naked and everyone can see me."

His arm snaked around her shoulders and he hugged her close. "On my honor, baby, this is just between us. No gossip. Not a word or a sly look will follow you after this. I know you want this, but I know why you're scared. That's one thing you won't have to worry about."

She cocked her head to the side and gave him a slow smile. "Oh yeah? So what will I have to worry about?"

His smile widened. "Walkin' bowlegged for a week."

Shanna couldn't help it, she snorted. Laughter spilled out. When they'd both quieted, she lifted her mouth.

Bo didn't have to be told what she needed. He gave her a quick chaste kiss. "Come on inside. The guys aren't gonna jump you. We can talk first." He reached for his door handle.

She reached for hers and opened her door. "This is embarrassing. I'm already imaginin' them all naked. They won't have a thing to be embarrassed about."

"Neither will you."

She slammed the door and met him around the front of the truck. "I'm too skinny. I've got no ass. And a sixth-grader has bigger boobs than me."

"You're slender. You've got the prettiest, softest skin, and your nipples are cherry-colored." He thumbed one of her little berries through her shirt.

Her pussy clenched. "Okay, I can do this."

Bo encircled her waist with both arms and pulled her into his chest. "Yes you can. I'll be right there with you. I won't let anything happen you don't want."

How could she tell him there wasn't likely to be anything she wouldn't want? She'd stored up a lifetime of sexual fantasies, never letting them loose because she hadn't wanted to be seen as anything like her mother. Even with Bo she'd stuck to plain vanilla, shying away from anything too wild.

She squared her shoulders.

Bo unwrapped himself from her and held out his hand. She took a deep breath and placed her trust in him. He'd never let her down. Never pushed her. He'd been the best friend a girl could have.

"It's gonna be okay."

When she stepped onto the porch stairs, the front door opened. Josh, the youngest of the Kinzie brothers strode out and clomped eagerly down the steps. He stood beside Bo and waited, staring her up and down.

"Be polite, Josh," Bo said.

"Can't help it," Josh said, eager as a puppy dog. "I've wanted to see you naked forever, Shanna Davies."

His lazy smile was infectious. Shanna couldn't help chuckling even while her cheeks burned. She let Josh take her hand and pull her up the steps.

Bo snorted behind her, but that only made her smile widen. He hadn't liked how easily she'd accepted Josh's hand, not after the fuss she'd made.

Inside the house, she glanced around, curious about the brothers' home. She'd never been to the Kinzie ranch before, would have loved seeing the corrals and horses during daylight, but the interior of the old house was pretty impressive too. Yellow stone and natural wood on the outside, inside the walls were a mixture of stone and plaster. Stone stretched along the far wall with a bump out for the huge fireplace. A cast-iron chandelier, shaped like interlocking longhorn cow horns, was suspended from a high ceiling. The floor was a warm yellow oak. The furnishings large and leather—masculine browns and golds.

"Everyone's out back," Josh said.

Everyone. She hoped to God he meant just his two brothers.

They walked through the living room to the French doors on the opposite side. The flagstone patio that surrounded a pool was enclosed by a tall wall and lit by tiki torches. Boulders at one end of the pool formed a natural waterfall.

"It's beautiful," Shanna said, stepping farther onto the patio.

Cade rose from a lounger beside the pool. Dressed in jeans, a tight tee and boots, his dark hair was slicked back, and he smelled of soap, like he'd just come from the shower. "Nice to see you, Shanna."

The deep rumble of his voice skittered along her nerve endings, causing her to shiver. She was doing this, really doing it.

His gaze didn't sweep her body like Josh's had in blatant sexual interest. However, the way he looked at her face, especially at her mouth, said sex was uppermost on his mind, too. And since both brothers had proclaimed their interest with a steady gaze, she eyed Josh and Cade, standing side by side, comparing the depth of the muscle that corded their arms and legs, the width of their shoulders. The youngest Kinzie, Josh, was tall and lean like Bo; his shaggy blond hair touched the tops of his shoulders. His face was beautiful, his chin manly, but the dimple in the center softened his look. Blue eyes twinkled but he held still beneath her perusal.

Something about Cade's expression settled her nerves. Made her feel safe. His energy wasn't as apparent as Josh's. His body was tight, his expression a little wary. His gaze was steady as she raked him with a quick glance, all she dared, because the silence was stretching uncomfortably among them. Still, he was the same height as Josh, a tad broader in the chest. His face wasn't pretty like Josh's, being more rugged and masculine, but he still had the power to leave her breathless.

Cade reached for her hand and pulled her deeper onto the patio, toward the pool where a figure swam laps from one end to the other, his long sleek body gliding beneath the surface and completely nude.

Her mouth dried as Ezra Kinzie reached the end of the pool at her feet and hauled himself out of the water.

She stepped back, her heart racing, and tried valiantly not to drop her gaze, but his cock was thick and wakening, demanding attention. He was large. Everything about him was bear-like and oversized—feet, hands, cock. Lord, her jaw sagged as the manliest part of him seemed to grow harder, bigger still, beneath her fascinated stare.

Ezra slid a finger beneath her chin and raised her face. "You're overdressed."

A groan leaked out, and Shanna covered her face with her hands. "What was I thinking?"

Ezra chuckled "Come have a seat. We'll talk."

"I can't. You're naked and I'm already drooling."

"Not a bad place to start," he murmured.

She peeked between her fingers and slowly dropped her hands.

Ezra raised a thickly muscled arm and combed back his wet, dark brown hair. Water ran in rivulets over his broad, tanned chest. He reached out sideways. "Need a pillow."

One was placed in his hand, and he held it for her.

Shanna read the challenge in his eyes. He thought she'd bolt. That she didn't have the guts.

She might be nervous, but she was more aroused, more curious—about what this would be like, what he'd taste like, how the other men would react once she knelt and took Ezra in her mouth.

Mostly, she wondered whether Bo would be angered or hot for it.

She took the pillow, stepped out of her shoes and knelt at Ezra's feet, not looking up, not moving for the longest moment, just letting the sound of her heartbeats and his breaths soothe her nerves.

The other men took seats, leaning back on lounge chairs.

"What're you waitin' for?" Ezra asked, his tone soft and even.

"For you to tell me what you want of me," she whispered, keeping her head bent, because it felt right.

"How did you know that would please me?"

She raised her face. "I didn't really... Maybe it was the way you looked at me..."

"How did I look?"

"Watchful. Waitin' for something. I thought maybe I should wait too."

His smile was slow, easing over his mouth and crinkling the corners of his ice blue eyes. He cupped her chin. His thumb slid over her bottom lip. "Open."

Her mouth fell open automatically, and he stuck his thumb into it.

She didn't wait for him to spell out what he wanted. She did what came naturally, what instinct drove her to do. She closed her lips around his thumb, swirled her tongue over the roughened tip and sucked.

Ezra gripped his shaft, pumped his hand up and down his length, then pulled his thumb free and pressed the head of his cock against her lips.

Shanna breathed in his scent, fresh and chlorinated. She opened obediently, widening when he pushed the blunt head inside, gliding against her tongue, thrusting toward her throat. Her lips tightened around him. She watched his face while she sucked him, never lowering her gaze.

Ezra spread apart his legs, and she reached up to cup his sac, rolling the twin orbs in her palm, then closing her fingers around them and tugging gently as she rocked forward and back, meeting his slow, steady strokes.

Large, rough hands reached around her body, unbuttoning her blouse and slipping it off her shoulders. Her bra was opened and it slid off one arm. She let go of Ezra's balls and the garments were whisked away. She felt a pang of disappointment when the hands left her body, because she wanted them to fondle her.

Ezra gripped the base of his cock, pumping. Her lips met his fingers with each long sweep. With his free hand, he gripped her hair and pulled her closer toward his groin, rocking on his heels, but still so quiet she wondered if she pleased him. Then he pulled quickly from her mouth, his breath catching. His come spurted in white ropes, striping her face and breasts.

She let him tilt back her head to receive it, his soft cap sliding in the come on her cheeks, making a sticky mess of her face, but she didn't care. She licked her lips, taking his taste into her mouth.

His smile was soft in his taut, reddened face. But at last, he stepped away, leaving her trembling on the pillow and wondering what came next.

Cade knelt beside her, wiped her face with a warm, wet cloth, and then stroked it over her breasts, cleaning her and exciting her nipples. He circled them, smiling at the way they popped eagerly to attention. Cade lifted her chin on a crooked finger and bent to kiss her mouth.

Innocent, so far as kisses went—if she didn't think about the way his fingers were teasing one of her nipples, scraping it with a nail, then clasping it and tugging, twisting. When she opened her mouth beneath his to gasp, his tongue swept inside, exploring the edges of her teeth, the rim of her lips. She passively accepted his attentions, only her shortening breaths betraying her excitement.

He drew back and pulled her to her feet. Hands reached around her waist and unbuttoned her slacks, pushing them over her hips to puddle around her feet. A tug at the lace bracketing her hips left her sex exposed.

Hands cupped her bare bottom and slid around, sinking between her folds to capture moisture, then pulling away. Josh walked around her, the finger he'd wet with her juices stuck in his mouth, his eyes alight with mischief. "Baby, I'm gonna eat you all up."

Liquid gushed between her legs, trickling down her inner thighs. She pressed them together to hide it, but she doubted they missed a thing that was happening to her body. Not the way they watched her—darkening blue gazes sliding over her, seeking out her secrets.

Cade pulled her hand, and she stepped out of her clothing then followed him to the lounger Ezra reclined on. The back was lowered to a forty-five-degree angle, and he opened his legs, making room for her to sit between them, her back against his chest. Cade and Josh undressed in front of her. The rustling of fabric, the snaps of waistbands opening, added to the visual feast as the two men stripped themselves bare then walked toward her.

Where Ezra's size and rugged beauty left her knees weak, these two were so handsome, so perfect in form that she felt inadequate. She stiffened, and Ezra turned her head toward him. "Open your legs."

She didn't hesitate although the move exposed her to two avid male gazes.

The foot of the lounger dropped, and Josh knelt between her spread legs, pushing them wider until they hung on either side of the chair, her sex completely opened.

He trailed a finger along the edges of her thin inner folds. "You're wet, Shanna. Why's that?" he teased.

Her tongue felt glued to the roof of her mouth, so she shook her head.

"I think you want me to play there. Want something hard coming up inside you. Am I right?"

Her body trembled, and she pressed back against Ezra, who tugged her hair and nuzzled her ear.

Cade sat on the edge of the lounger beside her hip and rubbed his hand over her mound. "Do you like having your pussy petted, Shanna?"

She pried her tongue from the roof of her mouth and swallowed. "I won't fuckin' purr," she said, surprised at the gravel in her voice.

Josh's grin split his face.

Cade's fingers plucked her short curls hard.

Shanna drew a breath between clenched teeth at the sharp pain. "Why'd I think you were the nice one?"

"Which one am I?" Josh asked.

"The player."

"And Ezra?"

"Just scary."

Ezra's hand caressed her breast, and he whispered in her ear, "Still think I'm scary?"

She nodded, and the men laughed, which didn't soothe her ravaged nerves.

Josh leaned toward her, his gaze glued to her pussy. His hands smoothed up her inner thighs, then slowed as they neared her sex. "Always knew those legs were long, but damn, girl." He tugged her outer lips between his thumbs and forefingers and spread them. "You're wet, sweetheart. Cream's all the way down your thighs. Did sucking Ezra do that to you?"

Chapter Three

"*Fuck,*" she whispered, then shot a sideways glance at Bo.

His shoulders were hunched. His hands planted on his knees. "Don't look at me. You wanted this."

"I never thought..." Suddenly ashamed, her gaze dropped. "Guess I didn't think at all."

"Want me to stop?" Josh asked. By now his expression had lost all humor, even his perpetual smirk had tightened.

"I ache," she admitted, her voice trembling.

Josh bent closer. "Wanna be fucked?"

She nodded, her mouth dry as dust.

"Too bad." He ducked toward her pussy, and his tongue slipped out and licked her from the bottom of her folds to the top, giving her clit an unsatisfying lap. "Ah hell." He bent closer and buried his face between her legs, his whisker-roughened chin driving into her folds, his nose nudging the hardening knot.

Shanna clamped her thighs around his head, dug her fingers into his hair and pulled as she curved to press her sex harder against his mouth.

Josh chuckled then concentrated his efforts around the turgid little knot at the top of her folds while Cade continued to tug her curls. Josh latched his lips around the sensitive knot, teethed it gently then suckled it hard before pulling back. But he wasn't done. Pressing two fingers against it, he swirled them around and around, giving her a devilish, dark look.

Half crazed with his teasing, she couldn't hold back the moan scratching at her throat. Her body convulsed, beginning the spiral.

He lifted away his fingers. "Not so quick."

"God, why not?" she gasped. "I was almost there."

"The longer I make you wait, the better it'll be. Promise."

"Don't care," she snarled. "Wanna come now."

The men laughed, low and dirty. Josh cupped his fingers together and swatted her pussy, the sharp slap landing on her clit.

Shanna jerked inside Ezra's hold. He hugged her closer and bit her earlobe.

Cade slid his free hand beneath her butt and curved his fingers, sliding them into the crevice that separated her cheeks. When he grazed the tiny hole, she froze and tried to turn her face, but Ezra bit harder. "No," he whispered. "No hidin', baby."

"I don't like it."

Josh thrust two fingers inside her pussy and twisted them, coming out with slick fingertips that he used to paint her lips. "You're lyin'. Taste your lies?"

"Bastard," she said, groaning again as Cade inserted one finger into her ass and twirled it in her hole.

She clamped the delicate muscles hard around the digit, trying to eject him, but he continued to roll it, gently, slowly, teasing her into relaxing. Her hips began to dance again, up and down, dragging on his finger. "Wrong, so wrong," she whispered.

Josh shushed her and drove his two digits into her pussy again, fucking her with them, in and out, while Cade swirled.

The sensations—the burning ache behind, the juicy heat in front—were tightening the tension in her core.

Ezra pinched a nipple and bit her ear again.

Josh kissed her clit while he fingered her. "Come for us. Do it now." Then he latched onto her clit and drove three fingers deep.

Shanna's back bowed, and she gave a strangled scream. The tension uncurled in one prolonged explosion that froze every muscle and forced the air from her lungs. She jerked and gasped at the end, then collapsed, drawing in deep breaths through her mouth, her eyelids fluttering down then squeezing tight because she wanted to protect herself from all the interested gazes cataloguing every response.

The two men playing below petted her gently, raking fingers through the down covering her mound, stroking her flanks.

Shanna gave a shuddering groan and was surprised by a nearly silent sob that shook her chest.

Ezra released her lobe. "That's it, baby. That's it. Shhhhh..."

She turned her head to the side, rubbing her cheek against his bare chest.

Cade's fingers withdrew from her rear hole, and he walked away. Josh kissed her clit and slowly pulled his fingers free.

Something warm and rough rubbed between her legs, and she felt the swipes of a washcloth, cleaning between her legs then slipping beneath her. Not until the cloth finished did she open her eyes.

Apparently satisfied, Cade tossed the cloth away and sat on the concrete beside the chair. He ruffled the hair sticking to her cheek. "What do you think, Shanna? Will you let us play some more?"

She laughed and groaned, wanting to hide her face. But really, they'd seen everything, hadn't they?

The men chuckled.

"What about you, Bo?" Ezra said, his voice rumbling pleasantly beneath her cheek.

She'd forgotten Bo was there, watching. Lord, what had it looked like to him? She'd come completely undone, surrounded by men, every orifice teased and filled at some point.

"I say we move inside," Bo said quietly. "Need something soft under us. And enough room to really get down to business."

Down to business. She turned toward him and stared. His face was tight, red blotches in the center of his cheeks, his eyes hot and hard.

Had he changed his mind? Did he think she was a whore like her mother now?

Josh pushed off his knees and followed Cade inside. Ezra gently leaned her forward and slid from behind her, leaving her alone with Bo.

She stayed silent, her gaze sliding away to stare at the edge of the pool.

Bo stood, his hands wiping down the outside of his thighs, but not speaking.

She didn't wait for him to decide he'd seen enough and leave. She rolled off the lounger, took two steps and dove into the pool, skimming along the bottom and kicking to put as much distance between herself and him as she could. When she surfaced, she shot up, gripped the edge of the far end of the pool and leaned her forehead against the rough concrete rim.

Footsteps trailed the pool, boots clomping closer. Hands cupped her shoulders then slid beneath her armpits. Bo lifted her from the water and set her on her feet in front of him. "Do you wanna leave?"

Water sluiced down her body and a gentle breeze caused her to shiver. "I don't know how to answer that."

"It's a yes or a no. Pretty damn simple."

"It's a helluva lot more complicated than that."

His fingers combed back her wet hair then gripped it to tilt her head. His expression was so hard she almost didn't recognize him—except for the heat in his green eyes.

"Do you wanna fuck us?" he asked, his voice gruff. "All of us?"

She shoved at his chest. "What's this all about? You proving to me that I'm just like my mama? Or do you want me to quit, back down now and choose you? Because that won't change a thing, Bo. I'm still leaving."

His eyebrows lowered into a furious scowl, a look he'd never worn around her before. "You're not a thing like your mama," he whispered furiously. "You don't fuck the one who can give you the most money or the better cars. You fuck because you're a healthy, sexual creature—and you're here because you're curious. I'm all right with that. I've pussy-footed around you since we were teenagers, never pushing you for more than you were comfortable giving, but I'm tellin' you now—I think you're a coward, Shanna. You want this. You want me. And you want to be used, to be commanded—you're dyin' to be taken."

Her mouth dried. "I thought I knew you."

"You do, deep inside. It's why you cut me off, why you try to stay away from me—because I know the woman you keep hidden deep inside." Shanna pushed him again, but he caught her hands and slid his fingers around her slender wrists, like steel cuffs. "I've been your friend. I've spent more time alone with you than any other person, including your kin. That doesn't mean I see you as my friend or as my little sister. I've wanted to fuck you since I was old enough to know what to do with my dick. I've wanted to call you mine even longer than that."

She tugged at her wrists, her body bumping against his, but he didn't budge. "If that's true then why did you do this? Why offer me this?"

"Because I want you to know how sexy you really are—and that it's okay to experiment." Bo slid a thigh between her legs, the coarse material chafing her pussy. "Me tellin' you it's okay isn't gonna make you believe it. So fuck them, blow them. Prove to yourself that you have it in you, that you're ready to explore everything you're capable of."

Shanna quivered against him, her breaths shortening. She'd never seen him this angry. Never thought him capable of manhandling her. When his thigh rubbed against her crotch, she stopped fighting him and settled onto it, welcoming the scrape against her tender flesh.

Bo crowded even closer, mashing her breasts against his chest. With his mouth hovering over hers, he whispered, "When you're done, I'll still be here. That's something you need to learn about me. I'm not in it for what I can get from you, Shanna. I'm not in it to make you mine. I'm here because I love you."

Shanna froze. Her gaze locked with his. She wanted to look away but couldn't. He'd said it. She wanted him to take it back.

Shanna didn't know why those three words infuriated her so much, but her skin heated, this time not because of arousal or embarrassment. She shoved her chest against his, pushing him. "Fuck you," she whispered. "You can't go changing on me. Fuck you to hell."

His hands tightened again; his jaw clenched. "I'm already there, baby."

Tears blurred his face and she blinked them away. "Then why do you put up with me? This isn't good for you. I'm not good for you."

Bo's eyes closed, so did his expression. "You ready to go inside?" He dropped his hands and backed up.

She spun around and walked on shaking legs toward the glass doors, determined to show him just how unsuitable she was. She slammed open the doors and entered the air-conditioned house. The cool air raised gooseflesh as soon as it sifted across her skin.

A shower sounded from deep inside the house, and she followed the noise, trailing down a hallway and into a large bedroom, Bo walking slowly behind her.

Inside the room, Josh lay on a king-sized bed, his blond hair wet, a towel wrapped around his hips.

Cade stepped out of the bathroom with a towel draped over his shoulders. He grinned at her and reached up to rub his head, drying his curls.

Which left Ezra in the shower. Giving Bo a scathing glance, she stepped into the bathroom and slammed the door shut behind her.

She could see the older brother's tall, broad frame through the clear glass of the shower door, his arms raised and his hands buried in his hair. Long ropes of soap slid over his back and along the curve of his tight, round buttocks. She opened the door and waited.

He glanced over his shoulder. "You two get it all worked out?"

"Hardly," she said, wrapping her arms over her middle. "He wants me to fuck you all to prove I'm sexual." She left out the part where Bo said he loved her, because she couldn't cope with it. Not right now. Not staring at Ezra Kinzie's hard-muscled body.

"Not the smoothest thing he could have said to a woman." His glance slid down, pausing on her legs. "I don't think you have a thing to prove."

"Why do you think he's doing this?"

Ezra shook his head. "He told you."

"It's bullshit. He ruined everything. He changed on me."

Ezra's expression didn't reveal a thing he was thinking as he studied her face.

She took a deep shuddering breath and glanced away. "Tell me the truth, Ezra. Any reasonably attractive woman would do for you and your brothers, right?"

He lifted his gaze and arched one dark brow. "For us to be interested? We're not man-whores, Shanna."

She blushed. "Is this something you do often?"

"Not at all. We experimented a bit when we were younger."

"Chrissi?"

"Just the once. I think we shocked the hell out of her." Ezra turned, his cock preceding him, drawing her attention to the insistent thrust of his long, slightly curved dick. "Look, the water's gettin' on the floor," he growled. "Come on in and we can talk."

Shanna blew out another ragged breath and stepped into the shower, remembering too late he was the most intimidating of the three brothers. "So you experimented. This isn't a regular thing?"

"We need the right girl to take us all on. We can't go around scarin' every woman in the county." One side of his mouth twitched, but she could see he was serious.

"I know you don't think I'm Ms. Right, so why do this?"

"Practice. And you're safe." His slow smile, when it came, took away her breath. The man's looks were deadly to a woman's peace of mind.

"Do you want me to understand that?"

"Not particularly. We live an isolated life here. Sure we get into town whenever we need to resupply, and when we need women, but we aren't seeking to make a reputation for being kinky sons of bitches. We tend to be attracted to the same women, which could have been problematic if we hadn't figured out we like sharin'. But we're waitin' for the right one to bring into our lives."

"You're lookin' for a woman to share on a permanent basis?"

"Yeah."

Shanna shook her head. "She'd have to be special all right. And have fantastic stamina."

Still smiling, Ezra plucked the washcloth from the rack at the far side of the stall. "Come here. You're too tense." He cupped one shoulder and forced her to face the back of the stall, then began to rub the soapy cloth over her back.

She braced her open palms against the wall and closed her eyes. Being bathed like a baby wasn't something she'd had on her list of things to experiment with, but she'd consider it an added bonus. Damn, the man had talented hands. "I didn't know this would be so hard. Being here with you and your brothers, that is. It's a little confusing."

"How so? All you have to do is give yourself to us. We make all the decisions, give you the pleasure. But you're talking about Bo, aren't you?"

Shanna sighed and closed her eyes. "He's different. Ever since he offered me this. Like he expects something in return."

"You don't like the change?" Ezra scrubbed in long, hard sweeps down her back.

Shanna swayed with the motion, relaxing. Something she hadn't thought possible in his presence. "I feel off-balance. I thought I knew him, but he's turnin' possessive," she said, wrinkling her nose.

"You think he shouldn't be?"

"It's not the way we are. It's the one reason I've always trusted him. He didn't get weird or jealous when I roamed."

His cloth-wrapped hand scraped over her buttocks. "You roam much?"

"No. I get nervous around men. Start thinkin' they think I'm like my mom. That that's why they're with me. Never lasts long."

"Then why is his possessiveness an issue?"

"I feel guilty about this, wanting you and your brothers, and about leaving him. I'm not stayin' in Two Mule."

"Ready to blow this town, are ya?"

"Yeah," she said, only for the first time, when she said it, she felt a little hollow. A little less sure.

Ezra tossed aside the cloth, and his bare hands smoothed up and down her body, massaging her. "What's so bad about Two Mule?"

Shanna moaned. Lord, he had magic in his strong hands. Every little knot, every hint of tension was draining away. "Small town, small minds," she mumbled.

"Tryin' to start fresh where no one knows you?"

She stiffened, sure he was going to mention her mother, but he started massaging her shoulders and upper arms then made his way slowly down her spine. When he reached the top of her buttocks, his hands opened, his palms pressing hard, his heels kneading the muscles until she was arching. "That feels really good," she groaned.

"Bo's gonna miss you," Ezra said, his tone accusing, but soft.

"I know that," she said, swallowing the lump building at the back of her throat. "But he's known forever that I can't stay."

"You gonna miss him, even a little bit?"

"I'll hate leaving him behind. He's the best thing that ever happened to me. We've shared everything since we were kids. Know each other's secrets. I can tell him anything, and he never looks at me like I've grown two heads."

"Not everything. You didn't tell him about your kinky side. How come it took you so long to tell him what you wanted?"

"I didn't want him to think less of me," she whispered. "Didn't want him to think I'm a whore."

"Have you kept other secrets from him?"

She shook her head, already regretting having told him so much. It wasn't like she and Ezra were even friends, but here she was running off at the mouth. She stiffened. "I can wash the rest."

"But it wouldn't be near as much fun," he drawled.

"This can't be fun for you. Your dick isn't getting any."

He gave one side of her bottom a slap. "Don't be ugly. I can enjoy touching you without my dick getting involved. It's not just about the orgasm."

"Really?" She turned, her shoulder gliding across his chest he stood so close. Then she glanced up, challenging him with a hard stare, and cupped his balls. With her free hand she traced the length of his cock, which was twitching into an impressive erection. "I'm gonna make a liar out of you."

"Let go, Shanna."

"Not a chance. You can pretend for Bo that this is all for me. But I know you're just another horny man and this time you've got the whore's daughter at your mercy. You just wanna see whether I'm anywhere as good as my mama."

His hands curled around her wrists and pinched.

She winced and let go of him.

Ezra raised his hands and slapped them against the tile on either side of her. "I never had your mother," he bit out. "And I never had any curiosity about being with her. She wasn't my type."

"She was every man's type."

"I like my women a little less used."

"Men like having a willing hole to poke. They just don't wanna marry it."

His gaze narrowed into angry slits. "You've got a nasty mouth."

Shanna raised her chin, relieved the anger flooding her was washing away her guilty tears. "I'm a realist. Every man's wired the same. Doesn't matter what you might like to think—that somehow you're different from any other guy. But when it comes down to it, if you're alone with something that's halfway decent lookin', your cock's gonna go on pussy alert."

Ezra turned off the water and pulled back the door. He stepped out of the shower, then turned and bent, shoving his shoulder hard into her belly, forcing air from her lungs while she crumpled over him. Upside down and sliding on his slippery skin, Shanna didn't know whether to hit him or cling to keep from falling.

When he walked into the bedroom, he flung her on the bed. The men inside the room glanced up, their gazes sharpening.

"You look pissed, Ezra," Josh said. "What'd she do?"

"She insulted us. Thinks we aren't all that particular about who we poke."

Josh snorted. "Those her words?"

"Yep."

"Damn, Shanna. If you'd said it to me, I might have let it slide."

Shanna sat up. "Don't know why he's so bent out of shape. Only statin' the bald truth. You're men. You don't have anything better to do on a Friday night."

Josh came up on his knees beside her, looming. "We don't have any other plans so we're doing you? That it?"

She gave a sharp nod.

"Think I'm pissed now, too."

She glanced to the far corner where Bo sat. He still had his jeans on, but the button at the waistband was open. His hands gripped the arms of his chair. His body was rigid.

She started to worry then and sat up. "Guess it's time for me to go. This just stopped bein' fun."

Ezra's hands fisted on his hips. "It's not always fun, Shanna—learning to obey. There's the bit about respect, for the man laying down the rules, and respect for yourself."

"I don't want anyone bein' the boss of me."

"You might not want it, but there's not a woman who needs it more, sweetheart." Ezra planted his palm in the center of her chest and pushed her slowly down to the mattress.

Her abdominal muscles burned as she tried to resist his inexorable push, but in the end she lay flat while his brothers stretched her arms above and her legs below, securing them to the bedposts with binding straps she hadn't seen before and leaving her spread-eagle on the mattress.

Angry, she pulled against the padded leather bindings, twisting every which way, but accomplishing nothing other than working up a sweat. When she finally relented, she panted, aiming daggers at their hides, but gritting her teeth to keep from screaming.

Ezra pulled open a drawer in the long built-in cabinet that stretched along one wall. He rifled the contents then drew out a long, thin dildo. He turned it upside down and flicked a switch on the base, making it hum.

Her knees turned inward, trying to close her thighs, but he crawled onto the bed between her legs, scooting closer and nudging her thighs wider apart. "Need some lube, Cade."

Shanna snarled and yanked on her bindings again, her heart starting to trip as she read the intent in his tightening features. He was going to punish her. Make her eat her words.

Part of her was thrilled, but the other part was appalled. She didn't like the thought that so many men would be witness to this. She had to resist, had to prove she wasn't weak, wasn't an easy whore like her mama.

Cade climbed onto the mattress at her side and leaned over her open thighs. His fingers smoothed between her folds and dipped inside. "Still wet as hell." When he glided deeper between her legs, between her buttocks, her knees stiffened, holding her legs straight, trying to deny him entrance by clamping her buttocks tight.

"Come on, sweetheart, tilt just a little bit so I can get inside there."

She shook her head, her upper lip beginning to tremble.

Ezra gave Josh a look, and Josh plucked the pillow from beneath her head, grabbed a second, and stuffed both under her stiff hips.

"Now there's enough give in the leg shackles you could raise your knees and tilt that pretty pink cunt at my mouth," Josh said. His hand cupped her mound. His thumb rasped over her cloaked clit. "You want my mouth on you, don't you, sweetheart?"

"Untie me," she whispered furiously, straining her neck to lift her head and deliver a deadly glare.

"Not a chance," Josh said with a small, infuriating smile.

"Bo!" Shanna wailed.

"He's not gonna help you," Ezra said, his voice dead even. "He knows you need this. You might be afraid, but you're also horny as hell. Think I can't smell how much you want this?"

Her face flushed hot with embarrassment. "I want you to stop. Right now."

"Really?" Josh's gaze met hers as he lowered his mouth over her pussy. "Really, Shanna? Want me to stop before I eat you out? Don't you want me to prove you want that dildo straight up your ass? That you want more? Every one of your sweet little holes filled and fucked?"

Liquid spilled from her pussy, and Josh's fingers swirled in it, proving her lies.

"God, I hate you."

"Only because I'm right. Now, tell another lie."

Ezra flicked the inside of her knee to draw her attention. "You want us to stop, we'll untie you. Bo here will get you dressed and you can walk right out the door. It's your choice, baby-girl."

"I'm not a baby," she said harshly, wanting to argue with something he'd said, but not wanting to say the one thing that would end this, because they were both right. She wanted to be forced, wanted them to take away her choices, but she didn't want to say it. They'd left her an out. But she wouldn't take it.

Ezra held out his hand. "That lube, Cade?"

Shanna turned her head to the side and didn't make a sound. Ezra's fingers, covered in gel, snuck between her legs, deep between her buttocks. He held her cheeks apart and rubbed her asshole then tucked a finger inside, twisting it to lube her untried hole.

Then the soft plastic head of the dildo pressed against her opening.

"Open up, just a little. Tilt your pussy, baby," Ezra crooned. "Give it to Josh."

She wondered if he got off on turning no into yes. If that was his thing. He did it so well.

Her belly shivered. Her thighs trembled, but she opened them, not too wide. Just enough that Joshua's hand cupped her, petting her fur. No doubt he'd have her straining against her bonds in minutes, trying to open as wide as she could because his wicked mouth was so very good.

His tongue stroked over her swollen lips.

Ezra eased the dildo deeper into her ass, twisting it slightly in the gel, the vibrations set too low to appease the heat curling inside her core.

Shanna gasped and closed her eyes tightly to hide the only part of her she could from the men closing in around her.

Chapter Four

A heavy hand stroked her hair. A warm palm cupped her cheek. A firm mouth brushed against hers—the taste familiar—and she groaned. Had to be Cade.

She peeked through her lashes and her gaze met his.

His mouth smiled against her. "Couldn't have you hidin' from us." He knelt on the edge of the bed, his cock sprung and tapping against his washboard belly.

Lord, it was a fucking cornucopia of pretty cocks. Every one individual in hue and bent. The Kinzie boys as a whole had round, knob-shaped cockheads, shafts curving slightly upward. Bo's head was more tapered, and his length perfectly straight.

She wasn't sure which she preferred, but thought Bo's would probably slip the easiest inside her ass. She wished it was him rather than the stiff dildo gliding gently in and out. She wondered why she'd never let him do it.

Oh right, they weren't supposed to be having sex.

Josh's lips pulled on her clit, and her thighs parted as though on command—the gates opening for someone to rush inside, only no one accepted the invitation.

She wanted one of those lovely, hard cocks pushing up inside her. *Now.* But she'd be damned if she begged. How could she entice them to forget about punishing her and get straight to business? What they'd given her on the patio had only whetted her appetite. The argument they'd just ended stirred the frustration more.

Fingers intruded, but only a quick slide up then they whisked away—Ezra, the bastard, checking her oil then sliding out the dildo. She didn't know whether she was relieved or not. Her ass burned, but she missed the tingling fullness.

Josh sucked her clit then released it, making a smacking sound and smiling. His eyelids drooped, lending him a sleepy charm.

When both men backed away, she glanced again at Cade, but he was bent over the side of the bed, picking up something from the floor beyond her view. When he raised it, she shook her head and her heart kicked into high gear.

He held a flogger with leather flanges. He tested it against his palm, and smiled when it made a crisp snap.

Her body tightened, and she tugged again against the bindings wrapped around her wrists.

Cade knelt beside her and trailed the fringes from her collarbone, around and around her breasts, then slowly down her belly. He lifted it and snapped it once against her belly, causing her to yelp, but only from surprise. The snap was more playful then painful.

He snapped again against her lower belly, just above her mound, this time a little harder. The tender flesh burned.

When he swept it over her pussy, stroking one outer lip then the other, she knew the leather came away wet because moisture gushed from inside her, wetting her cunt and soaking the already-damp bedding beneath her.

The dark, narrow look he pinned her with was her only warning. He lifted the flogger and snapped it against her cunt, stinging her labia, causing blood to zing south and swell her sex.

Fingers touched her, smoothing over her plump lips. "You'll have a nasty welt. Was that too much?" Ezra asked.

If Josh had asked she'd have told him to go to hell. But Ezra demanded a simpler, honest answer. "No," she whispered.

The flogger landed again, swatting, not snapping. Warming her flesh but not stinging. Causing a swell of sensation that superheated her sex and triggering an insistent throbbing she felt all the way up her channel.

Josh held open her lips and tugged them upward, baring her clit to the air.

Shanna sucked in a breath, shocked, because she knew what was going to happen. She tried to get a protest past her lips, but her mouth was dry and all she could manage was a pitiful mew.

The flogger swatted twice, landing directly on her clit, and she jerked against her bindings, nipples spiking hard.

"Too much now?" Ezra repeated.

She gave him a furious glare but tightened her lips.

Ezra jerked his chin. Cade tossed the flogger aside. His fingers slid down her slick, hot lips and rubbed, soothing...then lifted. The wicked glint in his eyes made her groan, a sound that was arrested when he spanked her pussy. Her sex was hot, swollen, dripping wet, and she couldn't hold back the moans piling one atop the other as she wrestled with the bindings, straining to lift her torso from the bed.

"Please...please," she begged, curving her hips to give him better access, because she'd come in just a second, just another swat...

Cade pulled his hand away, leaving her suspended in arousal.

"Please what?" Ezra said, a hard edge to his voice.

"Please fuck me," she said, so softly the men bent closer to hear.

"Anyone in particular you want?"

Her gaze sliced to Bo, but she stubbornly bit her lip.

"Don't think she's learned her lesson, do you, boys?" Ezra drawled.

Shanna saw them pull back, knew they meant to torment her further, and she took a deep breath. "Bastard. Fucking pervert!"

"Pervert?" Ezra tsked. "Who wanted us all? You can change your mind, quit any time you want, sweetheart."

"I hate you," she yelled, her voice cracking. Then she stopped fighting, stopped trying to hide the tears behind the anger and her smart mouth. She hung on the bindings, her chest shaking, tears leaking on either side of her face.

Ezra crawled next to her, stretching out beside her. One hand cupped her face and she nuzzled it, craving something tender. "Who do you want, Shanna? You're gonna have us all one way or another. But who do you want to cling to?"

She gazed at him, wanted to say him, but it would be a lie. And he'd know it. She closed her eyes and sobbed. "Bo. I need Bo."

It had taken every bit of Bo's self-control to keep silent and watch while the three brothers broke down his proud, stubborn woman. But from his perspective at least, the wait was worth it to hear the teary confession.

She'd chosen him. Above three other attractive prospects. Three men most females in the tri-county area sighed over every time they crossed their paths. Bo knew he wasn't exactly hound-dog ugly himself, but Shanna had already had him. Could have him anytime she wanted.

Still, she'd stuck with him. Had to mean something.

Ezra lifted a brow and rolled off the bed. "We'll leave you two alone for a few minutes."

Bo stood and smoothed his hands down the sides of his jeans. He didn't like admitting it, but he was nervous. They'd laid the groundwork. It was up to him to close the deal. He walked to the side of the bed and looked down at Shanna.

Her face was still blotchy and red from crying, her chest shivering with hiccupping sobs.

"Do you want to leave?" he asked quietly.

A frown dug a line between her eyebrows; her brown gaze darted away. "Will you think I'm a complete coward if I say yes?"

"I would never say that."

"Would you be disappointed in me if I said no?"

His mouth twitched. "Disappointed? Sweetheart, you've been amazing so far."

"Really?" She sniffed and glanced back at him. Her red nose was wet. "How?"

Bo reached for a tissue from the box on the nightstand and gently wiped away her tears and the dampness on her nose. "You're stubborn and strong. You took everything they threw at you."

"But I cried like a baby."

"You were overcome. But so passionate. Even when you were pissed."

She nodded. "It was intense."

He moved to sit beside her, but she shook her head. "I'm naked as the day I was born. It's not fair."

"All right." He unzipped his pants and winced as he peeled his jeans down his thighs. His cock was fully erect, aching.

He heard Shanna's quick intake of breath then looked over to find her lips parting, her tongue sliding along the bottom pink wedge.

"Don't look at me like that."

"Like what?"

"Like you want me to come down your throat."

Her lips twitched. "That has its own look?"

"Yeah. Think I would ever know when the time was right if you didn't telegraph?"

Her smile was a little shaky, but he wasn't quibbling. This was just the lull before the storm. Maybe she didn't know it, but he did. She needed to relax, recoup her strength.

"Do all my desires have their own looks?"

A smile tugged his mouth wide. He gave her a sheepish shrug. "Don't know about all of them. But I've never heard you complain. Or tell me what to do when we're naked."

"I never could read what you wanted. I'd be thinking, how do I get him to kiss me, and all of a sudden, you're pushing me against the wall and have your hands up my shirt before I even knew that's what I wanted all along."

Bo cupped her cheek and rubbed his thumb over her soft chin. "Think I got some kinda ESP?"

"I think you know me," she said, her eyes glistening again. "Wish I knew you that well."

"You could."

She shook her head and looked away. "No point. I'm not stayin'."

He pulled his hand away and curled his fingers tightly. "Jesus, you sure know where to twist that knife."

Shanna blinked. "I never led you on."

"I know. But I sure wanted you to. You could have used me all up and I wouldn't have cared."

"Why?"

"You don't know?"

She shook her head then turned her head aside. "I think I really do want to go home now."

Anger blazed inside him. And fear. She might slip away from him tonight, but not before she understood just how deep it went with him. "You're a coward, Shanna Davies. You had your chance to back out, but it's too late now. I have things I want to tell you. Things I have to do to you. With you tied up like a turkey, I can have you any way I want."

Her gaze snapped back. "Bo..." she said, her voice rising.

"Yeah, be worried, Shan," he said, narrowing his gaze and fisting his hand hard in her hair. "It's gonna be a long, long night."

A shiver worked its way down her spine, quivering through her, tightening her thighs and her toes. The slither of fluid from deep inside her didn't have a thing to do with the hard, angry cowboy hovering over her. Or so she told herself.

She'd seen Bo pissed off a time or two, but never with her. His anger shocked her—she'd hurt him more than she'd ever thought she could. But it also turned her on, and she wondered just how far he'd go to punish her for hurting him.

Bo shifted on the bed, coming up, his hand still wrapped in her hair. Her scalp stung. That's why tears were in her eyes again.

Damn him anyway for falling in love with her. She knew that's what it was that drove him. Felt the regret she couldn't return it deep inside her chest like a heavy knot threatening to choke her.

He tugged her head again then straddled her chest. "You're gonna take off the edge. 'Cause I have plans for your cunt that don't include shooting off too soon. *Open.*" The last word came out raw, rasping.

Shanna opened her mouth to ask him what the hell he was going to do about taking the edge off *her* lust, but he stuffed his cock into her mouth, muffling her complaint.

She shut her teeth to close him out, but he pinched her nose and she opened wider to gasp and drag air into her lungs. He shoved deeper into her mouth and pinched the sides of her jaws to keep her from biting down.

He may have control of her mouth, but he didn't have control over her glare, and she put every bit of anger and frustration and hurt into the look she speared him with, but Bo only smiled. Not a happy smile, no. But she felt the satisfaction rolling off him as he dominated her, forcing her to his will.

He leaned a hand against the headboard and bent over her, angling her head to drive his cock deeper.

Stuffed full of musky cock, her dry mouth moistened and she swallowed, then groaned, because she couldn't help rolling her tongue over the side of his shaft, suctioning harder to pull him deeper. Her pussy clamped hard, the hot ache growing until she knew she'd splinter into a thousand pieces if he ever let her come.

In the meantime, her eyes grew drowsy as she pulled and sucked, strangely comforted by the steady motion, appeased by the fullness sliding into her, the scent of his arousal and sweat, the sight of his hard belly flexing, filling her senses.

Tears leaked again, but this time they were in gratitude. He'd taken away her choice, not allowed her to reject him again, given her something precious to savor.

When his motions quickened, she moaned around him, suctioned with a little more desperation, wanting his come to bathe her throat, to nourish her soul.

Scalding spurts hit the back of her throat and she gave a muffled shout and swallowed again and again, until he quivered over her. His cock lessened. And then the caresses she gave him with her tongue and lips were meant to soothe, to thank him for the gift.

The bindings around her wrists loosened, but she didn't move, not until Bo pulled free of her mouth and scooted down, freeing her feet and then taking her into his arms. She raised her own arms, ignoring the tingling pain as blood rushed back. But she didn't care. She snuggled deep against his chest, pressed kisses against his collarbone and the corner of his neck.

He rocked her against him. Crooning words she couldn't understand, because she wasn't listening with her ears. She felt his heart beat beneath her cheek, the rhythm strong and comforting.

She didn't want the moment to end, for anything to intrude, but hands, not his, turned her onto her side. Latex snapped. Bo slipped away after pressing a kiss against her forehead.

A long male body eased up against her back.

Ezra lay down on his side in front of her. He smoothed a hand over her waist. "You okay?" he asked, his deep voice rumbling.

She nodded and gave him a small smile.

He blinked, his gaze dipping to her mouth. "I think that's the first honest smile I've gotten from you."

She knew what he meant. She felt fresh. New. Strangely innocent.

Ezra kissed her nose then took her mouth. A gentle rub of lips that left her breathless but reassured.

A nose nuzzled her ear. "Was Bo good to you?" Josh's voice, deep but a little anxious, tickled the side of her face.

"Bo loves me." She didn't know who was more surprised. She hadn't known that was going to come out of her mouth, but the soft chuckle that ruffled her hair, and Ezra's approving smile warmed her, seemed to put the stamp on the sentiment. Made it real and made her sure she'd meant it.

Ezra moved closer, and his long, thick cock pressed against her belly.

She waited patiently for him to tell her what he wanted.

When he guided her thigh over his hip and nudged between her folds, she sighed, although each gentle shove upwards stretched and burned. But she was wet. Soaked, really. Readied for this moment. A gel-covered finger circled her anus and she tightened her thigh on Ezra's hip.

"Relax," he whispered against her mouth. "It's going to be okay. I promise. We won't push you past what you can take. Not again."

She believed the solemn promise of his gaze and took a deep breath, trusting Josh as he stretched her, easing the tight muscles to accept two fingers then the soft, blunt cap of his cock.

Shanna mewled as he pushed, gently pulsing his cock against her, until at last, he eased inside her.

Air whistled between his teeth, and the arm he snaked around her chest held her tightly as his whole body shuddered. "Damn, you're tight," he whispered. *"Fuck."*

A breathy laugh escaped her, and she gave Ezra a heavy-lidded look, tilting back her head to seek a kiss which he pressed softly against her mouth. Then the men began to move in tandem. Easing slowly in and out. Time lengthened, measured by the easy back-and-forth rocking, like a pendulum set in motion, its soaring arc shortening with each stroke until the opposing forces halted.

Mute, breathless, Shanna allowed the men to shift her over Ezra. She snuggled her knees against his sides and leaned down, her nipples tangling in his chest hair, her bottom tilting slightly to accept the heavier jolts that rocked her ass, moving her forward and back on Ezra's cock while he kissed her, murmuring nonsense against her mouth—telling her how beautiful, how perfect, how pure she was.

Shanna basked in his praise, believing him because his cock was strong inside her, his hands roaming restlessly.

Josh bent over her back, bit her shoulder to still her movements and unleashed a storm, thundering against her, driving deep, building a burning friction that had her gulping air as tension tightened in her core. She couldn't breathe, couldn't move, couldn't see because an explosion of sound and light had her screaming as she came.

Josh pulled away and left the bed while Ezra's hands gentled her. He rolled her onto her side then pulled free of her. Her complaint was cut short when another cock thrust into pussy her from behind. She hadn't felt Cade's presence, didn't even know it was him until his hands smoothed around her belly and tugged the hair on her mons.

He pressed a kiss against her sweaty shoulder. "Can you do it again, sweetheart? Can you come for me?"

Still gasping, still quivering in the aftermath of the enervating orgasm, she started to shake her head, but the fingers gliding over her clit tapped her there, reigniting the flame. She pushed her ass into his groin, deepening the connection.

Then Bo stretched out in front of her and brushed back her hair. Cade didn't halt his motions and she rocked gently forward and back, her face heating as Bo watched her expression.

His eyes were smoky, the skin pulled taut over hardened features. He pressed closer, lifted her thigh and placed it over his hip. His cock dug into her belly and he leaned into her, kissing her hard. "You're gonna take us both, baby. I can't wait." He gripped his cock and looked down between their bodies, pulling her gaze with him.

Cade pulled out and slid the tip of his cock between her lips, letting them both see him there, then dipping an inch or two inside her again.

Bo stroked his cock, root to tip, then funneled it through his fingers while Cade reached around her and pulled her labia apart and up, widening her opening for Bo to insert his tapered cock and glide it along the top of his.

Cade cursed softly as their cocks crowded into her. His hand squeezed her breast and he snuggled closer to her back, his cheek gliding on her shoulder. "Up to you, buddy," he rasped.

Bo gave her an openedmouthed kiss, rubbing his lips over hers then drawing away. "Can you take it, Shan?"

"Fuck," she whispered.

"It's what we wanna do. Can you take it?" He kissed her again, this time touching his tongue to hers and pushing inside her mouth.

She sucked on it, pulling it hard, her lips closing as tightly around it as her pussy was clasping their cocks. Breathing hard, she pulled back, resting her forehead against his. "Fuck me, Bo. Fuck us both."

He gave a quick, tight grin, then clamped a hand on her hip, undulating his body, scooping his hips to push upward, driving hard against Cade, working them both inside her.

"No, no, no," she groaned, sure the two men would split her in two. Her pussy burned—so much pressure, so full. But then they were both stuffed deep inside, barely moving, their cocks pulsing in unison. The tightness was its own sweet torture, causing every part of her body to quiver and burn. She shivered between the two men, her breasts hardening painfully, her skin heating, sweating until her jagged breaths caused her nipples and her belly to stir in the moisture pooling between her and Bo.

"I want to move, baby. Cade, how 'bout you?"

Cade hissed breath between his teeth. "Shit, Bo. Have to do it together. Balls so fucking hard they'll burst."

"No, no, no," she chanted, clutching his shoulders and holding as still as she could because the last time she'd been this taut with arousal, she'd exploded, lost herself in a sensual haze. She didn't know if she could go there again, this soon. "It's not fair," she whispered. "You have all the control."

"Why does it matter?" Bo asked, his voice even, his expression carefully neutral.

"You think it doesn't?"

"I do, but I want to know why you think it matters."

She screwed her face into a grimace as her body fought her, beginning to convulse. "How can you talk?"

"By biting the inside of my mouth, baby." He bit her chin. "Tell me why."

"It's not fair because you're changing me. Capturing me."

Bo groaned and his fingers bit into her hips. "Cade, now!"

The men growled and moved in unison, pushing in and out, moving only a couple of inches, but the pressure made the friction quicken, the orgasm inescapable.

Shanna shattered into a million pieces, her moans lengthening, words spilling out in sobbing gasps, thoughts she couldn't hold, as her whole body convulsed.

Bo drove deep, raking over Cade's cock, cramming them both deeper, and she was lost, her pussy awash in cream churned to a thick, wet cascade that spilled across her thighs and trickled down her hip to the bed.

Shanna noted the sensations, but felt apart from herself, cocooned for a moment before her vision narrowed and she slipped away.

She awoke to find herself wrapped tightly against Bo's chest, his hands chafing her skin. "Baby, wake up. Shanna, baby, breathe."

She groaned loudly, the sound reverberating in her head.

"Shhhh... It's okay. It's okay."

"Stop," she mumbled.

"We did, sweetheart." He kissed her temple. One hand cupped the back of her head, and the other clamped around her back to hold her against his chest.

"Passed out?" she said, her voice scratchy and sore.

"You're safe. I've got you."

A sob racked her and she burrowed deeper against his chest.

"Baby, I'm so sorry. I didn't mean to hurt you. Swear, I didn't."

She shook her head. "Didn't. Love you."

"I know. I know. You never promised a thing. I shouldn't have expected it."

"No," she blurted, trying to get her hands between them, but he was holding her so tight. She strained her neck to look into his face. "I love you."

Bo grew still, his gaze boring into hers, green eyes blazing. His chest billowed around a deep breath. "Shanna, if you give me half a chance, I'll make all your dreams come true."

"This is where we leave you." Ezra's voice sounded far away, already moving toward the door. Footsteps padded, the door closed, the lock making a quiet snick of a sound.

The air cooled the sweat on her back, and she shifted, uncomfortable now that she'd said it. Hoping he hadn't changed his mind. "I didn't want to love you."

His snort sounded so normal, so "Bo", that she relaxed against him, letting the heavy thud of his heart quiet hers.

"I'm goin' with you," he said.

"Goin' where?" she said sleepily.

"Away. Wherever you want."

"But what about your job? You're up for foreman when Jed retires. You've worked hard for it."

"I can find something else. Who says I have to ranch?"

"You'd do that for me?"

"I'd do anything for you, Shanna Davies. I'd die for you. I'd marry you."

She wrinkled her nose. "Don't know whether to melt or laugh. Is marrying me gonna kill you?"

Bo snorted again. The hand cupping the back of her head pushed her face against his shoulder. He rolled to his back, taking her with him.

Shanna stretched out on top of him. "Was that a proposal?"

"I didn't do it right?"

"I'm not letting you take it back. But a husband has to be able to provide for a wife and family. I don't think I can let you quit."

His fingers tugged her hair, pulling to raise her face. He was frowning, his brows drawn into a straight, fierce line. "I'm not doing a long-distance thing. You're gonna sleep in my bed every goddamn night."

"Don't get huffy, cowboy." She bit her lip, and then locked her gaze with his. "I'm just sayin'...maybe we could stay here."

His scowl eased. "Thought you were all hell-bent to blow this town."

"I don't reckon I give a damn now what anyone thinks. Not when you think I'm good enough to be your wife."

Bo watched a beaming smile slide across Shanna's lovely mouth. She was a hot mess. Her hair in tangles and sticking to her face and shoulders. Her skin was shiny with sweat. Fatigue darkened the delicate half-circles beneath her soft brown eyes.

He bracketed her face with his palms, feeling like his heart would explode inside his chest because he'd held the hope for so long and finally, at last, she'd be his. Bo lifted his head and kissed her, the backs of his eyes stinging as he stroked into her mouth.

Her knees cupped his hips, opening her sex to rub against him. Her breasts were mashed against his chest. She pressed as close as she could get—without crawling right inside him. He recognized the sentiment, returned it a thousand-fold.

His cock filled again, pushing into her slowly, rousing as she began to rock gently, encouraging his invasion with sexy dips and swirls until he was fully embedded.

"Think they have their ear to the door?" he whispered.

"Bet Josh does," she drawled, then groaned. "God, I don't know how I'm gonna face them. The things I said to them."

"They're good guys, Shanna. They won't make you feel like a wh—"

She kissed his mouth hard, bumping against his teeth. "I'm not my mama. I hated her for being easy and embarrassing me, but I loved her too."

"I know, baby."

"Just because I like you to challenge me, to take charge now and then, won't mean I'm bored with you, or want another lover."

Bo nodded again, letting her make her intimate vows.

"I'll be a good wife," she said, her eyes sparkling with unshed tears.

Bo smiled and dug his hands into her hair, loving the warmth that wrapped around his fingers. He was surrounded by her loving heat. "I'll be the best husband. I swear to you, Shanna, you'll never regret being mine."

Josh eased his ear from the door, a small smile curving his lips. He tiptoed back to the kitchen where the brothers gathered to prepare a meal for everyone, sure the two lovers tucked into Ezra's bed would be starving the moment they came up for air.

Josh rubbed his belly. "Feels hollow."

Cade handed him a roast beef sandwich. "They doin' okay?"

Josh waggled his eyebrows. "I think we're gonna be best men."

Ezra snorted. "Then it was worth it."

"Tell me you didn't enjoy that," Josh said, eyeing his too-serious brother.

"Makes it hard to wait," Ezra ground out.

Cade nodded. "Yeah, think she'll ever let her guard down again?"

Josh leaned against the butcher block. "Didn't you learn anything from tonight?"

His brothers eyed him like he'd grown a second head. "So I'm not the smartest one, but Shanna just proved something. You can't back away from love. It won't come to you. You have to crowd against it, push it. Push *her*. Maybe scare her a little too."

"We did plenty of scaring. She hasn't spoken to us in seven damn years," Ezra said, his voice raw.

Josh shrugged. "She didn't press charges. We didn't leave a bruise on her she didn't beg for. She needs remindin' who owns her ass."

Ezra and Cade shared tense glances then turned back to Josh.

"If we try and fail," Ezra said, his voice still tight, "we move on. Find our own women."

Cade nodded. "She's worth the wait, but I agree. We have our whole lives ahead of us. I for one don't want to spend it without a woman in my bed."

Josh nodded slowly. "Since we're in agreement, we should make a plan."

The brothers migrated to the kitchen table. Beer bottles slammed on the table as they plotted.

In the end, all their hopes fell on Ezra, the one Chrissi Page had surrendered to the first time.

Breaking Leather

Dedication

To me. I need a medal for not self-combusting during the writing of this novel. ☺

Chapter One

Chrissi Page raised her cell phone in the air, staring at the screen. No bars. Not even a hint of one skinny, green nub. "Oh, come on," she moaned as her radiator hissed behind her. "Damn, damn, damn."

She'd been tempted to ignore the CHECK ENGINE light when it first appeared, wanting to take the chance she could limp back into Two Mule. However, the steam seeping from under the hood had pretty much killed that hope.

Today was not the day for her car to break down. Not so far from town. Not so close to *their* ranch. Any minute now one of the Kinzie brothers might happen by.

They'd stop because they'd never leave a woman stranded.

They might not let her go because of their shared past.

And she didn't know if she had the strength anymore to fight fate or her own inexplicable needs.

Macy Pettigrew, her best friend and boss, had sent her to the Dunstan house to make sure the owners had followed her suggestions to increase the house's curb appeal. Never mind that there wasn't a curb. Not really even a road—more of a caliche-covered goat trail that meandered up a steep hillside, rutted from runoff during recent summer storms.

Something must have happened to her car on the run up that hill. She'd heard the rocks pinging against her undercarriage but had been too busy thinking about Ms. Dunstan's handsome neighbors. She'd been afraid she'd pass them or that they might stop in to see old Lettie Dunstan, the widow selling off her roughhewn, century-old home.

Chrissi had forced a smile on her face, looked at the potted plants the old woman had placed in pretty window boxes and admired the paint she'd used to spruce up the weathered door and window frames. The junk the old woman's husband had accumulated, and that she hadn't had the heart to part with after his passing, was gone from the front lawn. And lo and behold, grass was beginning to grow to fill in the brown patches where engines and tires had lain.

Macy would be pleased. They had a potential buyer. One who'd relayed an offer via email, which had checked out with the mortgage lender. Details Macy had been eager to handle herself, leaving the showings to Chrissi.

Chrissi heard a powerful engine rev. She slowly lowered her arm and glanced nervously over her shoulder. A metallic sage pickup truck pulled off the road behind her, and her stomach dropped to her toes. She'd known the moment her CHECK ENGINE light had shone that this was going to happen.

And good Lord, it had to be Ezra Kinzie. His dark gaze narrowed on her through the windshield, the intensity of it feeling like the hissing heat of a brand against her skin.

He opened his door and stepped down, slamming it with a decisive shove. Everything Ezra did was deliberate. He never wavered once a decision was made.

Long ago, he'd decided he wasn't going to fight his brothers for her. If she wasn't going to decide among them, then she'd have to take them all.

And, Lord help her, she had.

She'd never gotten over that night, had never been able to push it to the farthest corner of her mind when she lay down to sleep. Just the memory of it made her hot, cold, *wet...*

And horribly ashamed. Anyone could have seen them beneath the bleachers at the homecoming game. Gossip hadn't followed, but that didn't make her any less self-conscious when she strode down the sidewalk on Main Street.

Someone might know. Someone might tell. The thought of that sordid night being revealed left her feeling nauseated. Her life had been circumspect ever since, her love life nonexistent.

They'd left her scarred. Unable to move on.

Not because they'd harmed her physically, but because she hadn't been able to shake off the terrible attraction that tempted her every single day since that fateful night.

Boots crunched on the gravel at the side of the road. The brim of Ezra's straw cowboy hat left his ice-blue eyes in shadow.

She straightened away from her car and squared her shoulders.

"Havin' trouble, Chrissi?"

"It just showed up," she said under her breath, determined not to let him see how flustered she felt.

One side of his mouth quirked up. He glanced up at the sky, squinting against the bright Texas sun before leveling that devastating stare on her again.

Her belly clenched, and she fought hard not to give him any clues about how he still affected her. Just the rumble of his deep voice always made her think of crisp, cool sheets and hot, slick skin.

Her glance flicked over his body-hugging dark tee, noted his well-developed chest, the bulge of his biceps, his taut abdomen. She started to sweat. "Will you call a tow truck for me when you get home?"

A frown dug a deep crease between his dark brows. "Get in my truck, Chrissi. I'm not leavin' you on the side of the road."

"I'm not goin' anywhere with you, Ezra Kinzie," she said tightly.

A muscle rippled alongside his jaw. "I'm just offerin' you a place to wait out of the sun. And a cool drink. Nothin' more."

His features were stern, his jaw rigid, but the heat blazing from his eyes mesmerized her, made her want to sway toward him. The intensity of that unblinking stare made her wish he'd take the decision right out of her hands. She'd never willingly take that first step. Her days of following his commands were over.

Chrissi swallowed hard and broke from his glance, looking down the road and praying someone else would appear over the crest of the hill. She needed rescuing from the deep emotions roiling inside her—from the temptation his large, hard frame embodied. However, only the shimmer of heat waves rose off the black tar.

A trickle of moisture dripped between her breasts, gliding along one curve—and just like that, her imagination replaced the slide of that hot little bead with the tip of his tongue. She turned away from him and dragged in a couple of deep breaths, trying to stiffen her resolve, but the only things hardening were the tips of her breasts. She crossed her arms over her chest and lifted her chin, then turned to aim a glare at the one man who had the power to make her knees quiver.

So many memories swamped her as she stared into his handsome, rugged face. So many regrets sat like soured milk in her gut. He'd been "the one" until she'd succumbed to a dark sensual greed.

Too bad she couldn't turn back the clock about seven years. She'd make damn sure she'd never let him take her hand and pull her into the shadows.

Ezra barely suppressed the urge to step closer and crowd her tall, lithe body against her car. He'd love nothing better than to snug his dick between her legs while he licked that trickle of sweat tracking down her chest, and then follow the curve of her sweet, round breast.

But he and his brothers had planned this abduction down to the last detail. No time now to let a hard-on get in the way. "I'm not leavin' you on the side of the road. It's a hundred damn degrees out here, sweetheart. Get in the truck."

"Don't call me sweetheart," she said, sounding a little breathless.

It did his ego good to know she wasn't unaffected. This was the closest they'd stood in seven years. Since he'd kissed her before letting her head to the girls' restroom to clean up after he and his brothers had her.

A sordid little chapter he was determined to remedy. If he could get her ass inside his truck.

However, Chrissi, stubborn as ever, jutted her chin high and crossed her arms over her chest. Did she know she was plumping up her breasts, drawing his gaze to the creamy tops? Her clothing stuck to the sweat coating her skin. Her light blouse skimmed close to her narrow waist. Her dark blue trousers pulled tightly as she braced apart her legs. Did she know how well they cupped her pussy?

Just that hint of a cleft was enough to add a spike of steel to his already raging erection.

"Maybe you'd let me use your cell phone?" she ground out.

Ezra let a hint of a smile curve the corners of his mouth. One thing he'd learned over the years was the value of patience. He'd waited a long time to be where he was, standing in front of the one woman who had the power to make his knees buckle. The one woman he'd gladly share if that was the only way he could have her.

"Chrissi, don't you think we've waited long enough?" he asked quietly.

Her breath caught, lifting her chest. "I've waited long enough for you to act the gentleman and do what I asked. I'll walk back to town." She dropped her arms, reached through her car window for her purse, then straightened.

She'd have to stride around him, and he guessed she was girding herself to do just that. Her gaze didn't rise above his shoulder. She sucked in a deep breath and gave him a wide berth as she brushed past.

Ezra let her go, easing a hip against her red Mustang and watching her walk away—on three-inch heels that stuck to the hot tar, making a sticky sound with each step she took. She made it only about ten feet past the end of his truck before she slowed.

Her shoulders fell, her head turned to the side, but not quite far enough for her to meet his gaze. "You're not gonna let me go, are you?" she asked softly.

Her profile, so pure and pretty, stirred a suffocating desire inside him. He steeled himself to pretend a strength he was far from feeling. So many hopes rode on the next few minutes.

"I'm just givin' you a few moments to make up your mind, sweetheart. I have every confidence you'll do the smart thing."

"Just a ride to your place to make a call?"

"And a cool drink. Whatever else happens will be up to you. I've always let you make your own choices. Even when you were dead wrong. Even when it was killin' me."

And even though she still hadn't moved, he straightened away from her car and walked to the passenger door of his truck. He opened the door and waited.

Chrissi turned her head toward the road, and Ezra held his breath, praying another vehicle wouldn't come along, praying he'd have the strength to do what had to be done, no matter how much she might beg him to end it later.

When she faced him, he couldn't read her expression. Her mouth was firmed into a thin line. Her chin tilted. Her brown eyes raked him up and down, and she stepped out, her body moving fluidly, hips swaying. Not a conscious invitation, but he knew if he touched her between her legs right this minute, she'd be wet.

He fought a smile of satisfaction as she walked toward him and stepped up into his cab. Before he closed the door, she laid a hand on his bare arm.

Was she reconsidering? He stared down at her short, peach-colored nails and slender, ringless fingers.

"I'm not stayin' any longer than it takes to make that call." Her fingers tightened on him, and then slowly dragged away.

That touch had felt like a caress. Like she couldn't resist the urge to test the muscle beneath his hot skin.

She turned to stare out the front windshield, her purse in her lap. Her hands crimped around the leather as though she might use the bag to defend herself.

He slammed her door closed and loped around the front of the truck, slid into the seat beside her and started the engine. As soon as it roared to life, he turned the AC knob to full. "That better?" he asked softly.

"Dammit, don't be nice."

Fuck, the last thing he felt was *nice*. He gripped the gearstick and slammed the truck into first, then a quick second and third, roaring down the highway toward the ranch. Chrissi Page sat in the seat next to him. He'd gotten her this far. Unless she wanted to eat pavement, he wasn't slowing to let her out until he had her at his home.

Aware of every little movement, every little sigh or nervous twitch, he watched her from the corner of his eye. He'd seen her from time to time over the years, but hadn't been this close.

She'd aged well. Time had trimmed the youthful roundness of her cheeks and honed the stubborn jut of her chin. Her dark eyes, her best feature as far as he was concerned, still held the wary innocence of a fawn. However, tension etched fine lines at the corners.

He'd always loved her eyes, loved the way her stare would follow him around the hallways at high school or while she sat atop a corral fence when he worked with a horse. He'd never felt uncomfortable, had warmed to her approval. In those days, all it had taken was a shy glance or a little half-smile to brighten his day. She'd trusted him then.

He wished she'd trusted herself as much.

The rest of her had matured just as well. Possessed of curves at an early age that could make a man weak at the knees, her body had only improved. High-set, rounded breasts, a narrow waist and full hips. He'd often caught a glimpse of her ass, twitching beneath her conservative clothing—round, plump, peach-shaped curves that were Cade's favorite feature.

And her legs... Josh had long ago decided hers were perfect. Long, slim, and beautifully curved at the calf and inner thigh.

Yeah, they each had their favorite Chrissi-part, one they wanted to claim for their own. Too bad she'd thought their attention was something dirty.

She was nervous. He could tell that from the way her fingers clenched her purse and then played with a wisp of dark brown hair that defied the clasp holding up the rest. And she should be wary. If she had any idea what lengths they'd gone to in order to engineer this rescue she'd have them all up on charges.

As it was, they might still wind up in jail if the plans they'd made ever came to light. They wanted this weekend to happen naturally, but they hadn't left anything to chance. Opportunity was there. She only had to have the courage to surrender.

"How have you been keepin'?" he asked, wanting to break the brittle tension.

"Fine. Yourself?"

Ezra clamped his fingers around the steering wheel, hating the tenor of her voice. It was a little high and strained, like she was afraid. "Been busy. We've had to move the cattle more than usual. Grass is dried up. We've shipped in hay from as far away as Iowa to keep 'em fed."

"Sorry about that. Everyone seems to be having similar issues."

Dammit, they sounded like a couple of strangers. "Still workin' for Macy Pettigrew?" he asked, although he knew damn well she was. He'd been in close communication with Macy, tendering the private offer for the Dunstan property.

Macy thought she was helping Ezra with a love connection. The fact there were three interested bachelors hadn't been mentioned.

"Yes. Three years now. Right after I got my realtor's license."

"Thought you wanted to be a teacher." Actually, she'd wanted to teach until she married, and then become a full-time mom, but he thought better of mentioning that.

Her mouth tightened. "I took business in college."

Had they been responsible for her change of heart? "Must be good at what you do."

"Why do you say that?"

"You've lasted. Macy's a bit of a shark."

"She's a pussycat if you're not afraid of a little hard work."

"I'll take your word on that."

The ranch's high arched gate loomed. Letting out a relieved breath that he'd gotten her this far, he turned off the highway onto the dusty gravel road that led through the gate. They bumped over the cattle guard grating, and he slowed as he approached the house. In the distance, he saw Josh, bent over his horse and riding at full tilt—coming from the direction of the Dunstan property line. Ezra almost smiled, except he caught Chrissi's expression as she watched Josh.

The longing in her dark eyes, and the way her mouth parted around her quickening breaths, had jealousy streaking through him. She hadn't reacted that way to him. She hadn't gone all soft and dewy. She'd turned up her nose and stiffened her back.

Ezra tamped down his sudden anger. He and his brothers had entered a pact. If one of them earned an advantage, they'd use it to help the others in this battle for her heart. They'd all thought he'd be the one to punch through her reserve. He'd been her first boyfriend. He'd been her first lover and the one who'd tempted her into sharing.

Maybe that was the problem. Chrissi blamed him for her fall from grace.

Chapter Two

Josh Kinzie watched the truck drive along the last hundred yards of gravel road before bumping over a cattle guard and into the fenced yard. He made out two figures in the cab—the bear-like figure of his brother and a slender, dark-haired feminine one sitting beside him.

Ezra had done it. Gotten Chrissi into the truck. With a little help from him. While Chrissi had been busy with Ms. Dunstan, he'd been busy making sure her radiator hose sprang a leak.

He pulled the reins to the right, whipping his horse around, and let out a loud "Yee-haw!" before racing toward the house. He pulled back when he neared the front porch and slid from the saddle to the ground in one fluid glide.

Cade sat on the top step, squinting against the sun as he watched the truck come to a stop. "We may still hit a snag, bro."

Josh glanced back at the truck. The couple inside appeared to be arguing.

"Not a good sign if he can't even get her out of the truck," Cade muttered.

Josh snorted, not too worried. He remembered how Ezra and Chrissi bumped heads in the old days. "Ezra may not be one for sweet-talk, but he does have a way of makin' the ladies do exactly what he wants. Eventually."

Cade grunted. "Chrissi's grown a metal-plated backbone."

"Our girl's all grown up."

They shared a glance, but turned to the sound of a door slamming.

Ezra crammed his cowboy hat on his head and walked around the truck, his features stern and his jaw grinding.

The sound of a click made Josh choke down a bark of laughter. "Did she just lock him out of his own truck?"

Cade grinned. "Won't do her any good. Though I think he's only givin' her a chance to behave. He's got the keys in his hand."

"Still, she's playin' with fire." Everyone knew you didn't defy Ezra Kinzie and expect to come out unscathed.

The two younger brothers watched, amusement growing, as Ezra cussed softly and tried the handle again.

"Chrissi," Ezra said, his voice deepening in warning, "thought you wanted to use that phone."

Even through the windshield, Josh could see the stubborn tilt of her chin.

Dark humor glinted in Chrissi's eyes. "I'm thinkin' I'd be better off usin' your truck to get back to town all by myself."

Ezra held up the keys. "Woman, how do you plan on doin' that? Do you know how to hot-wire a truck?" He tugged off his hat and raked a hand through his short, dark hair. "You were fine a minute ago. What the hell changed?"

Through the windshield, her gaze shifted to the two men on the porch and held.

Josh cussed under his breath.

Cade stood and brushed off his jeans. "Guess it might help if we made ourselves scarce for a couple o' minutes."

Josh grabbed up his horse's reins and spared one last look at Chrissi.

Her gaze met his, and her eyebrows furrowed into a fierce scowl. He tipped his hat to her and ambled toward the barn. Not looking back once.

It was hard pretending he was relaxed and indifferent to her anger. While she'd blatantly ignored Ezra and Cade over the years, she hadn't been quite as harsh with him, giving him the occasional subtle nod or tight smile.

He'd thought maybe she didn't hold as deep a grudge against him because he'd always been the one eager to soothe her bruised feelings, the one to coax a smile when things got out of hand with Ezra. And everyone always thought of him as the little brother, even though he and Cade had been born only minutes apart. That fact afforded him a little extra leniency with the ladies.

Josh cupped himself, readjusting his cock. Yeah, relaxed was the last thing he'd felt for days since they'd hatched this wild-ass plan. He tugged on the reins, pulling his trembling horse behind him. Sooner he turned him over to one of the ranch hands to walk, the better.

He didn't like leaving everything in Ezra's capable hands when Chrissi was on a tear—even though Ezra had always been the one who could bend a woman to his will, usually with just a look.

Josh ignored a pang of worry over the fact his brother's naturally dominating will didn't appear to be working at the moment. Chrissi was here. Within reach. One of them would shatter the armor she'd built around her heart.

Chrissi watched Josh lead away his tall roan gelding and breathed a sigh of relief. She'd thought her worst fears had already been realized when Ezra arrived to rescue her. Seeing Josh and Cade, in close proximity to Ezra, had sent her body into apoplectic shock, stirring up all those old memories.

Foremost in her mind, she remembered skinny-dipping in the river with them. Innocent enough since Ezra was her boyfriend and had approved. And how could she resist when the three brothers had eagerly shed their clothes?

Sweet Jesus, the three of them, so alike and yet so different... She'd gotten love-drunk on the sight of them.

Ezra, older by only a year than the other two, had always seemed so much more mature. His body even then had been broad and sturdy—ripped from his shoulders to his calves. His size and strength had always made her feel safe, except during sex—but then his largeness and sexual intensity thrilled her, frightened her almost, she'd wanted him that badly.

Cade had been the quiet one. The nice one. Always courteous, always respectful, but his slow smile, so seldom seen, had had the power to melt her to her toes. And although the most reserved of the three, the memory of being held inside the circle of his strong arms whenever she'd suffered a fright was a cherished one.

And Josh, dear God, Josh was the golden child. Blond where the other two were dark-haired, his tall, lean body and the wicked glint in his crystal blue eyes, as though he was always ready for an adventure, had never failed to make her hot. How many times had she smoothed her thumb over that dimple in the center of his chin and warned him not to break a woman's heart? Why hadn't she taken her own damn advice?

That day by the river, the sight of their tall, tanned bodies, lined up prettier than any Chippendales' review, had sucked the air right out of her lungs.

She hadn't been as eager to get naked, feeling a little insecure among so much perfection, but they'd teased her, joking with each other, jostling and shoving until she'd laughed at their antics and joined them.

Even then she'd felt their combined illicit allure. Her nipples had prickled, her sex had tightened—but she'd been relieved to know she wasn't the only one affected as each of the boys' cocks had hardened.

They'd laughed, as though it was the most natural thing in the world to watch each other get hard. Her stare had lingered as she assessed their size, the slight upward curve of their shafts, the ruddy tan color that gave way to a reddish-purple at their fat, round crowns. When they'd grown silent, she'd dared an upward glance.

Ezra's steamy blue gaze had locked with hers. "Not anything to be ashamed of, Chrissi. We're guys. It's what happens when we're around a pretty girl. Only you can't always see it when we're dressed."

She'd thought about that often, wondering how many men walked around with hard-ons inspired by a stray glimpse of an attractive woman. Not something she wanted to think about, considering she'd been living like a nun for a very long time.

"Open the door," Ezra repeated, his voice sounding as rough as gravel. She shivered at the quiet intensity of his order. Even after all this time, she wanted to do exactly what he asked. However, she knew where her submission would lead.

She folded her arms over her chest and looked away.

The locks sprung. The door slammed open. Startled, she glanced up, but Ezra already had her wrist inside his hand and was pulling her from the seat.

She slid to the ground, stumbled against him, and felt that rock-hard chest she'd sighed over for years. Resisting the temptation to explore, she shoved away.

"You always this stubborn?" he bit out.

She tossed back her head. "Guess you don't know me as well as you thought."

"I know more than you think, Chrissi."

She arched an eyebrow. "You don't know me. You haven't for a very long time."

"I know you're wet."

Her jaw sagged.

He turned on his heel and walked away.

"Am not," she whispered furiously. She turned to pick up her purse where it had fallen from her lap to the dirt and closed the cab door. Then, stiffening her backbone, she strode toward the porch.

The screen door slammed behind him as he walked inside without giving her a backward glance. She hated it when he did that, pretended his mama hadn't taught him any manners, because she knew it was deliberate. Something he did when she disobeyed him. A punishment.

And he knew she liked punishment.

She gave a silent moan and climbed the steps. The sooner she placed that call the better. Already she felt some of her carefully erected reserve crumbling away beneath the liquid heat her proximity to Kinzie testosterone generated.

Entering the house, she noted that not much had changed since Mr. and Mrs. Kinzie had moved to Padre Island to enjoy their retirement. That had happened after Cade and Josh graduated; Ezra had already been in charge for a couple of years.

And word was that Ezra was a capable rancher. Fair to his employees and as hard-working as any hand. So were Josh and Cade, although Josh liked his playtime.

She'd heard about his exploits, all the women he'd been through. Gossip about the other two had been harder to glean, but she knew they hadn't been celibate for long after she'd departed their lives.

Even though it had been her decision, she'd still been hurt. She'd nursed an aching heart for a very long time. However, she knew she'd done the right thing. There wasn't anywhere their relationship could go but straight to hell.

She glanced around, looking for a phone, but her attention was caught by the warmth of familiar surroundings. Wooden floors, yellow walls, brown leather sofas and Indian rugs were cozy and inviting, even if the tall, vaulted ceiling and huge iron chandelier hinted at their wealth. The Kinzies didn't act like boys who'd been born with silver spoons in their mouths. They'd been raised to work hard. Something she'd liked about them from the start. Raised by a single mom on a tight budget, she hadn't let her head be turned by their wealth.

"It's nice seein' you here again."

She turned to find Josh right behind her. How had he gotten here so quickly? He was a big man, as tall as his brothers if a little leaner, but he moved with a pantherish grace. "You still like sneakin' up on women, I see."

His lopsided grin made her heart do a flip-flop. The dimple in the center of his chin kept him from being too beautiful, and lent him a roguish appeal. She'd never been able to hold a grudge against him. His boyish charm was infectious and got him out of all sorts of scrapes.

"I didn't sneak up on you. You seemed lost in thought. You remembering us?"

"Remembering what?" she deadpanned.

He arched an eyebrow. "Remember who you're talkin' to, missy. I knew all your secrets."

Including one big fat secret that had spelled the end of all her dreams. "And you blabbed them to your brothers. You shouldn't have told, Josh."

"I am truly sorry about that. It wasn't the time. I know that now."

"There was never a right time for what we did," she whispered harshly. She glanced blindly around, looking for a telephone. "Dammit, I don't want to talk about it. I just want to use your phone."

Josh's gaze slid away, and he rubbed the back of his neck. "Well, there's gonna be a slight problem with that…"

She swung back. "What do you mean?"

"I mean, Ezra removed all the phones from the house."

"What?"

Josh reached behind him and pulled something from his pocket. When he held up a screwdriver, he gave her a sheepish shrug. "I was in charge of disablin' your car."

Her eyes widened, and her heart began to thump hard inside her chest. "And Cade?" she asked, her tightening throat. "What was his part?"

"Oh, Cade was in charge of gettin' the room ready for you."

"What the hell are you talking about?"

"We're kidnappin' you, kitten." His grin was wide, joyous even.

She stared at him like he'd grown two heads. "Are you insane?" she shouted. "You'll be arrested!"

"Only if you press charges. We're hopin' you won't."

She shook her head, dumbfounded. Her face was hot, her stomach lurching. Hadn't this been exactly what she'd been afraid of? "I think I'm gonna be sick."

His grin vanished. "Through here," he said, grabbing her hand and pulling her toward the bathroom just off the entrance.

Chrissi accepted the push of his hand at the back of her neck, bending over the bowl to empty her stomach. When she straightened, he handed her a moistened washcloth.

"Not the reaction we expected," he said quietly as she washed her hot face.

"What the hell did you expect?" she said, embarrassed and aiming a deadly glare his way.

Josh shrugged. "A lot of hollerin'."

"Ya think? Take me home."

He drew in a slow breath, all expression draining from his face. In place of his usual, affable smile, his tight features resembled Ezra's more than she would have believed. "I'm afraid I can't do that. We made a pact."

"A pact?" She knew she was echoing him, sounding stupid, but she still couldn't get her head around what was happening to her.

"All or nothin'," he said, nodding.

"All of what?"

"Us."

She didn't need it spelled out. She got his meaning in one hot second. "Then it's nothing," she croaked, her mouth drying instantly.

"We aren't acceptin' your answer. Not until Sunday. So don't even try to talk us out of it."

"You won't get away with this. When I don't show back up at the office—"

"Macy's in on it. She's not callin' the cops. She thinks Ezra's makin' a play to get you back. She thinks it's romantic."

"Macy doesn't have a heart. She'd never think a kidnappin' was romantic."

Josh's lips twitched. "They sent me to sweet-talk her."

"Bastard," she whispered, knowing exactly how Macy must have reacted. When Josh turned on the charm, there wasn't a woman who wouldn't melt. Even hardhearted Macy.

"You always said I had a silver tongue."

"But I bet it was your smile that did her in." She could have bit her lip for admitting that because his eyelids drifted down to give her a smoky glance.

"Does my smile bother you?"

"I'm immune."

"I don't believe you."

Yeah, she was a big, fat liar. She needed a little space to shore up those crumbling walls. "I have to pee."

He gave her a nod. "There's a new toothbrush in the drawer for you too. I'll be outside."

Listening? Like hell. "You don't have to hover over me. I'm not gonna throw up again."

"We aren't leavin' you alone this weekend. Not for a minute."

She shook her head, suddenly weary of thinking and of fighting the inevitable. "Why?"

"Because Ezra seems to think we bother you."

"Then wouldn't you want to bother me less?"

"Not that kind of bother. He thinks we still turn you on."

Chrissi felt ready to scream. Seven years, and they still read her like a book. "Ezra's an idiot. The only thing you three do is drive me crazy."

"Oh, I hope so, kitten."

She slammed the door in his face.

Cade sauntered up to Josh, who leaned against the wall next to the bathroom door. "How's she?"

"She threw up when I told what we'd done."

Cade grimaced. "Hell, do you think it's just food poisonin'?" Or could they really have frightened her so much she'd emptied her stomach? Cade didn't want to feel sorry for her. They had a plan they'd vowed to stick to no matter how pitiful she acted.

Josh grunted. "Think Ezra's right? That she makes a big show of avoidin' us because she never got over what happened?"

Cade glanced away and let out a deep breath. "Ezra knew her best. How about I take over now to reacquaint myself."

Josh gave him a quick smile. "Sounds like a good idea. She's a little perturbed with me at the moment. Where's Ezra?"

"Where do you think?"

"I might join him for a lap or two. Might relax me."

Cade watched Josh stride away to the pool, then leaned an ear against the door. He heard harsh mutters, a couple "dammits" and a "bastard". He felt a smile stretch his mouth. She couldn't be too scared if she was cussing rather than crying. The doorknob turned and he backed away, wiping his expression clear.

She glanced up, giving him a quick once-over before she met his gaze. "You the next shift?"

"I am," he said agreeably. "Thought I'd ask if you wanted a drink?"

"So you can loosen me up?"

"If you're afraid that's possible, I'll give you a soda."

Her eyes narrowed. "Only if I get to open the can."

"Are you afraid I'll slip something in your drink?" His lips twitched. "I think I'm almost insulted."

"You kidnapped me. I don't think there's much you wouldn't dare."

"Only when it comes to you, sugar."

Chrissi rolled her eyes. "Don't 'sugar' me. You are not gonna wear me down. I don't want to be here."

Cade ignored that last statement, taking heart from the fact her grumbling sounded halfhearted. "Would you like a drink? I'm havin' a beer. It's hot out there."

She let out a deep sigh, and he noticed the lines of tension around her lips. She looked tired.

"How about I promise that we won't make any moves. That we'll spend the evening just havin' a nice relaxing time. It'll be like old times, before..."

"Even if we wanted to, we can't go back." Her glance slid away, and her mouth twisted. "I missed us, you know. We were friends."

Cade barely resisted the urge to slide his hands around her and draw her close. If anyone needed a hug more, he'd never seen it. "You trusted us. We let you down."

"Yes, you did. But I should have had better sense too."

"See? We were young and stupid. We don't have to be enemies." When her expression eased, he gave her a small, coaxing half-smile. "Want a beer?" He held out his hand, holding his breath until she tentatively slid her palm inside his.

He'd always known he was attracted to her, that he'd yearned for her for years, but he hadn't really known how much he missed her until that precise moment. Her hand felt just right—small, slender, warm. He tightened his grip and gave her a guarded smile. Not enough to make her worry, he hoped.

He turned and pulled her behind him, like old times, drawing her deeper into the living room to the bar at the far wall. He opened the fridge and grabbed two Shiner Bocks, uncapped them and handed her a bottle. He held his up until she klinked her glass against it.

They both took a long draw from their bottles.

Her sigh when she set it down was louder than his. A faint smile tugged up one corner of her mouth. "It's been a long day. I needed that."

"Heard you were up at the Dunstan place," he said. "How's Lettie doin'?"

Her smile was tight, but it was a start. "Fine. She's eager to move in with her sister in town. They plan to go to bingo on Tuesdays and have pedicures every Friday." She gave a little laugh. "Don't get me wrong, I know she misses her husband, but she seems ready to move on."

"She deserves a little fun. Couldn't have been easy livin' out there, the two of them, for so long. Gets lonesome."

"Do you get lonesome?" Her lips pressed together. "Scratch that. It's none of my concern."

Cade leaned back against the bar, resting on his elbows, then gave her a waggle of his eyebrows. "Admit it. I'm gettin' to you."

She shook her head ruefully. "All three of you are *getting on my nerves*. I want to go home."

"And you will," he said, nodding. "Come Sunday—if you still want to."

Her face grew serious as she eyed him. "I don't believe you of all people went along with this."

"Because I'm so boring?"

"No, because you're the most honorable."

He remembered the biggest test of that honor—she did too by the shadow that crept across her face. He'd failed her, going along with his brothers. "There's not a day we don't regret what went down. The way it happened anyway. It was the wrong place."

"It was just plain wrong. Every part of it." She set her beer on the bar.

"I won't ever believe that."

"Why don't you all find some other girl to tag team," she bit out, an underlying tremor in her voice. "I'm sure there's a whore or two in town who'd be only too happy to oblige."

"That's what you think we made you?"

Her mouth trembled, the corners turning down, and she wrapped her own arms around herself. Giving herself the comfort he wished she'd let him offer.

Hoping to distract her from unpleasant memories, he pushed from the bar. "Day's nice. Let's head out to the patio and rest a spell."

She gave a vague nod, and followed him as he headed toward the French doors and the sounds of water lapping against the sides of the pool. Ezra would know how to reach her. She'd always trusted in his strength. No matter how bad things were now, he had to hope that deep down she knew she could lean on at least one of them.

Chrissi dragged her feet as she followed Cade to the pool. Another of those places that she'd just as soon forget. She remembered the time after Mr. Kinzie's heart attack, when the boys' parents had taken a vacation to reaffirm their gratitude to both be alive and together. Ezra had had a tough time, stepping into his dad's shoes, when the ranch hands and his brothers hadn't learned to respect an eighteen-year-old, no matter how big and smart he was.

She'd lived for the hours when he'd finished up working for the day. They'd escape to the pool, take a leisurely swim then lay naked in each other's arms on one of the loungers. It had been an unspoken thing between his brothers and him that those hours were his time, that no one was to interrupt.

She'd savored the attention and loved even better that he'd turned to her for comfort and escape from all his worries. She'd been deeply in love with him for years, but even though she'd been the only girl he dated, she hadn't been sure he returned the feelings, at least not to the degree she felt them.

Cade leaned against the boulder next to the pool, watching his brother skim below the surface, then turned his head to watch her.

Chrissi ignored him, glancing into the pool. Then she couldn't take her gaze from Ezra's honed body. She felt a moment's satisfaction knowing that he was bothered by what had passed between them on the road and inside his truck—that she'd driven him to this. Swimming was his release valve.

She wasn't surprised that he was nude. And right now, despite what she knew he wanted to have happen this weekend, it didn't feel like a gratuitous peep show. His powerful arms and thighs cut through the water, his face breaking the surface now and then for him to gulp for air. At the far end of the pool, he curled like the competitive swimmer he'd been and shot toward the opposite side again.

Chrissi watched him, her skin getting hotter, her belly cramping, not from any nausea but from desire so strong she knew she was past resisting.

She heard a scrape beside her, felt hands cup the notches of her hips and pull.

For all of a second, she resisted, and then she melted against Cade, her breath leaving in a long sigh. She didn't want to be this easy. But what was the point? "Cade?" she whispered, giving a little moan as he kissed her cheek, her temple.

"Yes, baby?" he said, gliding his hands over her belly, then up to cup her breasts through her clothing.

"Go away."

Chapter Three

As soon as Cade withdrew, she swayed, dizzying need swamping her. She caught herself, shivering, and wrapped her arms around herself for comfort as she watched Ezra turn and push off the side of the pool to return.

She couldn't help herself, she stared, her gaze roaming his tall frame, her mouth drying as his arms cut through the water, his powerful shoulders rippling with each slice.

The patio, partially shaded by trees and enclosed by a tall rock wall, had always seemed so cozy and safe. She inhaled the scent of chlorine, felt the slight breeze whispering through the oak trees waft against her hot face, and couldn't maintain her anger beneath the assault on all her senses.

This moment was inevitable. An itch that had to be scratched one last time before she could let go of the disappointment and yearning she'd harbored for all these years.

She slipped off her shoes and tugged her blouse from her trousers. She'd known where the day was leading from the first hiss of her radiator. Hell, she'd known she'd have to face up to this ever since she'd given Ezra the slip when he'd left her in the girls' bathroom after that fateful hook-up. She'd been running scared for a long, long time.

Ezra swam to the steps and stood at the bottom, water sluicing down his body. He wiped more water from his face and held her stare. "Baby, you sure about this? Are you really ready?"

The banked heat in his eyes, the tension revealed in the flex of his arms and chest muscles, set her heart fluttering. "Of course not," she rasped. "But I'm hot and bothered—by you, by your damn brothers. And I've had enough. We end this."

His ice-chip eyes darkened to a stormy gray. "That what you think this weekend is about? Ending it?"

"I don't care what you three think is supposed to happen." Not a lie, because she couldn't think of anything beyond the expanse of bronze skin, the crest of the cock rising from the water. "Right now, all I can think about is how much I ache," she said, her voice hoarse.

Chrissi unbuttoned her blouse and let it slide off her arms to whisper to the flagstones. She reached up and opened the clasp holding up her hair, and shook her head, enjoying the way the heavy fall trailed across the tops of her shoulders. Then she shimmied out of her trousers. When she stood in only her underwear, she stepped down into the pool, wading toward Ezra, whose hot glance raked her body, eliciting shivers that slid in ripples across her skin.

Standing in front of him, water lapping at her waist, she lifted her chin. "I don't want to make any decisions," she whispered. "I don't want to think at all."

Ezra nodded and slowly lifted a hand to grasp her arm and turn her. With her back to him, she breathed deeply while he unfastened her bra and drew it off, letting it float away in the water. Then his fingers slid beneath the band of elastic at her hips and pulled down her panties.

He walked around her, staring at everything he'd bared, then slowly lifted his glance to lock with hers. "You're prettier than I remembered."

"Was I so homely then?" she quipped, although she felt anything but humorous—her body was too tight, her need too strong.

He gave a harsh shake of his head. "You were perfect. No one's ever measured up."

"I don't want to hear that you've been with anyone else. It isn't any of my business. And I don't really wanna talk."

"I'm okay with that." He cupped her face between his large hands and bent his head to capture her mouth.

She didn't wait for him to come to her, she rose on her toes to meet him, her mouth slamming into his, her arms sliding around his shoulders to clutch at him, because she was afraid he'd hold back and tease her, and she didn't think she could take that and not fall apart.

Her heartbeats thudded, the tips of her nipples contracted into hard little beads, and she leaned against him to ease the ache, rubbing her breasts on him as his tongue pushed into her mouth.

He devoured her; her ragged breaths intermingled with his. She scraped her fingertips upward, sinking them in his thick, dark hair and pulling because urgency gripped her, coiling in her belly. Faint tremors radiated, rippling through her channel and tightening her pussy. She hiked up a thigh, and he dropped his hands to cup her ass and lift her against him.

She gave a little jump and slid both legs around him, locking her ankles low on his back as he began to rut, flexing his hips forward and back to rub his cock against her mound, all the while kissing her thoroughly, sweetly.

He broke the kiss and slid his cheek alongside hers. "Do you want it?"

She felt him smile against her skin and bit his earlobe. "Dammit, just do it."

"How bad do you want it, baby?" he rumbled.

How many times had he teased her like this? Making her beg for him to plunge inside her and ease the fever he built.

"Fuck, I ache for you, Ezra," she said, gasping. "I hurt."

He groaned and lifted her higher.

Eagerly, she slipped a hand between them, gripped his shaft and centered the tip between her folds. With their foreheads pressed together and their gazes locked, his fingers dug into her buttocks to move her steadily down his shaft. As he crowded into her, pumping shallowly to work himself inside, her mouth fell open and her head fell back.

She thought she'd remembered how it felt, but this was so much better. His water-cooled dick shocked her, causing sensual convulsions to work their way up and down her hot inner walls. "*Ez-raaaah.*"

Ezra's teeth nipped her jaw, bringin her back up. Then he rubbed her lips with his.

She gave a throaty groan, and her body vibrated. Her legs stirred, gripping his waist tighter. "Please...fuck me," she gasped. "I need it hard, baby. *Please.*" And she kissed his chin, his cheek, stroked her tongue over his firm lips.

He growled and his mouth opened over hers, suctioning, drawing on hers while he rocked forward and back, his thrusts gaining strength.

Her short, jagged breaths rattled her chest against his. She was quivering hard and whimpering. She jerked her head back to beg him again, but was caught by his expression.

His gaze was hot. His nostrils flared. His skin pulled taut across the sharp blades of his cheeks, making him look wilder, scarier. His movements were controlled, but she felt the tremors shuddering through him. He held back for her, to make the moment perfect, to stoke her desire when she knew all he wanted to do was slam deep inside and pound her like a wild thing.

"You don't have to be careful with me," she whispered.

"Sugar, you're tight. I don't wanna hurt you."

"You won't. I need you to move. Hard. Fast. *Please*, Ezra."

"Chrissi... *Damn*, Chrissi..." Ezra worked her up and down his cock, water churning around them. When a splash filled her mouth, he halted and shook his head. He pulled her against his chest and walked toward the steps, his cock still buried deep inside her body. He took the stairs slowly.

"Afraid if you slip you'll break somethin'?" she teased.

"I'm so damn hard, I'd fuckin' shatter," he growled. His body swayed with his steps, working him deeper. He cupped the back of her head and lowered her to a chaise.

With his face and shoulders above her, the blue sky blotted, she lowered her eyelids halfway, watching him begin the movements again, this time with better leverage to power into her. His strokes were strong, hard...getting faster.

Her breaths gusted at the end of each hard thrust, driven from her lungs and coming so fast she grew dizzy and lost in sensation. "Lord, it's been so damn long, Ezra," she moaned. "I forgot how good this feels."

His movements slowed, and his ice-chip gaze narrowed. "What about Kyle?" he asked, his voice dead even.

"Kyle?" she repeated, not understanding, and then she remembered the boy she'd dated after the incident. Kyle had been steady, reliable, but boring as hell as a lover. Far too careful with her body to satisfy her. "We didn't stay together long. Only until I left for college."

Ezra's movements stopped altogether, although his body shook with the need to thrust. "Who else?"

She undulated her hips to tempt him, to make him stop this line of questioning, but to no avail. "Who else what?" she bit out, beginning to get irritated because she'd almost been *there.*

"Who else did you take to your bed?"

Realizing he was serious, she silently fumed. By the tightness of his face, she knew he wouldn't relent, wouldn't give her what they both needed, until she told him. And pinned to the chaise by his heavy body, she had no way to escape his interrogation.

"Well, I didn't exactly take Kyle to my bed," she said acidly. "I was still livin' with my mom. It was more like the back seat of his Corolla."

His jaw clenched, a muscle popping and rolling along the hard edge.

She couldn't look away from the evidence of his tension. He was angry. Which nonsensically made her even hotter. "Did I ask for the names of all your lovers?"

"Why are you hedgin'?" he bit out. "Have there been so many you can't remember their names?"

It was almost funny, except the truth made her look pretty pathetic. She bit her lip and turned her face away.

Ezra growled and thrust his arms under her knees. He pulled her butt off the lounger and crammed himself deeper. Then he stopped again. "Names, Chrissi." The muscles of his forearms and shoulders bunched.

Maybe she'd pushed him too far. "There wasn't anyone else," she said, her voice small. "Not that it's any of your damn business."

"What?"

The hoarseness of his voice brought her gaze back. His disbelief was there in the deep scowl that forged a line between his heavy, dark brows.

She couldn't blame him for thinking she lied. She'd been such a horny little thing around him. She inhaled and fought to keep her mouth from trembling and letting him know just how humiliating this was. "It's been almost seven years since I've been with anyone," she said hoarsely.

Ezra's expression didn't change, but his chest rose and fell faster. His cock stirred inside her, and she couldn't help the little welcoming flush of liquid that seeped around him. Couldn't he tell how much she needed him to move? *Right. Fucking. Now.*

"Kyle wasn't what I wanted," she blurted. "And I couldn't think about bein' with anyone else because I knew it wasn't gonna work."

"Did he satisfy you?"

She glared up at him. "What do you think?"

Ezra grunted. "Was he too nice for you? Did he ask you if he could touch you first? Close his eyes when he fucked you?"

Good Lord, how did he know? "It's none of your goddamn business."

"He didn't do it for you. Guess I won't have to look him up and beat the shit out of him." Ezra pulled away, his cock sliding almost all the way out, but then he stroked back inside—easy as silk because she was so wet. "He didn't do it for you, did he, Chrissi? Not like I could."

"Never. It was never like this," she said on a choked sob. "Why does it matter?"

"You were mine. You could have been ours."

"I walked away. And you took lovers."

He circled his hips, dragging his cock around and around inside her. "Not many—and only when I couldn't stand it a day longer. I rubbed my fist raw before I sought any of 'em out."

Shifting her legs to ride higher on his waist, she tilted her pussy, trying to entice him to stop the teasing swirls. "I don't believe you. Any ole whore would have done."

His scowl deepened. "Stop it. Don't say that again."

"It's true. You made me this way. Made it so I'm ruined for anyone else."

"Because I do it for you?"

"Yes. Because you know exactly how to arouse me. Because you piss me off and walk away, and then I have to follow. I don't like bein' weak where you're concerned, but I am."

Ezra pulled out then slowly slid inward again, so slow a scream was building in her throat.

"What about my brothers?" he asked, his tone deepening. "What do they do for you?"

She shook her head. Not wanting to go there. "I never would have thought about it," she said past the lump building at the back of her throat. "Never would have looked twice. But you made me look—skinny-dippin' at the river. You put the idea in my head. Lettin' them hear us when we made love. Lettin' them come into the bedroom when we were done, sweaty and spent and still as naked as the day we were born."

"It made you hot."

Chrissi snorted. "Hell, yeah. Made me think that maybe you intended somethin' to happen."

"I didn't intend anything to happen, Chrissi. I wanted you to have fun. To love being with me. I wanted you to feel free with me."

"But I got scared because I thought you were just playin' with me. What man lets other men, even his own brothers, see his woman like that? So when you sent Josh or Cade to bring me to you, I didn't think twice about responding to their flirting. It's natural, you said. A man being aroused around a pretty woman." She took a shaky breath. She'd already revealed so much. Why not tell him everything? "Well, I was aroused too, and surrounded by Kinzies. I knew exactly what every one of you looked like naked, and when they got hard in their jeans, I knew what that looked like too. So when they flirted...I gave it right back."

Ezra's jaw eased. The cold blue of his gaze melted. "They thought it was just a game. A little competition to get under my skin, but Josh fell in love with you. Then Cade. They beat the crap out of me when you and I had a fight, because they didn't think I deserved you. They said any man would be glad to have you."

"Well, I didn't have them...not until you dared me into takin' all three of you."

How come I'm not enough? Ezra had gritted out all those years ago.

How's a girl supposed to choose, when one brother's prettier than the next? Inside, she'd begged silently, *Tell me you love me.*

Chrissi fell back against the cushions, relieved to have everything off her chest, but just as confused as ever about where she stood with this enigmatic man.

"So much time's passed," Ezra said, still braced above her, still sunk deep inside her body. "But I still think about us. Still miss havin' you around."

She gave up trying to still the tremor of her lips and chin. "I don't know what you expect from this weekend," she said, her voice thick from unshed tears.

He leaned down, forcing her knees higher, tilting her pelvis and delving deeper. With his mouth hovering over hers, he said, "I expect more of what you gave us that night. More of what it should have been."

She licked her lips. "Why? Is this your ultimate fantasy? The three of you sharin' a woman?"

"We've had that. You really think you were the only one?"

"Bastard."

"We were just practicin', sweetheart—makin' sure it was as good as we remembered. Makin' sure we remembered how."

"And was it good?"

"She wasn't you, but it was sweet. When we had her, there wasn't any tension between us. We functioned like a team. Like brothers."

"It's wrong, Ezra."

"You ready to choose one of us? To say you don't still desire all three of us? Can you say truthfully that you aren't dyin' to know what we have in store for you?"

Chrissi shook her head, but she was lying to herself. As always, Ezra Kinzie had her number. "I hate you...but I'll do this. I'll be with you and your brothers. But come Sunday, I'm out of all your lives for good, and you'll stop stalkin' me."

His dark brow arched. "You think we stalked you?"

"You checked up on me. Drivin' by the house..."

He grunted. "To make sure you were safe."

"Givin' the stink-eye to men when they asked me to dance at Shooters..."

"Because they wanted only one thing from you. You're better than that."

Blood suffused her face, heating it, making her head feel ready to explode. "You only want one thing," she railed, smacking his shoulders with her hands. "I'm a whore. I fucked all of you and gloried in it. Anyone could have seen us, and I'd have been ruined."

Ezra's jaw hardened, and he grabbed her wrists to stop her. "We didn't plan it that way. It just happened. But we were careful to make sure no one knew."

"Bo Crenshaw knew. He kissed me."

"Only because you were still being a smartass, liftin' that chin. You dared me into havin' him do it."

"But you sent him to keep watch. With his back to us. He heard everything."

"He wasn't into you, sweetheart. He's had his eye on another girl since they were kids."

"Would you have let him have me if he had been...*into me*?"

Ezra's jaw ground shut.

"Did that question confuse you, cowboy? Would you have let him have me too?"

"It wouldn't have mattered," he muttered, letting go of her hands and thrusting his arms under her thighs again.

"Why?" she asked, rising on her elbows. "Because I'm just some who—"

"I told you not to say that word again." He pulled back and lunged his hips forward, harshly, driving the breath from her in a sharp gust. Then he continued to pound fast, building friction, the tension in his body bulking out his shoulders and arms.

Chrissi fell back and gripped the sides of the chaise for dear life. She'd struck a nerve. He was angry. Not that she minded, because now he was mad enough to forget about punishing or interrogating her.

It was all about his dick now, and he wasn't stopping. Not for her, not for anyone.

With her knees drawn high, her chest restricted, she panted like a dog, unable to move. But he was stroking the right spots. Grazing her giddy-up spot, scraping her clit.

Soon, she was thrashing her head, murmuring, pleading—that he not stop, that it was too much...that she was going to explode...

And then she did, her body bucking beneath him as he hammered harder, his face an alarming shade of red, his lips peeled away from this teeth.

God, he looked feral, primitive—everything she'd loved most about fucking him.

"Yes, yes... *Oh fuck!*" She came—lights exploding behind her eyelids, her body racked with shudders, her pussy convulsing, squeezing hard around him.

He slowed. His mouth opened around a deep groan. He moved once, twice more, then pushed himself deep and held. With the first spurt of hot come, he shouted and pounded in short, spasmodic jerks, shoving the chaise with the strength of his uneven thrusts. Finally, he slowed and collapsed over her, his weight squeezing the breath out of her.

When he slipped his arms from under her knees, she wrapped herself tightly around him and buried her head against his neck.

"You cryin', sweetheart?"

A silent sob racked her and she nuzzled closer. "I won't ever cry over you, Ezra Kinzie. Not ever again."

Chapter Four

Chrissi groaned and slid her legs along Ezra's, resettling her head against his shoulder. He held her against his side, a hand smoothing up and down her upper arm while a breeze licked the sweat off their skin.

They hadn't spoken since she'd broken down. She didn't know what to say. Couldn't say precisely why she'd cried. She was relieved he didn't ask.

Footsteps padded their way. A figure, outlined by the sun lowering in the late afternoon sky, stood over them.

Chrissi blinked.

Wearing only a pair of faded jeans with the snap at the waist opened, Cade extended his hand.

She pressed her cheek against Ezra, closing out the sight of Cade's broad, naked chest. "I don't wanna move."

"I have a bath drawn," Cade said, his voice quiet but firm.

Ezra hugged her close, pressing a kiss against her hair. "Go on."

Embarrassment heated her cheeks, but her nude body wasn't anything Cade hadn't seen before. She wondered if he noticed how she'd changed, whether he liked what he saw.

She lifted her hand and let him pull her up. He held up her hand, turning her slightly as he looked her over.

"That bath?" she said breathlessly. Her nipples were prickling with arousal again. She hoped they'd start moving and he wouldn't notice, but his free hand cupped a breast and his thumb scraped the ripening tip.

"You're even prettier than I remember."

"She is, isn't she?" Ezra said, sitting on the edge of the lounger. "Give her a bath then bring her to us."

Bring her to us.

Fluid seeped down her thighs, and she gasped, remembering that she hadn't given a single thought to protection. She pressed her thighs together. "Ezra? We didn't..."

Ezra's eyes darkened. "We're all safe, Chrissi. I promise you that. And you've already admitted you haven't had sex with a man in years, so I'm assuming you're safe as well."

"But I'm not on the Pill."

"Do you want us to use something?"

He'd always left her with choices. He'd honor her answer.

Chrissi opened her mouth to give an automatic yes, but inside, she hesitated. Again, she didn't understand herself, why she'd be willing to take the risk, but they'd never used anything, never had anything between their bodies. She remembered the abandon, the freedom, the slick sensory delight.

"I'll take that as a no," he said softly, his gaze sharpening as he studied her face. He turned to Cade who wore a slight smile. "I don't wanna tell you again."

"Yes, sir," Cade said, his grin widening.

Just like the old days, Ezra liked to be in charge, liked his brothers to fall in line—if only when it came to sexy pleasures.

His brothers had never seemed to mind, falling in with his plans, whether it was shucking their clothes for a swim, or turning their backs when Ezra screwed her at the far end of the pool.

Cade tugged her hand and wrapped an arm around her shoulder as he led her away. Once inside the house, she glanced around, but found no sign of Josh. She took a deep steadying breath. One at time she could take without becoming a quivering mess.

They passed the stairs to the bedrooms above and walked down a hallway she knew led to the master suite.

"Ezra took it when mom and pops moved to Padre."

She nodded, but kept silent as they passed through the large darkened room to the bathroom.

When he opened the door for her and stood back, she sucked in a deep breath. The scent of roses, her favorite flower, permeated the air. The bath was filled to the top with fragrant bubbles.

"Go on and get in," Cade said.

She didn't look back, happy to sink beneath the bubbles and hide herself from view. Warmth enveloped her, instantly easing muscles she hadn't used in a long, long time.

Clothing rustled and her gaze swung toward him. Dark brows arched wickedly over dark blue eyes. He stepped out of his jeans and strode toward her. "Make room for me behind you."

Her breath hitched. Cade was broader across the shoulders than he'd been seven years ago, and his abdomen was deliciously ripped. A light smattering of masculine fur stretched between small brown nipples. His thighs, thick and muscled, flexed as he braced his legs apart while she stared.

His cock caught her attention. Rising from a nest of crisp, almost black curls, it was thick, veined, a ruddy tan along the shaft with a swollen purplish-red crown. "I'm just going to give you a bath."

"I can manage on my own," she choked out.

"Scared of me, Chrissi?"

"Course not."

"Then scootch up and make some room."

Lord, so this was how it would be, passed from one brother to the next. She should have been horrified, but deep inside heat blossomed again inside her. She wanted this. Needed it.

For closure, she told herself.

She scooted to the center of the large, rounded whirlpool tub.

He flicked a switch, sending the water swirling, then stepped inside, settling behind her.

When his hands cupped her shoulders and pulled her backward to rest against his chest, she fell against him, sighing. His cheek rubbed against hers, and then he bent to press a kiss against the top of her shoulder.

Chrissi accepted it. Not allowing herself to think about what was right or wrong. The scrape of his afternoon beard made her breaths come faster.

Something new. His whiskers had been softer the last time he'd kissed her. Cade was as much a man now as Ezra. Just as tall, just as hung. His cock was upright and snuggled against the seam of her buttocks.

"Why were you cryin'?" he murmured against her hair as his hands flowed over her. "Did Ezra hurt you?"

"He didn't hurt me. He didn't do anything I didn't want."

"Were you scared?"

She shook her head, not wanting to talk about it.

His hands cupped her breasts, his thumbs strumming the tips.

"I like that," she said quietly, lifting her chest, encouraging him to squeeze.

His gentle massage awakened the heat in her belly. She shifted, restless, but hoping he wouldn't notice.

Cade chuckled, his breaths soft, warm gusts against her moist neck. "Am I botherin' you?"

"It's just a bath. Maybe you should use some soap and get it over with."

"Eager for me to touch you elsewhere?" he asked, skimming a hand down her belly until his fingertips combed her pubic hair.

"No," she gasped, closing her legs and pulling her knees toward her chest.

"You know there's not a part of you I'm not gonna touch or kiss, darlin'."

"Why are you still talkin'?" she asked, her voice rising.

His chuckle shook against her back. "I've missed your sassy mouth."

She'd missed the way he always surprised her. She'd always considered him the safe one, until he did something like this. Something sexy and unexpected. He knew how to get to her. Through a back door. Not like Ezra's full frontal assaults. "You're sneakier than Ezra."

"Am I?" Long, thick digits slid through the top of her folds despite how tightly she clenched her legs together. They grazed her clit, sending a jolt of electricity arcing through her belly.

She rolled her head against his chest while his hand squeezed her breast harder. His fingers pinched her nipple while the ones hidden beneath the bubbles went to work on the swelling knot at the top of her folds.

Her knees slowly eased open, giving him room to work. He swirled and swirled while his body hardened against her and his cock twitched between her cheeks.

"If I turned you around, would you slide right down me, sugar?"

"I, ah... Don't call me Sugar." Her head lolled and her hips began to curl up and down, following his fingers, her knees falling farther apart. "Cade...?"

"Yes, baby."

His whisper, warm and husky, made her shiver. "Oh, hell." She gripped the handholds on the side of the large tub and lifted herself, then got her knees under her and turned with the assistance of his hands.

When her knees were tucked in close to his hips, he guided her forward. She reached into the water and pulled up his cock, aimed it between her folds, then slowly glided downward.

A long, breathless sigh sifted between her lips, and with her hands braced against his slick chest, she started to rock gently, mindful of the water lapping up the sides of the tub.

"Don't worry about gettin' the floor wet," he growled.

She clutched the tops of his shoulders and pushed herself up and down, looking anywhere but into his face, savoring the feeling of his thick cock stretching her. She made shallow thrusts, wanting speed rather than depth because friction was building and she could feel her orgasm coming on.

His fingers dug into her hips, forcing her down his shaft, not relenting until she was snug against his groin.

She whimpered, wanting to move, but he held her. She shot him a glare, then stilled, transfixed by the hardness of his features. He wasn't her old buddy—the boy she'd gone to talk to whenever she'd needed advice about how to handle Ezra.

Here, shoved deep inside her pussy, was a man, just as beautiful and rugged, just as arousing as his older brother. How had she missed the changes? They weren't subtle. Weren't things other women would have missed. She'd turned a blind eye. Stubbornly refusing to see that he was even more desirable than he'd been all those years ago.

Her breath hitched; her fingernails dug deep.

He raised an eyebrow, taunting her. "I'm not a boy anymore. Not your best friend. I won't pat your shoulder and send you back to Ezra. Not when I want you every bit as much."

"Cade," she said shakily, aware her pussy gave him a deep unmistakable caress. "Please let me come."

"Gonna close your eyes and pretend I'm him?"

"How can I? I want you. Fuck me, Cade. Do it."

He cupped the back of her head and pulled her hair, wrapping his hand in her length.

She tilted back her head and gave another gasp, her mouth opening around a long, fervent moan.

When he dragged her down, she scooped up his mouth, giving him open-mouthed kisses that pulled at his lips. Her tongue rimmed his teeth and stroked deep to taste.

When he sucked on her tongue and his fingers loosened around her hair, she broke away and began to move again, crashing down, sending the water sloshing over the edge of the tub, but now she didn't care.

Spurred by his husky chuckles and his burning gaze, she fucked him hard, building heat, her moans and grunts growing loud and lewd.

"Cade!" she cried out, her body slowing, consumed by the first wave of her orgasm.

Cade slid his fingers down her belly, and circled the tips over her distended clit, shooting her higher toward the peak. She screamed, her hips shoving forward and back, grinding down to take all of him. "Cade, Cade," she chanted. "Oh..."

She collapsed against his chest, her arms wrapping tightly around his shoulders.

His mouth glided along her shoulder and the side of her neck. He nudged her face upward and kissed her hard, while his body shook with tension against her.

"You didn't come," she gasped, rubbing her cheek like a cat against his.

He nipped her shoulder. "Turn around, sweetheart. Grip the edge of the tub."

She pulled away, letting his cock slip from inside her, then turned away, bending on her knees and gripping the porcelain.

Cade's fingers spread over her ass then delivered a slap.

Shock reverberated through her. The sound was wet, sharp, and she sank her back to raise her pussy. Fingers thrust inside her, swirling, rubbing against her G-spot, then quickly withdrew.

Cade place his cock at her entrance and pushed inside.

Again, she consumed him, an inch at a time, as he pumped, each thrust measured, even, controlled. He slipped a hand around her and touched her clit, rubbing it, then drawing away, then rubbing again—driving her crazy because she was still swollen and ultrasensitive, and he was teasing her into arousal again.

"Bastard," she groaned and pushed back, trying to force him deeper.

"Such a nasty mouth."

"You love my mouth. You'd love to fuck it."

"I would. And I will. But right now, I like this set of lips," he said, giving her a deep stroke. "Do you know how hot you are inside? Are you raw? Am I hurtin' you?"

"I'm hot, but only because you and Ezra don't ever quit."

"And Josh. Don't forget Josh."

"Dear God." That reminder was all it took to make her tremble and moan. They weren't done with her. Not by a long shot. Tender, hard, hot. They'd bring all that. But never respite.

She rolled her hot face against the cool porcelain. "How can you want this? I mean, I know a pussy is a pussy. But how can you want to share me?"

"I'll share because I won't go against my brothers. We know what we want, what we've missed and couldn't replace." His hands smoothed up and down her back then gripped the notches of her hips. "We want you, Chrissi. In our lives. In our beds."

"At your beck and fucking call?"

He slapped her butt again. "You like it like that. Admit it."

"Umm...never. I'm not a plaything. This isn't something we can sustain. It'd get out and people wouldn't understand."

"Why are you so worried about what other people think? Your mom's in Arizona. Who the hell else matters?"

"I have a job. Standing in the community."

"We'd take care of you."

"What about children? We aren't usin' anything. It could happen. How's that kid gonna be raised?"

"With three fathers who'll adore him."

"You're insane."

"We're not the first. The folks in Two Mule can take it."

"You're talkin' about Dani Cruz and her men. People barely speak to her."

"I'd kick anyone's ass who made a sideways comment to you."

"You can't ride herd over the whole town."

His hands smoothed up her sides and down again. "You won't need anyone but us. We'll be your lovers, your friends. We'll cherish you, sweetheart."

She rolled her head, wanting to argue, but so far gone she didn't have the strength. "Christ, just finish it. We have this weekend. To get it out of our systems. Come Sunday, I'm goin' home."

The bathroom door creaked open. Chrissi chose not to react. What did it matter if another of the Kinzies watched her getting screwed? She leaned her forehead against the top of the tub while Cade continued to hammer her pussy.

The continued silence of whoever had joined them finally drew her attention. She lifted her head, peeking from the corner of her eyes to see Josh enter the room and give Cade a look that asked permission to come inside.

Cade must have said yes. Josh stripped quietly at the door, and then walked toward the tub. When he stood in front of Chrissi's bent head, he raked his fingers through her hair and pulled to lift her face.

The waggle of his light brown eyebrows nearly made her smile. But she was being reamed from behind, her body rocked with Cade's forceful thrusts.

When Josh gripped his cock and stroked himself, she realized she'd been here before. Only then, they'd bent her over a low concrete wall, Cade fucking her from behind, getting her so hot she hadn't hesitated for even a second before opening her mouth to swallow down Josh's cock.

The only difference was that Ezra wasn't standing in the shadows, watching, stoking her desire with his hot stare. Seemed she didn't need it to catch fire after all.

Gazing down, his blond hair falling forward, Josh stroked himself again, then squeezed. A bead of precome bubbled up from his slit.

However, she wasn't the same girl, wasn't going to act the insatiable whore and offer him everything he wanted without a little show of resistance.

She pressed her lips together and glared.

Smiling, he bumped her mouth with his smooth, satiny head, smearing ejaculate on her lips.

She resisted the urge to lick it up, but he wasn't done.

With both hands, he calmly cupped her jaw and dug his thumbs into the corners, forcing her to open. Then he hooked a finger over her bottom teeth, fisted his shaft and drove himself toward her throat.

Chapter Five

Ezra stood in the doorway, watching while his brothers broke past every last objection Chrissi could manage—with her mouth full.

He felt a smile stretch one side of his own mouth. They were making a helluva mess. Soapy water rolled over the edge of the tub in waves.

He turned to the linen closet and grabbed towels, ready to mop up the mess once they'd finished.

Although pleasurably relaxed after the time he'd spent with Chrissi wrapped around him like a Band-Aid, he wasn't the least bit surprised when his cock refilled with urgent heat. Loving her had always been like that, an insatiable hunger.

Rocked back and forth by the force of Cade's thrusts, Chrissi's whole body was pink with exertion and sexual excitement. Her hair was plastered to her head, whether because it had been wet by the bathwater or sweat, he didn't know. Her eyes were closed, her expression agonized—the sweet kind, so he didn't worry that his two younger brothers were pushing her too hard.

No, she could easily handle them all. That's what they'd discovered long ago. Something that encouraged him when he'd begun to consider what it might be like to share her on a permanent basis.

For their part, his brothers' muscled frames were wired tight. Cade's gaze roamed her naked back and bottom. Josh gripped Chrissi's head and fucked her mouth, his gaze locked on his cock and her suctioning lips, looking as though he'd never done this before, but maybe he just felt that way because it was her.

Ezra knew he hadn't experienced the same intensity of arousal and emotion with any other partner since Chrissi had been his.

"Fuck, Chrissi. *Jesus*, suck it harder," Josh said, his face reddening. His mouth twisted as he blew fast between his lips. With a cry, he pulled away, his fingers wrapping around his shaft to pump, stripes of come erupting, hitting Chrissi in the face.

She didn't mind. Not by the way she tilted back her head and stuck out her tongue to catch the froth.

When Josh gave one last, strangled gasp, she slowly opened her eyes.

Ezra cleared his throat.

Chrissi's eyes widened as she glanced sideways to find him. She licked at the come on her lips, but otherwise didn't bother cleaning up the rest of the creamy stripes clinging to her cheeks and chin.

Good Lord, she looked like a porno star.

Ezra stepped closer, edging Josh out of the way to kneel beside the tub.

Chrissi's wide brown gaze clung to his, slightly unfocused. Her nostrils flared. She was a wild, primal thing. Completely different from the prissy, collected woman who'd stood by the side of the road with her cell phone in the air.

"Any second now," Cade warned, still thrusting hard against her bottom.

"Lean up a bit, baby," Ezra whispered to her.

Holding his gaze, Chrissi swallowed, then pressed down on the edge of the tub to raise her torso. Her arms shook, which made her generous breasts quiver.

Ezra stretched his arm, sliding his palm along her belly until his fingers curved around her mound. Her pussy was stretched tight around Cade. Ezra tucked into the top of her folds and tapped her clit, then rubbed it hard. "Can you come again? For me, baby?"

"What the fuck am I doing back here?" Cade groused.

"You're the lube job," Ezra said, narrowing his eyes, daring her to take offense.

"Who's got the potty mouth now?" she said, just as quietly.

Their glances locked and she didn't look away, even when her face reddened and her features grew taut.

"Almost there, sweetheart?" he asked, pinching her clit between his thumb and forefinger.

She nodded swiftly, her breaths jagged. A whimper broke and she threw back her head, silently riding the crest.

Ezra aimed a glare at Cade. "Enough."

Cade grunted and thrust twice more, then hissed between his teeth as his hips jerked. He pulled away, sitting back in the water, his arms stretching over the rim of the tub. "Fuck me," he said, breathing deeply. "Fuck."

Ezra gave Josh a sideways glare. "Make yourself useful and mop up the water." Then he picked up a washcloth, wet it in the tub and began to wipe away the streaks on Chrissi's face. "Close your eyes."

She did so, so sweetly obedient, that he couldn't resist kissing her swollen mouth. Then he smoothed the terry cloth over her cheeks. "You have some on your eyelashes," he warned her before wiping over her delicate lids.

When he was done, she kept her eyes closed.

"Are you hiding?"

"If I can't see you, you can't see me," she said, smiling impudently.

He grunted, amused. "Are you hungry?"

Her eyes popped open. "Starved."

Ezra reached for a towel and stood. "Up you go."

Chrissi rose, a little unsteady, but she righted herself and stepped out of the tub to stand in front of him.

With efficient rubs, he dried her hair then her body, spending a little extra time between her legs.

"I think I'm dry now," she said, her tone wry.

"Wanted to make sure." He dropped the towel on the floor.

"Do you have anything I can wear?"

"Didn't I tell you the rules?"

She combed her wet hair back with her fingers. "Rules?"

"For the weekend. No clothes." He turned to leave the bathroom, confident she'd follow.

"You'd have been so fucked if I were on my period," she muttered from right behind him.

Cade and Josh chuckled. Ezra's mouth quirked. "Think I left that to chance?"

She groaned. "Macy?"

"Uh-huh."

"The bitch."

Not stopping as they walked into the bedroom, he glanced back, grinning.

Her head canted as she returned his stare. "You don't do it often enough. Smile, that is."

"How do you know?"

"I've seen you around."

Ezra strode to the dresser and picked up a hairbrush. "I could say the same for you." He didn't have to say a word, just pointed to the edge of the bed.

Chrissi arched an eyebrow, but sat, pressing her thighs together as she gripped the edge of the mattress. "I've been busy getting on with my life. There hasn't been a lot of time for fun."

"There's always time for that." He started at the bottom of her tangled hair, careful not to pull too hard as he slowly brushed her hair.

"Then how come you always look as stern as a hangin' judge?"

"Been busy, sweetheart. Runnin' a ranch and waitin' on you." He paused to see how she reacted to that last bit.

Her dark eyebrows lowered, forming an impressive scowl. "Stop sayin' that. It's not true."

"You think I haven't been haunted too?"

"Not like me," she said, her voice thickening. "You don't have any idea."

Ezra sighed and sat next to her. He wrapped an arm around her shoulder and pulled her stiff body against his side. "Then tell me, sweetheart. Make me understand."

Slowly, her body relaxed. She lifted an arm to wrap around his waist and snuggled into his side. "That night," she said, dipping her head to hide her face, "when you left me at the restroom..."

He kissed her hair. "Yeah, I remember," he rumbled. "You ditched me. Left me waitin' there. I didn't know what the hell had happened."

"I wasn't alone. Remember Stacy Holder and Mariana Lopez?"

"Sure. They're both fat and have a half a dozen kids between 'em now."

"Well, they were in there. Talking about you and me. Pretendin' they didn't see me come in."

He could feel the tension in her body. Her arm tightened around him. Her breaths slowed. "Baby, what did they say?"

Chrissi huffed a breath. "'Did you see her?'" she said, mimicking Mariana's high-pitched voice. "'I bet they just did it. Her hair's all messed up and she stinks.' And then Stacy started in, 'Think they did it under the bleachers? Or in his car? I'd let him. He's so cute. Hell, I'd do them all.' And then Mariana laughed," Chrissi said, her voice barely above a whisper. "She called Stacy a slut for just saying it." She raised her face, her eyes shimmered with tears welling in her soft brown eyes. "But I did it. I did all of you. I was the slut. And I think they knew."

An ache settled in his chest. He hadn't known she'd carried this around all this time. No wonder she'd run. "No one knew about us, sweetheart. They might have suspected, but no one saw us. I promise you that."

"Didn't matter. I couldn't face you. I thought, what guy does that with a girl he likes? I dragged the trash can under the window and crawled up on it to climb out."

"I was worried. I waited a long time, knowin' I'd handled it wrong. That I shouldn't have pushed you. All because I was jealous. Because Josh told me you had fantasies—about the three of us. And because I didn't want to admit that the idea was one that'd been keepin' me up at night too."

She blinked, and a tear trickled down her cheek. He caught it with his thumb and licked it away.

Her nostrils flared again, her gaze dipped to his mouth, and that was all the invitation he needed.

Ezra bent to kiss her softly, framing her jaw with his palm, combing back her hair as he pressed his lips against hers and rubbed in slow circles until she followed him, a thready moan seeping into his mouth.

Pulling away nearly killed him, but he and his brothers had an agenda. A bigger goal than slaking the lust they'd hoarded for years. He kissed her forehead and smiled at her expression. "You look like Sleeping Beauty wakin' up to a kiss."

"Think you're a prince?"

"Nah. Just a cowboy."

"Not 'just' about it." She dropped her arm from around his waist. "You were kiddin' about the rule, right? I can't walk around naked all weekend long."

"Not embarrassed, are you?"

She wrinkled her nose. "No, but I do feel really...vulnerable. How about just a shirt. Anything of yours would fit me like a dress anyway. And please, have Josh and Cade wear some jeans. I can't hold a conversation when I'm droolin'."

Ezra smiled at the hint of tart humor, relieved she'd found her footing again. Their intentions were to break her down this weekend, but they wanted to protect her pride as well. "I'll find you somethin' to wear."

Josh flipped a steak on the grill, watched the meat sizzle and then splashed it with the beer he was drinking. "Should be done in a few minutes, guys," he called over his shoulder.

Cade was busy lighting the Tiki torches surrounding the patio and had already plugged in the bug zapper to handle any flying insects.

Ezra and Chrissi were making a salad in the kitchen. The two of them had been glued together since big brother had removed her from the bathroom. Josh wasn't worried though. Chrissi always gravitated to Ezra when she needed to absorb a bit of strength. He and Cade had pushed her hard. Left her shattered.

While they'd cleaned up the bathroom, they'd listened to the quiet conversation and learned why Chrissi had bolted all those years ago. Why she'd ruthlessly cut off their relationship. And while he understood how she'd felt, he couldn't help feeling a little angry with her that she hadn't trusted them enough to talk to them about what bothered her.

Not that he, Josh, had ever been someone she'd turned to for comfort or counsel. They'd been playmates. Teamed up to play practical jokes on the other two. Fussed and prodded and teased each other like crazy, but they'd never confided in each other. Except when it came to their fantasies. He still remembered confiding that he'd had a thing for long, sleek legs, just like hers. How Shanna Davies's legs had always done it for him too. She'd laughed, told him to go for it, then had this odd expression on her face.

"Tell me. I know that look," he'd prodded.

She tucked a lock of hair behind her ears, and her gaze evaded his. "What look?"

"The 'I'm thinkin' something so wicked I'll burn in hell' look. Have to tell. I told you my fantasy."

She shook her head and laughed, but it sounded strained.

"Chrissi?"

"You'll tell."

"Tell Ezra?"

She nodded. "I don't want him mad."

"It'll be our secret."

Her face had screwed up in a grimace. "Sometimes, when I'm in bed and thinkin'...I wonder what it would be like."

"What?" he'd asked, thinking he might already know from the blush coloring her face.

"What it would be like to be with you and Cade and Ezra...together."

His heart had thudded against his chest. His cock had jerked inside his jeans then started to fill. He cleared his throat. "You think about it often?"

She nodded, ducking her head. "I know. Makes me sound like a skanky whore, huh?"

"Nothing wrong with fantasies. I've had the same one."

She'd blinked, then her gaze locked with his for a long moment before she'd broken away and shrugged. "So that was my fantasy. Yours is doable. So why haven't you made a move on Shanna?"

"'Cause my best friend, Bo, wouldn't like it much."

And just like that, she'd put the idea in his head. He'd talked to Cade first, who'd warned him not to say a thing to Ezra because he didn't need Ezra getting bent out of shape.

But things had changed. They'd both started watching Chrissi with more than just a male's casual appreciation. They'd begun to think of her as a potential partner. It couldn't be helped, even if they were straying into their brother's territory.

All it had taken to make things blow up was a conversation that exploded into blistering argument in the truck while they drove to the Homecoming game.

"Penny for 'em," came a soft voice, pulling him back into the present. The object of his fantasies stood next to him, her smile shy but her chin lifting to let him know she wasn't gonna let a little thing like a blowjob make her feel less sure of herself.

Warmth crowded into Josh's chest. "I ever tell you how much I love that sassy mouth of yours, sweetheart?"

She laughed, her cheeks turning a lovely rose. "When it's full or when it's dishin' insults?"

"I'm equally impressed. Grab that plate and I'll get these steaks off the grill before they're overdone."

"You made mine—"

"Like shoe leather, yeah, I remember. Not a hint o' pink."

Chrissi picked up the platter and held it while he stacked the thick steaks.

"It's nice havin' you here," he muttered.

"So you all keep sayin'."

"It's true."

"I know that. And I have to admit, it feels kinda natural bein' here again. Like I never left. Makes it harder, I think."

"To say goodbye?"

She nodded, then bit her lip. "I'll take these to the table."

He watched her walk away while he turned off the propane and closed the grill. She'd let her guard down at last. Was talking to them again, enjoying herself. He knew what they had was good. Ezra told them she hadn't had a lot of partners over the years so her sensuality wasn't something she spread around. It belonged to them. How could she even consider cutting off that part of herself? It didn't make sense.

Walking toward the glass table, he watched Cade hold out her chair and her laugh at something he said, ducking her chin then glancing at Ezra as though seeking affirmation that it was okay for her to enjoy his brother's attentions.

And that's when it struck him—what they had to do. Ezra had thought that maybe they should go easy. Make her comfortable, remind her gently how good it was be among them. Cade had been the one to quietly prepare the playroom, the one Ezra had said she wasn't ready to enjoy.

Josh glanced at Cade who'd seen Chrissi's little "tell". He gave him a nod. The next round, Ezra wouldn't be the one in charge if he wasn't willing to give Chrissi everything she needed to make the right choice come Sunday.

Chapter Six

Cade kept mostly quiet throughout the meal while he studied Chrissi. Her manner was more relaxed than it had been when she first arrived, but there was still a wall that she kept carefully erected between herself and them, or maybe between herself and her desires. Cade knew it was up to him to figure out how to breach it.

Ezra could tempt her, could momentarily push her past her comfort zone. She'd crumbled beneath his full-on seduction. Josh was a buffer. A playmate who could tease a smile from her or gentle her anger with a teasing jibe.

Cade knew he was the dark horse, the one she thought of as a Steady Eddie. But if he was quiet it was only because he liked to suss out a problem, think of all the ways it could be fixed, before he made a move.

The problem with Chrissi wasn't gonna be fixed by fucking her straight through the weekend. Not by trading her off, one brother to the other. They'd only be confirming her fears, tightening her resolve.

Chrissi needed something new. Something to shock her past being able to regroup and reestablish her defenses. He and his brothers had only played with domination with Chrissi in the past. They'd let Ezra be the boss of things, and she'd always blossomed for those brief moments. But Chrissi needed to have a little training. Reinforcement and refinement. She needed to be shown what she really was, what she needed deep in her heart of hearts.

Chrissi was a submissive in need of a strong Dom, maybe a pair of them. Ezra wasn't going to like it. He thought she needed a gentle introduction, that schooling her would be part of a long-term campaign, but Cade was solidly with Josh now.

Ezra sat beside Chrissi, his hand cupped around hers as she sipped her iced tea.

Cade nudged his foot under the table.

His older brother shot him a questioning gaze, then narrowed his eyes, guessing from his expression that something was afoot.

"I'm taking Chrissi to bed," Cade said quietly.

Ezra arched an eyebrow.

Chrissi blushed.

He noted the dark shadows beneath eyes that still managed a hint of sparkle at the thought of another sexy interlude.

"Sweetheart, hate to disappoint you, but you need rest. You look done in." To the guys he said, "Take care of the dishes and see to *the room.*"

She didn't appear to hear the special inflection he added, which was a good thing. She'd need rest for what he had planned for her.

Ezra's hand tightened around Chrissi's, but he leaned toward her and kissed her cheek. "Go on with Cade. He'll take care of you."

She gave him a nod then shot Cade a glance that was at once a little hesitant and trusting.

Cade felt a like heel, knowing she'd look at him in an entirely different light come morning.

Chrissi straightened her shoulders. "Hate to rain on your parade, but what's happenin' with my car? I can't let it sit on the side of the road all night."

Josh grinned. "A friend of ours took care of that already. He had it towed to your house."

"A friend?"

"Bo Crenshaw."

Her expression clouded. Reminded again of that long-ago night. Cade hoped like hell that one day she'd forgive them for

Delilah Devlin

being thoughtless and crass. That night had colored their past, tainted their friendship and stolen years.

"Any more worries?" he asked, keeping his tone even.

She shook her head. "Guess not."

Cade pushed up from his chair and circled the table to stand beside her. He held out his hand and she slid her delicate one across his palm. With a gentle tug, he pulled her up and slid an arm around her waist. "Promise. Sleep only," he whispered against her ear.

"Thanks. I didn't know until this moment just how tired I am."

Cade nodded to Ezra and Josh and watched the tightening of their faces. They knew he was through waiting. That he'd taken the lead. For now.

Inside Ezra's bedroom, Chrissi stood beside the bed while Cade pulled the oversized shirt over her head and turned down the covers.

"I need to use the facilities," she said quietly, feeling awkward again to be standing naked next to the quiet Kinzie.

Cade might be the quiet one, might be the one she'd always thought of as the most grounded and kind, but there was something different about him now. Something watchful. She didn't know why, but something of his stance and enigmatic expression put her to mind of a wolf, a patient, intelligent predator.

He gave her a nod, his permission to leave, which made her bristle. She didn't need any man's permission to do a damn thing, but here she was allowing him to take charge. Still, she left him to take care of business in the bathroom and brush her teeth.

When she let herself out of the bathroom, she saw his jeans draped over the armchair in the corner, and Cade lying beneath the covers with two pillows wedged behind his shoulders. He patted the bed. "I didn't change my mind. We're just sleepin'. But I'm gonna hold you."

The thought was too delicious, too seductive to a woman who'd slept alone for so many years, for her to even pretend she didn't want it. She slid beneath the covers while he turned off the bedside lamp, then let him turn her to spoon her body against his.

She rested her head on his arm and scooted deeper against him. His cock was semi-aroused and pushing against her butt.

"Can't help that," he whispered, humor in his tone. "Ignore it."

"Easy for you to say," she grumbled, hiding a smile.

"Nothin' easy about having you here in my arms and not doin' a thing about it. But I don't wanna prove you can't trust what I say."

"I never doubted you were an honest man, Cade." She turned inside his arms. His gaze, which glinted in the moonlight, was still shuttered, wary. "Maybe you can make me understand."

He pulled away a lock of hair that clung to the moist corner of her mouth. "What can't you quite grasp?"

"How you of all people can be okay with this. Don't you want a woman of your own?"

"Truth be told, I've never found another you, Chrissi."

"But I wasn't your girl. We weren't intimate before that night. How could you know?"

"Didn't you know the truth? Even before we did it? Why else would you have told Josh what you did?"

She sighed. "I didn't see it as something permanent. Just a fantasy. Like fucking Brad Pitt. Not something I truly aspired to."

"I knew because every time I watched you with Ezra, I burned. I was so eaten up with jealousy, I stayed horny and mad and ready to pull teeth because I wasn't the one you wanted. I didn't like what it made me feel about my brother. I didn't like that my fantasy had to do with stealing you away, fucking you in front of him. Now, I love my brother. I'd die for him. But I'd fight him for the right be with you."

She swallowed hard. The uninflected way he said it, the steadiness of his gaze said he meant every single word. She turned away, but let him pull her snug against him, let him smooth his hands over her body, avoiding her breasts, never straying between her thighs—soothing jumbled thoughts and a worn-out body.

She felt sorry for herself that she didn't feel the same sense of conviction that he did. Couldn't be as selfless about her needs. She might desire all three of them, but she needed peace of mind. Needed self-respect. Needed to know that her future wasn't going to be something sordid and sinful, and ultimately flawed. When she took a mate, she wanted it to be forever. Not just for now.

And she seriously didn't see how this could work in any way, except as a short-termed fling.

"Go to sleep, Chrissi. Stop worryin'. It's gonna be okay."

"You sound like Ezra. You both like bein' in charge. How does that work with him managin' the ranch?"

"He's got the final say, but I'm the foreman. He has to listen to my advice."

"Josh doesn't get a say?"

"He doesn't want the responsibility. He likes bein' a cowboy, ridin' the range, wranglin'. He'd as soon spend his days mendin' fences and pullin' calves from arroyos than figurin' out when to move the herd or send 'em to market."

She stayed silent for a few minutes, thinking about everything he'd said. "You really think this could work?"

"I know it can. You just have to trust that we've got it all worked out among us. That we can truly share. Now sleep, sweetheart. You're gonna need your rest."

She smiled softly at that last bit. There was a warning couched in his quiet command. And while her body warmed to his insistence, her mind was shutting down, drifting. Dreaming about three sexy cowboys who loved her. Who wanted her for always.

Why was she fighting them? They made it sound so easy, so inevitable.

For the first time, she let her dreams follow where her heart led. As she fell asleep, Cade's large capable hands soothing away her stress, she thought maybe she was ready to believe.

As soon as her breathing evened in sleep, Cade pulled away from Chrissi's warm body. The ache in his groin had to be seen to before he sought out the others. He thought maybe he'd gotten through to her, made her reconsider her stubborn stance, but he wasn't going to leave anything to chance.

He headed to the bathroom, started the shower and took himself in hand, working his cock in his fist. The rhythmic motions were steady, punctuated by his deepening breaths, while he thought about everything that had happened that day. Especially about how sweetly she'd surrendered in the tub. How lovely she'd been in all her distress. He ached for her, wished he could think of a way to make her acceptance easier, but Chrissi Page was a complicated woman.

She thought she needed control. Thought she needed the trappings of a traditional marriage to feel complete. She hadn't a clue how wrong she was. How unsuited she was to that kind of life.

Her sensual nature was capable of so much more. Any one man would leave her unsatisfied. She was needier of attention, of physical loving, than any one man could provide.

He'd sensed it all those years ago when Ezra had taken up with her. She'd demurred whenever his big brother had pushed her beyond her natural modesty, but she'd embraced every adventure with her loving, open heart.

His arm tensed, stroking harder. His balls drew up tight against his groin, and he moaned as the first explosion rocked him, sending hot spurts against the tiles. He remembered her face, striped with Josh's come, the pearly white foam clinging to her cheeks, her eyelashes. She'd been beautiful, wanton. So near to perfect, his chest had frozen.

A soft knock sounded on the door. He let go of his shaft and hung his head for a moment to drag soul-cleansing breaths into his lungs before flipping back the curtain to greet Josh.

Josh's eyes danced with amusement. "Heard you all the way into the hallway. Don't know how she slept through that racket."

Cade gave him a stinging glare, which only widened Josh's grin. He reached for the towel hanging from the peg beside the shower and wrapped it around his waist. "You try having that ass snuggled up against your dick."

Josh grunted, then his expression changed, turning sly. "Everything's ready. The room's arranged. I tucked a blindfold under the pillow."

"We'll let her sleep a while."

"Ezra thinks we should all catch some shut-eye."

"Ezra's not wrong. You wanna keep her company? Can you wake without an alarm?"

"I'm always up with the roosters. You don't have to stir until I come for you."

Cade nodded and stepped quietly back into the bedroom. Josh stripped off his jeans and edged under the covers, taking up Cade's former spot.

Chrissi's breathing didn't change as Josh pulled her close and tucked his face into the corner of her neck and breathed. "She smells like heaven," he whispered reverently.

Smiling, Cade tiptoed out of the room. Ezra was finishing up the dishes, a towel draped over his shoulder. He glanced back as Cade walked inside. "She asleep?"

"With Josh. She was out like a light."

Ezra let the water out of the sink and leaned his butt against the counter. "Tomorrow's the make or break day. If she's not ready, she'll bolt."

"How much do you love her, Ezra?"

Ezra's face darkened with anger. "What the fuck kinda question is that?"

"I have to ask. Do you want her for her, or for what you think she'll bring to our lives?"

"There hasn't been a day since I first laid eyes on Chrissi that I haven't wanted her."

"But do you love her? The real her?"

"What are you gettin' at?"

"Chrissi's not all surface. She's beautiful, sassy. But deep inside she's not that secure."

"You think you know her better than me?"

"I've spent years watching her. My mind's not clouded with doin' a whole hell of a lot. She's soft at the center. You saw some of that when you pushed and she broke down. We can hurt her. Or if we're careful, we can bring out her strengths, help her embrace the woman she could be."

Ezra's lips twisted. "You been reading too much *Cosmo*."

Cade smiled. "Maybe. But I'm right about this, Ezra. Let's play tomorrow. But let me be the one to call the shots. We both want the same thing. We want her to be ours. No reservations."

Ezra crossed his arms over his naked chest. "I need a swim."

"You do that. But then you get some rest. I don't need you cranky."

Ezra turned to lean both hands against the counter and stare out the window at the night sky. "You sure we're doin' the right thing?"

"Yeah. More than ever. It's like breakin' in a new pair of leather boots. You have to wear 'em, stress 'em a bit, before they really fit."

Ezra raised a brow. "Did you just compare Chrissi to a pair of cowboy boots?"

Cade shrugged, then pulled a beer from the fridge and popped the top before heading to the playroom at the far side of the house. The room he and his brothers had worked on off and on for months. Not knowing exactly when it would come into use, but hoping.

They'd each had their say in what would be in there. They'd each practiced with similar toys and equipment over the years, learning how to ply a flogger or wrap a rope around delicate skin. But never together.

When they'd accepted Bo Crenshaw's challenge to give his girl Shanna one memorable night, they'd plied some of what they'd learned, but they hadn't brought her here. Hadn't wanted any one woman to experience it with them but Chrissi.

Cade pulled a flogger from a drawer in the hand-built cabinet against one wall, and rifled a finger down across the edges of the suede flanges. Chrissi would love this one. Once she got past the shock.

Chapter Seven

Chrissi woke in stages, swimming through exquisite layers of sensation. At first, she thought she dreamed. Feather-soft touches stroked her skin, eliciting delicate shivers before drifting away again. She slept on...to be enticed again with smooth glides of firm lips. Two pairs. One starting at her toes, the other at her nipples.

She smiled to herself as she dreamily blinked her eyes.

The room was still dark. Not a glint of moonlight coming through the window, not a gleam of artificial light around the edges of any door. She wasn't sure which of the men was nibbling at her toes, but she wondered what he might do if she kicked him. When he slid his tongue between her toes, she curled them, trying to capture the sensation rather than deflect it. She hadn't known her toes were an erogenous zone.

The more obvious delight, the lips latching gently around one hardened nipple, had her clutching at warm thick hair, a shaggy mop she recognized immediately as Josh's. she pulled to bring him closer, to deepen the sucking kisses that didn't satisfy, only teased, but he released her nipple and glided lower, sucking the tender skin at the underside of her breast.

She'd have a trail of bruised love bites if he kept it up, but she didn't really mind. The only ones who'd know would be the three cowboys who had set their minds to her seduction.

Chrissi moaned then breathed deeply, feigning sleep again. They'd have to work a little harder to get her to admit she was fully awake and enjoying the attention.

A calloused fingertip scraped up the back of her calf, tickling behind her knee, and she couldn't help the giggle that escaped.

"I knew it," Cade drawled. "You're playin' possum."

"Was not."

Josh chuckled, warm air gusting against her upper belly.

"Hell, I just closed my eyes," she grumbled. "Thought you guys needed me rested."

"Aren't you?"

Breath blew against the tender skin just above her mound and her thighs tensed in anticipation. "Guess so," she whispered.

"We're gonna play a game," Cade said, his voice deepening.

Again, the roughening texture of his voice hinted at a masculine dominance that had her stirring restlessly on the mattress. "What kind of game?"

"Wouldn't be as much fun if we told you."

She huffed. "Fun for who?"

"Think we don't mean to give you all the pleasure you can stand?" A finger traced through the hair on her mound to the top of her folds and tapped her hooded clit.

Sweet Jesus, was that all it took to get her hot? "Umm… I'm game."

"Josh…" Cade murmured.

Josh kissed her nipple then withdrew. A whisper slid across the sheets… The glide of a hand? Cade tugged her wrist, bringing her to a sitting position, and Josh's hot skin moved in to cloak her back. Fabric slithered over her face then tightened around her eyes.

"A blindfold? But it's dark already."

"We have someplace to take you," Cade said, his tone brooking no arguments. "Get on up, Chrissi."

The bed dipped around her, both her hands were clasped. The brothers led her from the bed, through the hallway, the living room, to somewhere beyond. The old workout room? She didn't mind the silence or the gentle grips of their strong hands. "Is Ezra already there?"

"Ezra's waitin', sweetheart."

Good Lord, she wasn't sure what she felt about the sound of this. "Maybe I'd rather see where I'm goin'."

"Think we're givin' you a choice?"

She tried to tug her hands away, but both men tightened their grips.

A door creaked open, and she was swept inside. The sounds inside the room, their footsteps, her excited breaths, seemed muted, like the walls had better insulation here. She turned her head to try to catch the sound of another male inside. "Ezra?"

Hands slid around her waist, sweeping up and down her belly, then cupping her breasts while thumbs rubbed the spiking tips. "Trust us," he whispered in her ear. He framed her hips with his large hands and propelled her slowly forward. "Stop here."

Hands guided her, picking up a foot to slide it along something wooden behind her. She stepped onto it. They guided her other foot onto another step. Bands wrapped her ankles. The scratch of Velcro made her jump. Her arms were raised at her sides and her fingers were wrapped around a grip before her wrists were tied as well.

Then all the hands, all the warm support, withdrew. There was a creak, and suddenly the thing she was fastened to tilted back, at an angle, not completely horizontal, but enough that the padded supports under her arms, legs and torso, took her weight.

The supports beneath her legs were opened, spreading her thighs. Something stroked up the inside from below her knee to just beneath her folds then back down again.

Heat closed in at one side of her face. Minty breath gusted over her cheek. "This is how it's gonna be, sugar," Cade whispered. "I'm gonna stroke your skin, and here and there, I'm gonna give you a pop. Not enough to leave a mark. Not unless you want me to. You have to be honest. Tell me if I hurt you. Or tell me if you want more."

"You're gonna hit me?"

"Stripe you, baby. You'll see." She heard him move around to stand between her spread legs.

"You've got a pretty pussy. And it's wet." A finger burrowed into her, withdrew, then rubbed her mouth with her moisture. "Suck it clean, sweetheart."

Her pussy made a moist clasping sound, and she tried to draw her knees together, but that was the point of the bindings. Nothing would be hidden. Not a single reaction. Her lips parted, ready to tell him to go straight to hell, but he rubbed her mouth again and her tongue touched him, liked the flavor he shared, and swept out to curl around his finger until he stuck it into her mouth to let her suck. When he pulled it out, she licked her lips, then bit them, because something was snaking up her inner thigh again, something soft and trailing.

It lifted off her skin, then flicked, stinging her inner thigh.

She gasped and pulled against her bindings. Before she could form a protest, the strands were stroking her belly, her breasts. Her nipples reacted, contracting. Her flesh tingled and goose bumps rose. The flanges lifted and struck one breast. "Shit!"

"Too much?" Ezra was beside her ear.

But the flanges were moving again, down her belly, between her legs. Her knees lifted, fighting the bindings at her ankles, but all she could manage was a slight outward turn.

"You like that?" Ezra whispered. "Do you want Cade to flick you there?"

Her body was beginning to shiver. She nodded quickly, and the flick, a divinely sharp, stinging glance, landed on her outer labia. Blood surged south to make them swell.

She was squirming now, her skin heating. "Is it a whip?"

"A flogger," Ezra said. "Soft suede. Cade knew you'd love it."

"Jesus," she breathed.

The flanges lifted from her skin, but didn't strike. "You're gettin' used to knowin' where it'll land," Cade said—like that was a bad thing.

"Shouldn't I know? To prepare?"

"Then you'd have some control over how you react." The flogger struck her belly, her mound, her knee, then swirled around and around one breast in delicious, soothing swirls while she struggled to even out her breaths.

The flogger disappeared. Fingers plumped her breast then lips latched around the turgid tip, pulling hard and eliciting a deep groan from her.

"Like that?" Ezra said.

"Yes," she hissed, wondering who was sucking at her breasts.

Fingers pinched the tip and pulled then released, then repeated the action, squeezing harder.

Liquid oozed from inside her, dribbling from her pussy.

Fingers sank into her and pumped in and out, then withdrew.

"God, you're killin' me."

Laughter, low chuckles sounded all around her. The men were moving, changing places. Something cold closed around the tip of one nipple, tightening, pinching hard.

"Too much?" Josh asked.

She bit her lip, but shook her head. The pain was delightful, causing her womb to clench. The clamp cinched tighter, and she hissed between her teeth, but didn't complain.

Her other breast was plumped and kissed, the nipple tortured with lips, fingers, then another cold clamp was applied. When both were tight, fingers toggled the tips, rasping over them. "So red," Josh said. "Beautiful, baby."

A quiver shook up her spine, and she grew rigid against her supports, arching her back. "Please," she begged, but she didn't know what she wanted other than to be filled, for them to ease the ache growing inside her.

"Get her off the cross," Cade said, his voice deep and hard-edged.

She liked the way it sounded, then liked even better the way the men followed his command. Her body responded with more shivers that racked her belly and inner thighs.

The bindings at her wrists and ankles eased, and the cross was adjusted until it stood upright. A strong arm encircled her waist, and she leaned against a hard chest while she was moved a few feet. Her knees bumped against padded leather. The arm at her back pulled away. A hand pressed between her shoulder blades, and she gasped, afraid she'd fall forward, but her belly landed on leather squabs and an upholstered bench cushioned her knees. The edge was just below her breasts, which left them to sway beneath her. Her nipples tightened and the clamps pinched harder.

Folded over the bench, her bottom raised, she knew what was coming next and hung her head. She couldn't form a complaint or a question. Waited quietly while hands smoothed over her legs and bound her again to the bench. Fingers thrust through her hair and lifted her head. A mouth closed over hers and kissed her.

So drunk on endorphins rushing through her veins, she couldn't wonder who kissed her, didn't really care, only that a tongue mated with hers, suctioning her lips while hands massaged her ass.

Those hands lifted, and she held her breath. A slap rocked her, and she sucked hard on the tongue inside her mouth, her body tightening, jumping with each hard, successive smack.

Her bottom grew hot, her pussy swelled, fluid trickled down one thigh but the slaps continued against one side then the other, and then right between her spread legs, against her pussy.

The shock pushed her into an orgasm that made her whimper and mewl, and the mouth grinding against hers left, leaving her sobbing.

More slaps landed, but her mind was wrapped in a haze. Something soft butted against her mouth and she opened, welcoming a thick musky cock.

Fingers combed through her hair then pulled. "Suck harder, baby," Ezra said, his voice tight. Tight like it always was just before he blew.

Her lips closed around him. She opened her jaws a little wider and sucked him down, encouraging him to deepen his strokes.

She gurgled and groaned around him, not caring how desperate she sounded, only that she obeyed, that she pleased him. The hands warming her backside smoothed over her buttocks then gripped them hard. A cock nudged her folds, and she screamed around Ezra when it stroked deep, thrusting toward her core in a single drive that pushed the air from her lungs.

Again, her womb tightened, her body writhed, pleasure escalating as the men fucked her mouth, her cunt, stroking in opposing rhythms. When the man behind her began to thrust harder, his belly slapping against the moisture spilling from inside her, Ezra's strokes shortened, quickened. Come hit her tongue, the back of her throat. She swallowed around him, taking it down.

The man behind her bounced against her ass and a shout sounded, deep, agonized, and the mystery man powered three more times before withdrawing. Hot fluid landed on her ass. The cock stroked over it, spreading the sticky goo.

Both men pulled away, leaving her bent over the bench, all strength gone.

She lay, limp as a dishrag, unmoving, even when fingers traced the crack of her ass. She gasped as they swirled around her tiny hole. Footsteps circled behind her. An ointment was squeezed against her hole, the tip of the tube entered her, and more gel filled her. When it pulled away, she groaned, not sure she was ready for this, but unwilling to voice her unease. A finger eased inside her slowly, and she tensed her thighs, her buttocks.

"You have to relax," Cade said, his voice soothing now. "Let me in, sweetheart. You'll like this with me. I promise."

His finger pulled free. Latex snapped—the first hint of a condom she'd heard or seen. Then he was back, the blunt head of his cock pushing against her. His hands gripped her buttocks, thumbs easing her open, spreading her hole. His cock surged against her, pushing against her tight ring.

She whimpered, but pushed apart her knees, as far as she could and tilted up her ass. Giving her silent acceptance to the invasion.

"Fuck, Chrissi," he said, his voice strained. He pushed again, and popped through, surging deeper as her muscles eased around him.

She sobbed. She burned. And when he began to pump inside her, she flung back her head and drew sharp, shattered breaths. He was deep, his groin pounding against her cheeks. Something she'd never done before. Never considered sexy, but here she was, with Cade reaming her, and her loving every moment.

She ached, but she was on fire. "Oh please, please."

"What do you want?" Ezra said beside her ear.

"Rub my clit," she gritted out.

His chuckle sounded strained, but moistened fingers came up between her legs and swirled on the hard, distended knot.

"Gonna come, baby," Cade warned.

"Please, please, please," she chanted.

When he powered harder, sharper, the slaps loud and lewd, a mouth closed over hers. A tongue thrust inside.

Good Lord, they were all three here, all working her. She could see it in her mind, and the picture was beyond dirty. The tight coil of arousal burst, and she gave an agonized groan, her whole body going rigid as wave after wave of shivering convulsions swept through her.

She barely noted Cade's shout. Didn't demur when the fingers between her legs left her. Josh kissed her mouth, her cheeks, and she lifted her face to accept his blessing and murmured praise.

A warm wet cloth cleaned between her legs and buttocks. The fastenings melted away. She was urged to the ground on her knees. Her hands were pulled behind her and made to wrap one around the other. Her head was pushed down.

"Like this sweetheart. We want you to wait like this," Cade said, kissing her shoulder then moving away.

The blindfold fell away and she blinked, keeping her head down and pulling in deep ragged breaths.

Three sets of large feet were lined up in front of her, and she couldn't help the tired grin that stretched her swollen mouth.

"She's smiling," Josh said.

One of them grunted. Had to be Ezra.

A hand cupped her chin and lifted her face. Cade was bent over her, his gaze studying her expression. "Are you quiet because you're tired?"

Her lips parted. She was tired. That was true. She shook her head.

His smile was slow and eased up one side of his mouth. "This is what we want from you. Here in this room. Obedience."

She licked her lips and nodded, beyond exhausted, completely sated.

"You can speak."

"When we're not in here...?" she asked, her voice croaking.

"We expect sass. Lots of it. Get it out of your system before you come inside."

Her lips trembled. "How'd you know I'd like this? I sure as hell didn't."

Cade's grin widened. "Because we wanted it. And you're made for us, Chrissi."

Chrissi thought about that for a moment, then felt moisture well in her eyes. She felt as though a weight had lifted from her chest, as though the fear and shame she'd carried around for so long had simply floated away. "I was made for you," she repeated slowly.

Cade dropped his hand and held it out. She slipped hers inside and let him pull her to her feet. She swayed, and Josh stepped forward to slide an arm around her back. He lifted her in his arms and held her against his chest, a huge smile stretching across his face.

She glanced across at Ezra, the man she'd loved first. His expression was stoic. Her heart thudded dully against her chest. "You haven't said anything," she said softly, hoping with all her heart that he hadn't gotten a glimpse of their future and decided he'd made a mistake.

Ezra stepped closer, and his gaze trailed from her face, along her body, then swept slowly back. He cleared his throat. "I'm the one marryin' you. We decided."

"Were you gonna ask?" she said drily, her heart stuttering and quickening again.

"You don't get a say. Not in here."

She narrowed her eyes. "Josh?"

"Yeah, baby."

"Take me outside."

Cade and Josh both chuckled, but Ezra's jaw strained. His eyelids fell to a scary squint.

She wasn't scared. Those last few feet to the door, she leaned up and wiggled her calves. "You can let me down."

Josh set her on her feet at the door, and she stepped across the threshold, straightened her shoulders and stalked away.

"Where's she off to now?" Josh said.

"She's mine," Ezra ground out.

She heard his feet slap the wooden floor behind her, but she pretended she wasn't intimidated. She headed through the living room straight to the master bedroom. Before she made it to the hallway, her arm was grabbed, and she was turned and folded over Ezra's broad shoulder. Her clamped nipples hit his back.

Her breath left her, but she didn't fight his hold. She was exactly where she wanted to be, being manhandled by the one man who could go caveman on her ass any time he wanted because she loved how primal he got with her, how desperate he got when he couldn't find the right words to tell her how he felt.

He dumped her onto the bed, then climbed right over her, his hands snagging her wrists to push them above her head, his knees digging between her legs to make her spread them.

When he settled, his big frame pressing her into the mattress so hard she could barely draw a breath, only then did the tension in his face ease.

Chrissi didn't wait for him to say a word, she lifted her head and kissed him. Words weren't what they both needed now. Right now, they both needed reassurance they were doing the right thing.

When she fell back, his eyes gleamed. "You can fight me now."

She scoffed. "You have me pinned to the bed. How'm I gonna do that?"

"You can tell me all the reasons why this won't work. You can talk and talk, and I'll listen. But you'll wear down. Eventually. And when you run out of reasons why it won't work, I'll show you again all the reasons why it will."

"Show me?"

His hips ground crudely against hers. "Again. And again. As many times as it takes."

"You're gonna fuck me into submission."

"I'll do whatever it takes."

She shook her head, then pressed her lips together. But the shaking of her body gave her away.

"Are you laughing at me?"

"If I am?"

"Chrissi, I'm dead serious."

"I know, she said, snickering. "That's what makes this so damn hysterical."

Chapter Eight

Ezra glared down at Chrissi. Didn't she know how close to the edge he was? "You think this is funny?"

"Yes!" Chrissi's laughter bubbled over. Her whole body vibrated with it.

Pulling back his hips, he centered his cock between her folds and drove straight up her sweet, tight cunt.

Her laughter faded, but her smile didn't. She waggled her eyebrows. "Did you think I was mockin' your manhood or something?"

"We have to talk," he ground out.

"I'd rather you did something with the tree trunk you just shoved up inside me." She wriggled beneath him, but he lowered his body, crushing her beneath him.

"Dammit, I have to know." He clenched his jaws, and waited for her to settle down.

Chrissi fell back, eyeing him with a hint of wariness, at last. "You said I had until Sunday—which is tomorrow."

He gave her another hard stroke. Masculine satisfaction eased over him as her mouth rounded and she gasped. "I'm not gonna sleep a wink until you give me an answer."

"You never asked a question, cowboy," she said breathlessly.

"Are you gonna stay?"

"How long do you see this lastin'?"

"All our lives."

"Doesn't seem like enough to me."

He stroked to a standstill. "You want more men?"

A wicked gleam entered her gaze. "Would you give that to me? The freedom to have anyone I want?"

This was not going the way he'd expected, and her stubborn chin was tightening, jutting out at him.

"Chrissi, are you serious?"

She snorted. "Course not. When I said it didn't seem enough, I meant, a lifetime didn't seem enough. I'm a greedy, horny woman. I don't want just a lifetime, I want forever."

Ezra blew out a deep breath and felt his whole body relax. "You'll stay?"

She arched an eyebrow and strummed her fingers across his shoulder. "I do have a house to sell."

"We'll pack up everything you want to bring."

Another strum and that damned arch curved higher. "I have a job."

"You can quit—" He paused when he saw both brows shoot straight up. "Or not. I'll make space for you in my office so you can work from home, if you like."

She shook her head. "I don't think I'll have enough energy to work outside the home. You're gonna have to support me."

Ezra felt his mouth twitch. "I thought you were bein' a little ambitious. We're a lusty bunch."

Her smile slid across her face again, softer this time. "You're gonna have to be my whole world. You know that, right? People won't be so accepting of me once they get wind of how we live."

"You'll have friends."

"Gonna find some for me?"

"You already have three. Right here in this house."

She tilted her head. "I do, don't I? I missed that, Ezra. I missed you all so much."

He released her wrists and came up on his elbows.

Her breath billowed out of her chest. "Wasn't gonna say it, but you've gained some weight." She wriggled beneath him again, but this time it was to free her legs and wrap them around his hips. "You can move anytime."

"Maybe I don't want it to end just yet. I like where I am."

Her fingers pinched his chest. "I'll let you sleep like this, your dick snuggled up inside me, but you have to move now."

"I do?"

"Yeah. And I want you to do it like you mean it."

"Don't I always?" he drawled, liking how her desperation was rising.

"No holdin' back. No tryin' to make it perfect. I want you there with me."

"I'm right here," he said, flexing his ass to pull out, then stroking deep again. "You get bossy when you're horny."

"I know what I want. At last."

"You've known all along or you would have found someone else, sweetheart."

Her eyes grew misty. But her smile didn't dim.

As he began to rock against her, he gave her everything he had, his passion and his heart. With her brown eyes watching him come unraveled, he felt like a much more powerful man. Complete. Chrissi Page belonged to them at last.

Late afternoon on Sunday, a door slammed in the distance. Chrissi stirred in the chaise where she'd been lying in the shade nude, a margarita on the table beside her and a man painting her toenails.

Josh glanced up and grinned. "Looks like we've got company."

She lifted her foot to admire her pedicure. "You missed your callin'."

"Always liked red toenails."

"As long as you paint 'em, it'll be my favorite color too."

Setting aside the bottle, he stood and stretched, then reached for the terry cloth robe beside her.

"Maybe I should get dressed," she said, beginning to worry about being caught like this—naked in the middle of the day.

"Maybe you should remember who's in charge," he growled.

She gave a snort. "It isn't you. Besides, I can't greet anyone in my birthday suit."

"Bet they wouldn't mind a bit," he said under his breath, but held out the robe for her to slide into it.

She belted the waist and pulled her hair from under the collar, then headed into the house in a hurry, or as fast as she could hobble walking on her heels to protect her toenail polish. She was determined to slide into the bedroom before whoever came inside.

But she was only three steps inside the living room when the door was flung open. Bo Crenshaw stepped inside.

Her back stiffened. Her toes dropped to the floor. Lord, would she ever be able to look at him and not feel ashamed?

Bo's glance narrowed on her, sweeping briefly from her hair to her red toenails. He gave her a swift nod. "Afternoon, Chrissi."

She returned the nod. "Bo."

Ezra and Cade came in behind him, their chests rising and falling swiftly. They'd run from the barn where they'd been mucking out stalls.

Ezra fisted his hands on his hips. "Bo, thought I told you I'd pick up the keys from you later."

Bo's gaze didn't leave her. He tucked his fingers into the front pocket of his Wranglers and pulled out her key ring. "A girl has a right to a choice, Ezra. Even if it's a bad one." He stepped closer and held them out. "If you like, I'll give you a ride back to town."

Chrissi couldn't let go of what he'd said. That she had a right to a choice, even a bad one. He was talking about that night. Her cheeks burned with the memory of what he'd witnessed. She wrapped her fingers tightly around the keys, at a loss for what to say when he was staring so intently.

A throat cleared. A surprisingly feminine sound. Chrissi peered around Bo's shoulder. A small hand shoved at Ezra's arm to push him aside. Shanna Davies stepped up beside Bo.

He glanced down, giving her a frown. "I thought I told you to wait in the truck."

"Four against one," she said to him, while she stared Chrissi up and down. "I don't think so."

Chrissi raised a brow. "You think he's gonna have to fight his way out of here?"

Shanna rolled her eyes. "No, I mean four cowboys full of testosterone. Hardly seemed fair to let you face them all alone."

Chrissi sighed. "Is there anyone in Two Mule who doesn't know what went down this weekend?" Even though she complained, for the first time, she didn't feel the horrible shame she would have just a couple of days ago. Had she changed that much? Bo's dogged willingness to be her champion, if she needed one, took the bite right out of that particular bone.

Shanna gave a little chuckle. "Bo doesn't keep secrets from me. We're engaged, you know. Thanks in no small part to your three beaus."

Chrissi's gaze snapped to Ezra. "Your little practice session?" she bit out.

Shanna's mouth dropped, then snapped shut. "You don't have to worry. Or be jealous. I'm crazy about Bo. We're gettin' married in a month."

Chrissi gave her deadly glare. "Josh always thought you had killer legs."

Shanna blushed. "Well, I guess he should know."

Chrissi stepped closer and raised her hand to wrap her fingers around Shanna's wrist. "You boys have your little talk. Shanna and I are gonna get to know each other." She turned and goose-stepped Shanna toward the doors leading out onto the patio. She stifled a tight grin when she heard Ezra cuss softly behind her.

Ezra turned on Bo. "What the hell were you thinkin'?

"That Chrissi might need rescuin'."

"Did she look like she was unhappy? Did she look like we've abused her?"

Bo shrugged, his expression neutral. "I didn't do right by her all those years ago. I should have said something to stop the three of you. If I'd known how things would turn out—"

"They've turned out just fine," Cade ground out. "She was comin' around."

"Well, maybe she should have some space. I don't imagine the three of you have left her time to think since Friday, have you?"

Ezra raked a hand through his hair, and pulled away a piece of hay. Damn, he didn't need this. Not now. "We don't need your interference, Bo. Chrissi's stayin'. Said so last night."

"Well, I'll want to hear it from her. Without you hoverin' over her."

"I didn't know Chrissi could be so jealous," Josh drawled, as though there wasn't enough tension in the room to pressure cook a stew. "It's kinda sexy."

Cade gave him a baleful glare. "I don't think it's a good idea to leave those two alone too long. Chrissi's got a twenty-five pound advantage."

Ezra stepped around Bo and stalked toward the French doors, the other three on his heels.

When he stepped out on the patio, his gaze swept it, then slammed into a sight that made him stumble.

Josh barreled into his back. "What...? Oh, hell."

Ezra felt the corners of his mouth twitch into a grin. The girls were seated at the edge of the pool. Their backs to the door. Their very naked backs.

Ezra noted the differences. One slender as a reed. The other curved. The dimples riding the upper curves of Shanna's ass were deep as her bare bottom hugged the concrete.

Chrissi glanced over her shoulder. "Didn't seem fair, you know. The fact you've had her. That she's had all four of you, and I don't even know what Bo looks like nekkid."

"Thought you were fine with just the three of us?" Ezra groused, although he wasn't really that perturbed with her. Chrissi was being Chrissi. Smart-mouthed. Savagely witty. Her eyes sparked with challenge. Lord, he'd missed that look.

"It's natural, you know," she said, her voice filled with lazy amusement. "Skinny-dippin' with friends."

She emphasized the last word, and Ezra's gaze cut to Shanna who gave him a winsome smile. "It was all her idea."

"I never doubted it, Shanna." Ezra walked to a chaise and sat on the edge, then bent to tug off his dusty boots. "I hope you know," he said, giving Chrissi a glare, "I'm gonna paddle that sweet ass of yours later."

"I'm countin' on it, cowboy."

"Just how far are you willin' to let this go?"

Chrissi rolled her eyes. "As you've told me repeatedly, I don't get to make those decisions."

Shanna groaned. "Bo, what's keepin' you, honey?"

Bo's chuckle was low and dirty. Then Josh's joined in. And Cade's.

Ezra held Chrissi's gaze while he stripped off the rest of his clothes. He shoved up off the lounger and strode to the pool, not the least embarrassed that his cock was hard and bouncing between his legs.

"Mmm-mm," Shanna said, turning to Chrissi. "You do know how lucky you are, right?"

"I do indeed."

"Most of the women in Two Mule are gonna hate your guts," Shanna said grinning wickedly.

"I figured that would happen." But Chrissi didn't sound like she cared.

"They'll all be jealous as hell."

"You won't be?"

Shanna grinned. "I had 'em. It was a present from Bo. Best present I ever had."

"What about that ring I gave you?" Bo asked, his voice deepening with displeasure.

Shanna giggled and held up her hand. "Ever see anything that pretty?"

The ring caught the sunlight and sparkled. Ezra eyed the large stone, then arched a brow at Bo.

"So it'll set me back a bit," Bo said. "She deserves to be spoiled."

Chrissi held Shanna's hand and oohed over the sparkling gem. Ezra gave Cade and Josh a pointed glance. Tomorrow, they'd head to San Angelo to rectify that little oversight.

Ezra dove into the water and swam beneath the surface to the far end, made a quick turn and returned. When he reached Chrissi's dangling feet, he wrapped his hands around her ankles and pulled.

She toppled into the water and sputtered when she came up for air. But a wide smile curved her lush mouth.

He bent and kissed her, snuggling his dick against her belly. Her appreciative groan was everything he could have asked. He broke the kiss. "You don't wanna watch, you'd better get the hell out of here," he said, not looking up to see how his warning was received.

Chrissi gripped the tops of his shoulders and gave a little jump. His hands cupped her butt while she wrapped her long, sleek legs around his waist.

"Shanna and I are gonna be real good friends," Chrissi said slyly. "We've decided."

He gave her a hard kiss. "How good?"

Chrissi lifted her chin, pointing to the side of the pool. A naked Bo was sliding into the water next to his girl and holding out his arms. Shanna laughed and reached for him, her legs closing quickly around his waist.

"Damn, seems a little crowded," Josh complained.

"Never stopped you before," Chrissi said, a wicked glint in her eyes.

Josh tore at his clothes. Cade laughed and settled onto a lounger, his gaze taking in the scene as he leaned back.

When Josh surfaced behind Chrissi, Ezra didn't feel the least bit crowded or annoyed at the intrusion. The light of happiness glowing in Chrissi's eyes was everything he'd ever hoped for. He kissed her mouth. Josh cupped her shoulders and glided his lips along the top curve.

"Slide down my cock, Chrissi," Ezra said.

"You tellin' or askin'."

"Which do you prefer?"

"I love it when you make me, cowboy."

He growled again and gripped her ass hard, centered his cock between her folds and shoved her all the way down.

Her eyelids fluttered, then slowly closed. "Oh my," she breathed.

Ezra caught Shanna's glance from the corner of his eye. She was peering over Bo's shoulder. Shanna's eyes glittered with delight, then she gave a wink. But it wasn't directed at him. He looked down to catch Chrissi's sly wink before she looked up and shrugged.

"We didn't leave you two alone that long. What did you two hatch up between you?"

Chrissi gave him a look that was all innocence. "I told her as how it didn't seem fair that she'd had all of you."

"Uh huh?"

"And we decided, seeing as how we're all gonna be such close friends, that we'd better even things up, just so I wouldn't feel so awkward around Bo. There's something about watchin' a man come that levels the field."

"That what she said?"

"I might have said that."

"That all you two have planned?"

"I'm never gonna tell."

Shanna laughed, then squealed until Bo pushed her head beneath the water.

"Serves me right," Bo groused. "I shoulda left her at home."

"Like I was gonna let you," Shanna said, coughing. "Most excitin' thing to happen in Two Mule—"

"I thought Dani Cruz's marriage was that."

"Guess there's more happenin' in our little town than I ever knew."

"Still happy you decided to stay?" Ezra asked Shanna, trying to keep his mind on the conversation, just to aggravate Chrissi, whose legs were tightening and whose fingers were twisting in his chest hair.

"I can't imagine a life now without Bo in it."

Bo's expression was taut, his eyes darkening with pleasure.

Ezra smiled. He knew the feeling. He turned his attention back to the woman who was rubbing her back like a cat against Josh's chest.

Chrissi wrinkled her nose at him. "Well, you weren't payin' me any attention."

"You need to learn a little discipline."

"You can teach me some—after you let me come."

Ezra lifted his chin to Josh. "Think we can take the starch out of her tone?"

"If you're not squeamish."

Ezra grunted. Then he wrapped his arms tight around Chrissi to hold her still.

Chrissi kept her gaze locked with his, but her mouth dropped open.

Ezra felt the nudge of Josh's cock. He raised Chrissi enough so that only the crown of his remained inside her.

Josh's cock aligned with his, and he pushed. Together they crammed upward.

"Sweet Jesus," Chrissi said, her eyes widening in alarm. "That's not gonna work."

"Have a little faith," Josh murmured beside her ear. "Relax, sweetheart. You owe me for those pretty red toes."

Ezra held still and let Josh take her hips and move her in short, grinding pulses up and down.

Chrissi reached one hand behind her and sank her fingers in Josh's hair.

Ezra palmed a breast and squeezed the nipple hard between his thumb and forefinger.

Her face screwed up in sexy anguish, a slow mewling whimper broke. "Move! Move now."

Water churned as he and Josh began to stroke, bouncing her on their cocks in short strokes. Chrissi flung back her head and screamed.

"Damn."

Breathing hard, Ezra turned his head, to find Shanna's avid stare trained on them.

"Wondered what it looked like. Damn."

But he couldn't have cared less that they were the center of attention. His balls were cramping, ready to burst.

Josh let out a deep groan, pumped her twice more up and down their cocks, then sank his face into the corner of her shoulder.

Ezra gave him a few moments to recoup. When Josh pulled away, Ezra walked to the steps with Chrissi held tightly against his chest. At the first chaise, he laid her back, braced his arms on either side of her and began to thrust—hard strokes, gliding faster, and faster. Her legs crept up, and he paused to settle them over his shoulders and then he hammered her again. When her eyes squeezed shut and her body bucked against his, he let go.

When he came back down, it was to Chrissi's hands smoothing over his chest, his shoulders. Her mouth peppering his face with kisses. He slumped over her, then crawled fully onto the lounger and didn't move.

The sexy convulsions caressing his shaft waned. Chrissi sighed beneath him, and snuggled her face against his neck. "I like this part too," she whispered.

"You're not goin' back to town tonight."

"No. I'm stayin' right where I belong."

Ezra kissed her, putting all of himself into the kiss—all his hopes and desires.

When he pulled back, she gave him a sleepy smile. "I can't believe I'm here. That I'm this happy."

"You won't want for a thing, darlin'. Not ever."

"I believe you. And I'm sorry."

He shook his head. "Don't be. Took us a while to get here is all."

His cock slid from inside her, and he rolled to his side, coming up on an elbow to look around the patio. Bo finally had Shanna's full attention. And by the froth the two were stirring in the water, they'd be done in just a few moments. Josh lay on his belly on a towel beside the pool, his head cradled on his arms. Cade met his glance when he finally got to him.

Cade gave him a little satisfied nod. "Not too shabby, bro."

Whether it was praise for his performance or for the fact they'd really done it, lassoed Chrissi for good, he didn't know. But he smiled. He didn't doubt there'd still be adjustments to be made. Trying to figure out the sleeping arrangements, how they'd share her, but he had no doubts they'd work it out.

If Cade and Josh felt even a fraction of the joy that he did, they'd make it.

Chrissi stirred, turning to spoon against him. "Think we could have sleepovers?"

Cade's laughter rang out, and Ezra grinned, then lifted a hand to smack Chrissi's thigh. "Only if you're very, very good."

Chrissi smiled across at Cade, sharing her pleasure. Cade's gaze warmed, his mouth eased into a one-sided grin. He hadn't been part of the shenangigans in the pool, but he'd liked watching. She could tell. She'd have to dream up more opportunities to take care of that proclivity. Maybe she could cajole Shanna into something wicked another time.

For now, he'd have to be content knowing he'd have her complete attention later when he took her to *the room.*

With Ezra cupping a breast, his skin and the sun warming her through and through, she couldn't imagine a more perfect day. What had been dirty and sordid had been repainted with all the colors of her passions. And deep inside, she didn't harbor a single doubt that this would work for all of them. That feeling of inevitability was stronger than ever.

"Happy?" Ezra murmured in her ear.

"Yes." She didn't need to say anything more.

His hand squeezed her again, then smoothed over her hip. "I love you. We all love you."

"I know."

He pinched her nipple and she grinned over at Cade. "I love you all too. But you already knew that."

Cade gave her a waggle of his eyebrows. "How those boots fittin' now, Ezra?"

Ezra grunted behind her. "Those boots are feelin' just fine."

Chrissi shook her head, wondering what the heck Cade thought was so damn funny, but she let them have their little joke. Probably at her expense. "Think Macy will be surprised?"

"Not a bit. Josh told her you wouldn't be comin' back."

Chrissi huffed. "You were sure of yourselves."

"You can't fight somethin' this strong."

"Don't think I'll always be this easy."

"Baby, told you before. I like you sassy."

"Better hold on tight. Because I have years of sass stored up just for you."

His hand smoothed down her belly and slid between her thighs. The caress he gave her made her moan. "So do we, babe. So do we."

A Four-Gone Conclusion

Dedication

To my fans. You motivate me, nag me, and push me to be better. Thanks for the emails, the letters, and the FB love!

Chapter One

"It's time you boys found yerselves a wife." Sam Logan made his pronouncement then waited, watching the four younger men seated at the table from the corner of his eye. He didn't have to wait long for his words to sink in. They exploded in the room with the force of a silent grenade.

Johnny's jaw closed with a snap, and he laid his spoon down on the scarred oak table. His black winged brows drew together, nearly meeting over his dark eyes as he raised his head.

Sam suppressed a smile. That look could make the toughest *hombre* gulp, but Sam wasn't the least bit concerned. Johnny tended to look mean when things changed. His oldest boy hated any kind of change.

If any other man had said what he had, Johnny would have cussed under his breath and aimed a piercing, silencing glare. However, he respected Sam, trusted him as much as he could anyone. That trust and respect were the only things that kept his butt on the bench beside his brother Killian.

For his part, Killian's eyes narrowed. The corners of his lips twitched. Likely he was amused by Johnny's reaction and didn't want to let him off the hook too quickly, but was already lining up all the reasons why Sam's idea was ludicrous. He was quick that way.

Sam calmly ladled the hearty stew he'd made into his mouth and let his gaze roam to the twins. Jason was coughing into his napkin while Mace gave him "helpful" taps between his shoulder blades.

Mace caught his stare and grinned. "*A* wife, did you say?"

Sam grunted, ignoring the one word that had caught his son's attention. "This is the third time this week we've had stew," he murmured. Not to change the subject, but to point out a glaring fact.

"I like stew just fine," Johnny muttered.

"This house misses a woman's touch." There, he'd said it. Sat the big gorilla in the room right at the dinner table. Impossible to ignore.

"Gracie can't be replaced," Killian said softly.

The permanent ache next to his heart echoed that truth. Sam nodded. "She's gone. Three years. I miss her every day. Know you do too. But life goes on. You're men now. You have an obligation. Ranchin's a family business. Y'all need families."

Johnny cleared his throat. "No disrespect intended, Sam, but you didn't get sons the old-fashioned way."

"Not because Gracie and I didn't try. And in the end, we had no regrets. We both loved you all like you was our own."

"So, you'd rather saddle us with—"

Sam aimed a quelling stare. "Think I felt like Gracie was a noose around my neck?"

"No sir, but..." Johnny's hands fisted on the tabletop. "Hell, how're we to find someone like her?"

Sam understood what he meant. Gracie's passing had left a hole in all their hearts. The boys had loved her. Took to her the very first day he'd brought each of them home. Gracie had been born to be a mother, and she'd showered them all with the things they'd needed most—acceptance and unconditional love.

"Boys, Gracie wasn't born a rancher's wife. Truth is, she didn't know a bull from a cow and damn near poisoned me with the first meals she cooked. But she learned. Find a woman willin' to learn, one you kin love and who'll love you back."

"You said, '*a wife*'." Mace wasn't gonna let that slip of the tongue go.

Sam shook his head and gave the twins a faint glimmer of a smile. Those two could always see the humor in any predicament. "Thought I'd give you two options. I know one can't piss without the other goin' too. And there are damn few single women to go around these parts. 'Nough said?" When all of them nodded, he cleared his throat. "I'll be out of town for the next four days. Auction in Abilene. The house is yours."

Johnny glanced around the dinner table at his brothers, whose attention had been snared from the first moment Sam had made his firmly spoken pronouncement. They were accustomed to eating quietly, filling their hollow bellies at the end of a long, hard day's work. Sam's words echoed in the silence that followed and hung in the air like a sour-smelling cloud. At least to Johnny's imagination. The thought of taking a wife, keeping a woman around on a permanent basis, made him itch.

The suggestion that they find "*a* wife" had come out of the blue. But the look on Sam's face said he'd thought long and hard about it and would brook no arguments. His sly mention that the twins might share one should have been shocking but wasn't given their recent escapades, as well as the unconventional relationships springing up like chokeweeds all around Two Mule, Texas.

The glint of humor in Killian's eyes forewarned he was about to say something sly. Johnny grunted and shook his head. Now was not the time to make a joke.

Killian snorted. His lips twisted, but he gave a shrug to indicate he'd behave.

Johnny didn't like the turn of the conversation, but it was Sam Logan giving the advice. When Sam spoke, which was seldom, they all listened.

After all, they owed Sam everything.

Jason leaned away from Mace and grabbed at the hand that been pounding his back. "Can we draw straws to see who gets saddled with one?"

Sam's eyes narrowed. "Strange things been happenin' around this town. Fact is, I don't care whether you all find one woman to take you on or four. But it's time for you boys to settle down."

Johnny knew what this was about. From the flinty glint in Killian's eyes, he did too. Apparently so did the twins, who shifted uncomfortably in their chairs, cheeks flushing a dull red.

"I'm not sayin' it was a sin, what you two boys did," Sam said. "The girl was willin' and yer young. But word gets around. Decent folks'll keep their women away from ya. Best to make your move fast before everyone hears the gossip and doors close in your face. This is a hard life. A man needs his comforts. Do I need to say more?"

All four younger men shook their heads.

"No sir," Johnny muttered. Sam's pronouncements weren't suggestions. He folded his napkin and laid it beside his plate. He'd been hungry before his foster father had spoken, but now his food sat like a cold lump in his belly.

A woman. He had to find a woman. He'd offer no arguments. Just like any other chore, he'd get to it with quiet efficiency.

"If you'll excuse me," he said, glaring at the twins as he pushed away from the table. "I have business in town."

Sam eyed him, then solemnly nodded. "You do indeed. Good luck, son."

It didn't take long for the other three to find him. The bathroom door opened as he slicked back his wet hair. Mace sidled inside while Killian leaned against the doorframe and Jason stood behind him with his hands in his pockets.

Mace grimaced as he sat on the edge of the bathtub. "Think he was serious?"

"When is he not?" Johnny said, keeping his tone even.

"You gonna do it? Just like that? Find yourself a wife?"

Johnny squared his shoulders. "It's what needs to be done."

"Because Sam said so?"

Johnny turned and shot out a hand to grip the collar of Mace's shirt.

Mace met his glare with one of his own. "Didn't mean it that way, bro. But hell, a wife? Shouldn't we take our time? Do this thing right? It's a big damn step."

Johnny hardened his glare. "You two may have been the ones to draw attention to the problem, but we've all done plenty to answer for. If we've embarrassed Sam, it's time we manned up."

Mace's lips firmed then he released a deep sigh.

Johnny let him go but stood with his hands fisted on his hips.

"Guess you're right," Mace muttered. "So, what's the plan?"

Why was it they always looked to him for a plan? In this instance, he was the least qualified one to decide. But as always, Johnny gritted his teeth and kept it simple. "We find a woman, someone we all don't object to, 'cause she's gonna be underfoot. Then one of us has to marry her."

"Think it'll be that easy?"

"'Course not. But since when have we shied away from a challenge?"

"We'll go in two separate trucks," Killian said, straightening away from the door. "Cover twice as much ground."

Johnny turned to the mirror and gave his appearance once last look. Wasn't much he could do, but at least his hair was combed and his breath was fresh. He glanced over his shoulder as the twins headed down the hallway, laughing and shoving each other toward the stairs. "Don't know why I'm suddenly scared to death," he muttered.

Killian laughed. "Yeah, those two with a mission. Boggles the mind."

The trip into town was made in silence. The way he liked most things. From the corner of his eye he could see Killian glancing his way, like he wanted to say something, but Johnny didn't give him any encouragement. He was mad as hell it had come to this.

Up to now, they'd had it good. Sure, the work was backbreaking but the ranch was all he had, all any of them had. Sam was planning to leave it to them, but only if they managed to keep out of trouble, learn to ranch, and be good citizens. Learning to ranch had been the easy part. They'd all taken to it like ducks to water, thriving on the physical challenge, learning to rope and ride. Learning how to break a horse to saddle, how to birth a calf.

That had been the simple part. The being good citizens part had been tougher. None of them had had the greatest examples of manhood in their lives to model themselves after. Not until Sam. And Sam had his issues. He was damn near a hermit. Grumpy as hell around other people. Even more so after Gracie had passed away.

Johnny had grown more like Sam than the others, but hadn't realized it was a problem until it came to dealing with the opposite sex. While the twins and Killian never had any trouble finding willing partners, Johnny had bedded few. His straight stare seemed to scare women away.

And if they weren't put off with the way he looked at them, he didn't have a silver tongue. In fact, he couldn't seem to put two coherent words together, much less figure out a way to put a woman at ease in his company.

Still, he wasn't all that worried about Sam's pronouncement. The others would have a better chance of finding a woman willing to take them on. He'd do his duty, give it a try, set an example for the others, but he knew his chances of finding a suitable woman who could overlook his flaws was slim to none. No, he didn't have an ounce of charm, had two left feet and a face as rugged as a mountain. Given those facts and his history, what woman would look his way and want to make a family with him?

Not that the thought of having children didn't cause his chest to fill with a lonely ache.

"I could help you, you know," Killian said, his tone casual.

Too casual. Johnny grunted. "With what?"

"Gettin' you a wife."

His hands tightened on the steering wheel. "Worry about findin' your own."

"It's not how it works, bro. We're brothers."

"We're not blood."

"Blood's not what counts."

Which was a sorry damn truth they all knew too well. Blood had failed them all.

Johnny cussed under his breath. "How would you help? You gonna chat her up for me? You gonna tell her what a catch I am?"

"Well, you are. You stand to inherit a fourth of the Double Tree. And I've seen the way women look at you."

Johnny snorted.

"You're not a bad lookin' guy.

Johnny aimed a blistering glare his way. "You gonna ask me out?"

Killian grinned. "Just statin' the facts. You're not hard on the eyes. And you're tall. Girls like that. And they like your hair. They like you fine until you give 'em that thousand-yard stare like you're sightin' down a rifle barrel."

Johnny gave him his meanest glare. "This isn't gonna work."

Killian gave a waggle of his eyebrows. "I'll help. What're brothers for?"

"You're just hoping I'll snag a wife and that'll be the end of it. You'll be off the hook."

"Maybe."

"You think this is funny."

"Watchin' you tryin' to sweet talk a woman—yeah, it'll be the most fun I've had in while. So where do you wanna start?"

Johnny didn't answer but he passed up the most obvious place. The saloon's parking lot was already full. Instead, he turned onto Main Street and slowed as he searched for a parking place.

Killian straightened in his seat. "You're not thinkin' of Ellie, are you?"

The way Killian said it intimated he thought Johnny had lost his mind. Maybe he had. But she was the first woman he'd thought of when Sam had mentioned the stew. "She can cook."

Killian gave an exaggerated shudder. "But she's mean."

"Should be perfect for me then, don't you think?"

Killian gave a bark of laughter then crammed his cowboy hat on his head.

Johnny raked his hair with his fingers and wished he'd thought to bring a rubber band to tie it back. However, Killian had said girls liked his long, straight hair. He didn't know why he'd kept it. It was the one most glaring trait that set him apart from his brothers. The last vestige of the heritage he'd thrown off when he'd run away from life on the reservation.

He trailed behind Killian, who stepped out with a bounce in his step, likely grinning his ass off that Ellie Harker was the first woman who'd come to his mind. What he didn't know was that Johnny had been working up the courage to ask her out, sitting in the diner week after week, but never quite finding the right way to do it.

Killian pushed through the door of the café. Johnny caught it before it slammed in his face, but didn't say a word. Already, he could feel his body tensing at the thought of talking to the woman.

She'd taken over the running of Katie's Diner when Katie's belly got too big and her husband, Cutter Standifer, had insisted she hire a cook until after the birth of their first child.

Inside, the smell of freshly baked apple pie assailed him, and his belly rumbled loudly. There could be worse things than being hitched to a mean woman, especially when she could cook almost as well as Gracie.

The place was busy. Wade Luckadoo's girl, a college kid home for the summer with blue streaks in her white-blond hair, glided out of the kitchen with a tray balanced on one hand. "Someone'll be right with you. Take a seat if you can find one."

Killian headed to the counter and slid onto a stool then patted the empty one beside him. Johnny felt his face harden to stone, his usual mask in public, as he sat. From this vantage they had a view straight into the kitchen where Ellie was working.

One glance and his body stilled, breath leaving in a quiet sigh. She was a pretty woman, although her looks weren't flashy like most men might prefer. Pale blonde hair, pretty milk-colored skin, and he didn't need to see what stretched below. Her well-padded curves were burned into his memory.

Right now, her cheeks were rosy, a fine sheen of sweat glistening on her brow. Johnny stared, wondering, not for the first time, whether she'd taste like everything she cooked.

Ellie pushed back a lock of her pale hair that fell over her hazel eyes with the back of her hand and then glanced up. Her startled gaze met his for a second then quickly darted to his brother before falling away.

He kept right on staring, wondering how long it would be before she'd come out to check on the customers first-hand.

Killian leaned toward him to whisper. "See? She was lookin'."

"She looked at you too. Would have looked at Ole Win's ugly face if he'd taken a seat right in front of her."

"But she wouldn't have blushed."

"She's cookin' over a stove. Of course her cheeks are pink."

Killian grunted. "You are the stubbornest man I've ever known. She's interested."

Johnny didn't like the little thrill of hope that warmed him. No use getting excited when Killian was only trying to warm him up to the challenge. "She looked at you too," he repeated under his breath.

Killian arched a brow. "We could follow in the twins' footsteps..."

"I'm not sharin' a wife with you."

"Only one of us can marry her, but seein' as you're a little stunted in the courtin' arena, you might need someone watchin' out for your interests. I can close this deal for you, bro."

Johnny thought about all the times he'd rehearsed the perfect opening line but sat tongue-tied when Ellie's attention landed right on him. He might need some help all right. "Say I was to agree to let you help. No one else would have to know?"

Killian's lips curved in a sly arc. "No one other than Ellie."

Johnny ground his teeth. "I might need a little help. The woman ties my tongue into a knot."

"You just do what you always do. Play the silent Injun. Be mysterious. Leave the rest to me."

Johnny didn't like it one bit, but he didn't see another way around it. And the last thing he'd admit to Killian was that Sam's pronouncement had given him the nudge he'd needed. He'd had his eye on Mean Ellie Harker for weeks but hadn't gotten up the gumption to do anything about it.

He nodded, then instantly regretted agreeing when Killian's mouth stretched into a wider grin.

"Not a word to the twins," he said, gritting his teeth.

"It'll be our little secret."

The kitchen door swung open and Ellie breezed out, a towel over her shoulder and a pitcher of water in her hand. She grabbed two tumblers from under the counter and set one in front of each man. "What can I do for you boys?"

Johnny bristled. No one called him a boy except Sam these days. And the way she said it with that wicked glint in her eyes told him she knew he didn't like it.

Killian leaned over the counter and tilted back his head. "Sweetheart, how come no one's married you out from under this place?"

Johnny stepped on Killian's boot and ground his heel into his brother's toe.

Killian grimaced but didn't turn away from Ellie's narrowing glance.

"Guess I've just been lucky," she said, her tone brisk. "What'll it be? We've got meatloaf and mac tonight."

"Just pie. Johnny here's been goin' on and on about how good your pie is."

"Has he now?" Her razor glance flicked to Johnny, and he felt its scrape against his cheek. She leaned closer, her face inches from his. "What do you say, cowboy? Want me to top it with cream?"

He gulped at her throaty purr. Not a sound he'd ever heard her make. His dick stirred and his cheeks heated. "Vanilla," he ground out.

She tsked. "A shame. Not what I had in mind at all."

His mind went blank for a second. "Um, you meant whipped?"

She gave a wicked chuckle, and his skin burned like fire.

"Now, that's more like it," she said, her voice deepening into husky purr again.

Beside him, Killian choked on laughter.

Ellie straightened and raised both brows. "Pie comin' up. À la mode." She turned on her heel, but not before he saw a hint of a smile on her face.

"Not bad, bro. Not bad at all."

"Not bad?" Johnny growled. "She thinks I'm an idiot."

"She was flirtin' with you."

"She knows I can't get a word out that makes a lick o' sense around her."

Killian turned his gaze from the sashay of her pretty bottom. "She knows you're interested."

"How long we gotta sit here?"

"'Til this place closes down. Don't eat that pie too quick."

"It'll be soggy."

"Then get another slice."

Johnny ducked his head and turned to watch Ellie as she refilled glasses, pausing to share a word or a quick quip. She had a way with her customers. A sassy flare. With her other customers anyway. Most times, she just ignored him. Or teased him, like tonight, until he couldn't think he was so damn hard.

Her head tilted back in laughter at something a couple said to her, then turned to catch him watching her.

For once, he didn't let his glance skitter away. He held her gaze, let her note where he looked, and then burned a slow trail down her body.

This time, he saw her throat work around a gulp.

Killian nudged him with an elbow. "Not bad, bro. Not bad at all."

Chapter Two

Ellie hoped like hell that anyone looking at her now would attribute her pink cheeks to the fact she'd been working over a hot stove. The last thing she wanted folks to guess was what a powerful effect the two men sitting at the counter had on her.

The moment they'd slid onto their stools, she'd felt their gazes burning like brands against her skin. Before she'd entered the dining area, she'd been tempted to comb her hair, wash the perspiration from her forehead, and slick gloss on her mouth. But she couldn't let them know they had that sort of power over her—the ability to rob her of good sense.

They made her feel girlish, breathless—wildly aroused. And they probably took it for granted that every woman who crossed their paths felt the same way too.

It didn't help her peace of mind that they were so different. Two sides of a savory sandwich. Which was exactly where her mind went every time she saw them together. Both were thickly muscled and tall, but Killian's face was classically handsome while Johnny's darker visage was savagely blunt. Killian's brown eyes always held a sparkle of sexy glee while Johnny's black ones were so intense her toes curled just thinking about what it might be like to have that gaze slide over her naked skin.

And lord, Johnny's hair... She couldn't count the number of times she'd gone to sleep imagining running her hands through the silky black strands.

For her, Killian made better sense. He'd be easy to be around. Easy to flirt with. Johnny scared her half to death. His silences and stoic expression gave away little of what he thought, and were why every once in a while she gave into the urge to tease him, mercilessly, until his jaw sawed closed and stayed that way. The spark of anger, whether for her or himself, was at least a reaction. Proof that she got to him.

Tonight, she'd been just a little meaner than usual, her mood fueled by her intense attraction to both brothers. Killian Logan had flirted with her in front of Johnny, but drew attention to his brother. Why had he done that? It unsettled her. Made her itch. So she'd turned it back on him by going after the brother, making sure she made Johnny so uncomfortable his brows drew together over that feral glare, and his face hardened into stone. Even his skin was a darker, redder tinge. Maybe she'd gone too far.

Still, Johnny had been watching her as she walked away. They both had.

Trouble was brewing and Ellie was just desperate enough to welcome it. If she could manage to play it cool and pretend she wasn't a mass of scorched nerve endings, anxious and aroused.

It wasn't like she had tons of options. She was pushing thirty. She dated, sure, but she hadn't found that spark in any of the men she'd stepped out with.

Maybe her standards were too high.

Which had her wondering again, why these two men turned her head. Everyone said all four brothers were trouble in boots. They'd come to Two Mule with juvie records. Even ten years later, town folks were slow to let go of their initial suspicions that they'd run off with the silverware if they weren't watched closely. Or worse, their women.

It didn't help that each of the four was intensely attractive in his own way.

Maybe that was it. She was discovering a latent attraction to bad boys inside herself. Or maybe she just needed to get laid and they seemed the easiest bet.

Ellie made a pass around the room, the pitcher of water her excuse to take her time before coming back to the counter and dishing out pie to the two rugged cowboys still watching her the way a pair of lazy cats might a mouse.

When the last glass was filled, she straightened her spine, deciding that boldness was the smartest defense against their allure. She came around the counter and did her best to ignore them as she divvied up two generous portions of her pie then plucked an ice cream scoop from beside the sink and bent deep into the freezer to get the ice cream.

A slow, quiet whistle had her popping up to aim a glare over her shoulder.

Killian's mouth kicked up at one corner. His brother's gaze was pitch black, his lips tight. She shook her head, suddenly self-conscious of the size of her ass, but bent again, hoping the chilly air inside the freezer would cool her cheeks.

Two rounded lumps of ice cream later, she slid their plates across the counter. "Coffee?"

Johnny nodded, then cleared his throat. "Please...*ma'am.*"

Lord, with any other man she wouldn't have reacted, but the raspy gravel in his voice made her nipples tingle. Would he sound like that in bed?

Fresh out of tart gibes, she gave a quick nod and poured them both steaming cups. When she set a cup in front of Killian, he reached for it, his sand-paper rough fingers sliding over hers before she had a chance to let go. She damn near dropped it.

"Easy. It's hot," he said, covering her hand with his, cupping it against the mug.

"Hotter than you can handle," she quipped.

"You sure about that?"

"Killian..." Johnny ground out.

Ellie licked her lips. Temptation wrapped around her, choking back the smart retort that flashed through her mind.

"Wanna find out?" Killian asked slyly, his eyelids dipping in a sexy tease.

Her tongue stuck to the roof of her mouth and she swallowed hard, unable to get a word out. Apparently, he didn't really need an answer, or something in her expression betrayed her.

His curt nod was at odds with his previous teasing. "Make sure you close up on time. We'll be waitin' out front."

Her gaze darted between Killian and Johnny. Killian's sharp gaze and the slight curve of his mouth was a dare she was tempted to take. Johnny's harsh features seemed etched in stone, like he at least waited for her answer.

Good lord, did they mean what she thought? Images of the three of them, naked and writhing on a bed had her breaths shortening. *Dammit, don't faint now.*

Ellie took a deep breath and eased her hand away to wipe it on her hip. "I've got customers," she said, shocked at the breathy whisper she managed.

"We won't keep you. Go on now." Killian picked up his coffee and gave her a wink before he took a sip.

Ellie backed up a step, and then whirled and hurried to the kitchen.

As she walked away, she heard Johnny whisper, "She didn't say yes."

"She sure didn't say no," Killian replied just as softly.

Inside, she leaned against the metal counter while she willed her heart to slow down. She'd lost her mind. That was the only thing she could believe, because she was already thinking of ways to clear the diner by seven sharp.

Her belly trembled; her fingers felt icy cold. Her nipples... She palmed them, giving them a squeeze to ease the taut, nearly painful sensation. Well, she'd wanted sex. Looked like she'd have more than she could handle.

At six thirty, Ellie gave another surreptitious glance at the clock. Johnny and Killian had stirred restlessly on their stools and then left, promising to see her when she closed. At least she hadn't had to pretend she was oblivious to the tension swirling in the room.

Ole Win was the last customer. She hadn't managed to hurry him to the door. His newspaper was pulled up to his nose, but his gaze rested on her. Had he heard Killian Logan's bold invitation? The old curmudgeon was the biggest gossip around. If he waited long enough, he'd see her leaving with the two men and her reputation would be in shreds.

Cindy Luckadoo topped off the last saltshaker. "I'll give the tables a quick wipe," she said smiling.

Any other time, Ellie would have appreciated the girl's diligence. "Thanks, Cin. I'll take the trash out to the dumpster. Then we're closing."

The glass door of the diner swooshed open, and Ellie's heart fluttered, but it was another set of Logan boys, the twins. She had yet to be able to discern between them they looked so alike. "We're getting ready to close," she said, hoping Winston would get the hint too.

"Can we get some pie? We won't keep you long. Promise," one of the boys said with an innocent smile.

"What is it with you boys and pie?" she muttered. "Sure," she said, smiling tightly, knowing it'd take more to cajole them out the door than just serve them the damn pie.

She busied herself behind the counter dishing it out. Damned if she'd offer them cream too. Quicker they ate, the quicker she could get out the door and see if Killian and Johnny had been serious.

As she watched both men mill into their desert, eyes closing in ecstasy, she shook her head. They were beautiful. While Killian and Johnny were cut from a more rugged stamp, these two were blond Adonises. A matched pair that could make any woman sigh.

"You busy tonight?" the one with the smile asked around a bite of pie.

"As a matter of fact, I am."

"Gotta date?"

Ellie arched a brow. "What business is it of yours?"

The two men shared a devilish wink.

"Whatever's goin' through your minds right now—"

"Just makin' sure you're available."

"Well, I'm not." *At least, not to you two tonight. Maybe.* "And you need to hurry it up because I'm closin' in five minutes."

The one with the smile pushed away his plate. "I'll be outside," he said to his brother, then gave her a quick wink before turning toward the door.

Lord, there'd be a whole damn family reunion in front of the café.

She raised her head to spear Ole Win with a last exasperated glance. "We're closin', hon."

He set aside his paper. "See ya for breakfast. You be careful, hear?" He ambled out, but with a glance over his shoulder as he left, like he was afraid he'd miss something.

Anticipation set her heart pounding. Ellie glanced toward Cindy who was straightening napkins in a holder while she tried to be subtle about watching the cowboy still seated at the counter.

Ellie cleared her throat. "Cindy, can you take this one's money while I take out the trash?"

Cindy blushed, but nodded.

She gave the remaining twin a pointed look. "Hope you enjoyed your pie."

"I did indeed." His grin was blissful, but something in his eyes hinted at mischief.

Ellie returned to the kitchen, wrestled with the trash bag lining the large bin then headed outside. As soon as the door closed behind her, she strode toward the dumpster next to the chain-link fence.

A scrape sounded behind her, the fence jangled. She glanced back, but something dropped over her head, blinding her. Hands grasped her wrists, and she let go of the trash bag and tried to turn around, but she was dragged backward against a hard chest. Before she could suck in a deep breath to scream, her hands were released, and strong arms enfolded her midriff, cutting off her air.

"Shhh, it's me, Mace Logan," came a teasing whisper beside her ear. "We're gonna play a little game."

"A game?" she squeaked.

"Yeah, promise we mean no harm."

We? Ellie wriggled hard inside his embrace, but his steely arms didn't give an inch. "Look, dumbass, you'd better let me go now before this goes too far. Don't think I won't press charges."

"No cause for that, now. Swear we won't hurt you. We won't do anything you won't want."

The way he said it, so cheerfully, calmed the fear that had had her gasping. Would a serial rapist sound so blithe? "Did Killian put you up to this?" Was this what he'd had in mind when he'd told her to be ready?

Masculine chuckles rumbled next to her ear. "No, but it looks like we all had pretty much the same idea."

Ellie stomped her loafer on his boot, whirled inside his arms then tried to wriggle down his body to escape, but he gripped her waist and tugged her higher, sliding her body up some interesting bulges.

"You're insane, you know," she said, trying to catch her breath.

"And you're not an easy woman," he mumbled.

"Does this actually work for you?" she said in a harsh whisper.

"First time I ever decided to kidnap a girl. Wouldn't have thought to try it, but Sam did mention he was tired of stew."

"What?" she asked, trying to make sense out of what appeared to be a kidnapping in progress.

"We asked at Shooters—who's the best cook in town? The best *unmarried* cook? Your name was mentioned more than once."

"So you're kidnappin' me for my pie?" she asked, her voice rising.

"Not just your pie. You're pretty too."

Ellie gave an exasperated growl. "Of all the cockeyed ideas. Get this sack off my head!"

A hand soothed up and down her back. "Promise we'll treat you nice. We just didn't think you'd say yes."

Ya think? "To what?

"To spending time with us. Getting to know us."

Her body reacted to the low rumble of his voice as well as the hard body she was pressed against, softening inside, warming. Yup, she'd completely lost her mind. "That's all you expect?"

"Well, we're not gonna attack you or anything. Not unless you want us to." And then he chuckled again.

Ellie couldn't help it. She laughed. If there was a note of hysteria in her voice, well who'd blame her? She'd been bored. Thought her dating options were drying up. But in the space of one night, four handsome men had sought her out. Not in a way she would ever have imagined it happening, but she stopped wrestling, resigned that whatever came to pass, it was going to be a very interesting night.

Johnny pulled in front of the diner just in time to see the Luckadoo girl heading to her Corolla. The sign on the diner door read *Closed*. "Get out and see if she's ready."

Killian gave him a crooked smile. "You're grumpy when you're horny."

Johnny grimaced. "Don't say that word to me. What I am at the moment is mad. This was a dumb idea."

Killian laughed and stepped down from the cab. He ambled to the door. He tried it then glanced over his shoulder and shrugged.

Johnny hit the steering wheel with his hand. She'd run. He guessed that was answer enough.

Killian cupped a hand over his eyes and peered through the glass before walking back to the truck and climbing inside. "Know where she lives?"

He did, but he wasn't telling Killian. She'd made up her mind. "Let's go home."

"You're gonna give up? Just like that?" His mouth pursed, then his head swung back toward Johnny. "Maybe she wants us to give a little chase so we appreciate her when we catch her."

Johnny shook his head. "She's not the type to play games."

"She's got a smart mouth. Maybe she does."

He gripped the steering wheel tighter. "Let's go home."

Killian sighed. "I'm sorrier than I can say this didn't work out. I was really lookin' forward to rumplin' her starchy hide."

Johnny shot him a killing glare and put the truck in reverse, backing up then making a U-turn in the middle of Main Street to head home again.

Killian grunted then turned in his seat. "You're not gonna give up that easy, are you? What about Sam?"

"Sam can hire a damn cook."

They passed the saloon on the left. The music was loud enough to be heard above the rumbling diesel engine.

"Want to get a drink before we head home?"

And have some yahoo make a comment about Indians and their liquor? Johnny knew his limits. His sour mood guaranteed he'd be hauled to jail after a fistfight. "No. You can come back later, by yourself, if you wanna drink."

"All right. I give up."

Thankfully the trip home was quiet. Darkness fell with the quickness of light blinking out.

Rolling up to the garage, Johnny noted the twins' truck parked at an angle in the center of the driveway.

"Guess they were in a hurry. Must have got lucky."

Johnny didn't reply. For a short while as they'd killed time in the Feed and Seed, purchasing supplies while waiting for the diner to close, he'd felt lighter, anticipating an evening spent with a warm, willing woman. An attractive woman with rosy cheeks and a sharp-eyed gaze. Now he'd have to listen to the sounds his brothers made as they entertained a girl. And it would be *a* girl, he thought sourly.

He and his brother piled out of the truck and walked through the breezeway and straight into the mudroom off the kitchen.

Voices sounded from the living room. One voice in particular caught his attention, the feminine edge so familiar his body grew instantly taut.

"I am not sleeping with you! Get it out of your head right this minute."

What the hell was Ellie doing here? And with the twins? And what the hell was she talking about—not sleeping with them? Had Mace and Jason succeeded where he'd failed? He glanced back at Killian whose eyebrows rose high.

"Is it because of our reputations?" Mace sounded like he always did—on the brink of laughter. "Not all of it was earned, I swear."

"And that's supposed to make me feel better?"

The edge of sarcasm in her voice pushed him into action. Women went soft and giggly around the twins. However, Ellie wasn't treating them any differently than she had him and Killian.

Johnny slammed through the swinging door—and ground to an abrupt halt.

Ellie sat on a kitchen chair, her hands behind her as though bound. When her head swiveled his way, her eyes snapped with anger and a furious blush colored her cheeks.

Johnny's head felt ready to explode. "What the hell is goin' on?" he shouted.

Mace and Jason glanced up from where they knelt beside her, tying another knot.

"She tried to bolt and take the truck back to town," Mace said cheerfully.

"Why the hell is she here?"

Ellie's chin shot up, her mouth thinning. "*She* wasn't given a goddamn choice!"

Jason shrugged. "We asked nicely. First. But she said she was busy."

"Maybe you should have believed her."

Killian swept past him and circled behind Ellie. "Nice knots."

Ellie sputtered. "Nice knots? Do you know how many charges I could bring against these two idiots?"

Johnny's anger cooled in an instant. He narrowed his gaze on the disheveled woman. "Law's not comin' anywhere near them," he growled.

Her eyebrows lowered and her lips pushed into a stubborn pout. "Untie me now."

Johnny glanced at Killian whose expression was bemused. His brother cleared his throat and knelt at her side. "You know they don't mean any harm," Killian said, his tone even and for once without a hint of sly humor.

"That doesn't excuse the fact they kidnapped me," Ellie said with a firm nod.

Johnny strode forward and gripped the arms of the chair and turned it hard, jerking it to face him directly. Then he bent so close he was nearly nose to nose with her. "What has you maddest? The fact they kidnapped you? Or the fact that it wasn't Killian and me?"

Mace's eyebrows shot up. "It was you she was gettin' busy with?" He started chuckling.

Jason's laughter was full-bodied, and he hugged his belly and dropped onto his ass on the floor.

Johnny shook his head, waiting for them to quiet while his fingers tightened on the chair's arms.

Mace held up a finger. "We'll stop...promise. Gotta hear the rest of this."

He felt a tic pulse beside his eye. Anger and frustration, even a little fear for the twins, bubbled up inside him.

Her frown eased and her hazel eyes widened, staring at the tic. She wet her lips with the tip of her tongue.

Silence enclosed them at last as the twins' laughter faded. He knew they all stared at him, waiting to see how he'd solve this problem. His focus narrowed as he loomed over her. This was between the two of them. Regardless of how it had happened, this moment had been inevitable. For once, the right words spilled out. "Maybe they didn't go about it right, but it doesn't mean this has to end bad."

Her gaze locked with his.

His trailed down her body.

Her chest moved with her shortened breaths. Her nipples beaded against the thin tee stretched taut by the position of her arms.

"I don't approve how they got you here, but you're stuck here now. Until we figure out a way to make this right."

She snorted, but her expression softened as though she wasn't quite as self-assured as she'd been moments ago. "You wanna make this right?" she said softly. "You take me home now."

Killian eased closer and pushed a mussed strand of her hair behind her ear. "Tell the truth, Ellie," he whispered. "You kinda like this, don't you?"

Her head pulled back. "You're all insane."

Killian tapped her nose. "The truth now. This is the most fun you've had, isn't it? Or it could be."

More than a little shocked at the implications, Johnny fought the sudden surge of heat roaring through his body. The sight of her, trembling with rage, tied and vulnerable, shot lust straight through him. What the hell did that say about the kind of man he was?

He cleared his throat to get their attention. "Ellie, we're already in too deep now. Look at me."

Her head hung for a minute then slowly lifted. Moisture filled her eyes, but her chin firmed again as she met his glance.

"They went about this all wrong. But they don't mean any harm. None of us do."

"What do you want from me, Johnny?" she asked, her voice husky.

His throat worked as he drew moisture into a mouth gone dry. Christ, he was really gonna say this. "I want anything you're willin' to give."

She gave a soft gasp.

The impulse was there, and since he was already damned, he didn't resist. He bent toward her, satisfaction blazing through him when she raised her mouth to meet his.

Chapter Three

Ellie drowned in that kiss, pulled under by the ebb and flow of his firm lips.

Already breathless with excitement over her unusual predicament, the way he'd waded into the room, taking command of the situation, and of her, melted her resolve.

What woman could resist? *Seriously?*

Four handsome men hell-bent on having her? Ellie Harker? If this were a romance novel, like the naughty ones she preferred, the heroine's resolve would wilt beneath their strong wills right about now.

Why did she think she had to fight? How could she now? His lips circled on hers, tugging at her mouth, pausing to bite her lower lip until she gasped and opened. Then he was inside her, stroking deep. Every bit as determined as the hard edge of his jaw had appeared as he'd strode toward her.

Why not surrender?

The thought seeped into her mind, eroding the walls she'd erected around herself when she'd thought they only toyed with her, flirted with her like they would any other woman, not meaning it.

When his tongue stroked hers, teasing her in a sensual play no one else could see, she was sorely tempted to give way.

But then where would she be? A single sordid night with the Logan boys? A soiled reputation with little hope of finding a decent man willing to overlook the stain? She clamped her teeth around his tongue and bit, then opened her eyes.

He grunted. His eyes slammed open.

"She just bite him?" one of the twins said then laughed.

Johnny's hands clamped on her shoulders, giving her a firm but gentle squeeze of warning.

She opened her jaws and let him retreat.

A kiss pressed against the side of her cheek. Killian tipped her chin his way and gave her a wink. "She's just reminding us she's got choices even if she is tied to a chair, aren't you, sweetheart?"

Johnny pushed away from the chair and straightened, his tall, thickly muscled frame looming like a dark shadow.

Ellie dragged in deeper breaths, relieved he wasn't so close he clouded her mind.

"Our intentions are purely honorable, you know," Killian murmured.

She gave him a wide-eyed glare.

"As it so happens, we're in need of a wife."

"*A* wife?"

The twins shared a glance then burst into dirty chuckles.

"How about we do a trial run?" Killian said, his tone cajoling. "You can see what we're like to be around. Then you can choose."

"A trial run..." she parroted dumbly. Had he really just said that they wanted her not as a plaything but as a wife? "*Choose?*"

"Which one of us you marry."

She shook her head. "You're crazy."

"But the thought isn't a huge surprise, is it? Tell me that we haven't tempted you."

She turned her head, taking in the sight of the men—the grinning twins, Killian's wicked half smile, then last, Johnny's quiet glower. Her gaze darted back to the twins. Safer territory, or so she told herself. "What if I don't choose any of you?"

One of Killian's dark reddish-brown brows rose. "Then we all walk away. We won't bother you again."

She grunted, not believing his easy charm, as glib as any used car salesman trying to unload the lemon on his lot. "You say that, but you seem pretty sure I won't."

His expression softened. "Sweetheart, you're full of sass, but I've seen the way you look at us. The way you looked when Johnny kissed you."

He'd noticed that? Lord, she'd all but melted into a puddle. "You must think I'm a big whore to even consider your proposition."

"If you were a whore, you wouldn't have been our first choice. We want children, and we want to know they're ours."

Despite his assurance, she felt more than mildly insulted. "Let me guess. It's all about my pies."

Killian's smile stretched wide. "That's where it started. But the way you've handled this, us...now that's even more of a turn-on."

Ellie relaxed against the hard back of the chair and closed her eyes. For privacy. Since they'd allowed her none. She knew they awaited her answer.

She knew what her answer should be, what a good girl would say, but then she'd be back to square one—wondering when the rest of her life would begin. And this felt like a new beginning. Even though she told herself this was probably just an elaborate, sexy trap to lure a woman into a foursome, hope stirred inside her.

Would this be the start of something wonderful or was she going to make the biggest mistake of her life?

She opened her eyes, seeking Johnny's gaze first, as though it was natural to look for his approval.

"Untie me," she said quietly.

He let out a deep breath, his mouth twisting, but strode toward her again and slipped behind her. The knots eased instantly, and she pulled her hands in front of her, rubbing her wrists although they didn't really hurt.

She stood shakily and all the men stood and backed up a step, their expressions, for once, all looking consistently grim. "I'm hungry. I haven't had my dinner yet," she said. "Show me the kitchen."

Johnny leaned his butt against one of the counters, watching as Ellie took control of the kitchen, stepping up like a general as she called for pans and pots and ingredients, which the men eagerly leapt to provide.

Not him, though. He watched, staying silent. Tense inside, because he was fighting arousal. Someone, maybe several someones, would be sharing her bed once she'd made her choice. He understood that she was asserting herself now so they'd know she wouldn't be pushed into anything she didn't want.

He was fine with that. At least, she'd stopped harping on bringing them all up on charges. Not that a night or two in jail wasn't a bad idea for his two younger foster siblings. Mace and Jason had gone too far. As they always did. Pushing the limits of folks' tolerance for their free-spirited shenanigans.

And yet, Ellie seemed at ease with them, had them hanging on her every word and gesture like puppies eager for a pet or a scratch behind the ears.

Which of them would she choose in the end? How would the contest be decided? Would it come down to who was best in bed? Who was kindest? Who treated her most like a queen?

He'd lose for sure because he couldn't be any other way than how he was. For her, however, he yearned to be the better man. He wanted to be the man who called her "wife".

Killian stood at the stove stirring a creamy sauce for a stroganoff while Mace and Jason cut vegetables for a salad.

Ellie glanced up then gave him the look. The one that had the other men scurrying to do her bidding.

He arched a brow.

"Maybe you could set the table," she said, sounding breathless.

She'd worded it as a request rather than an order. He shoved away from the counter and gathered plates and utensils. In minutes they were all seated at the table and tucking in to the meal she'd created from scratch. Sam would have no complaints about her cooking.

"Sam'll have no complaints," Killian said around his food, echoing his thoughts.

"Sam'd have all our hides for what those two yahoos did," Johnny muttered.

"Sam's your foster father?" Ellie asked, a tentative note in her voice.

Johnny nodded, hoping she wouldn't continue down that particular road. He wasn't comfortable talking about how he'd come to be here. It was past. Better not revisited.

"Sam never adopted you all," she continued when no one jumped to answer her question.

Mace glanced at Johnny.

Johnny knew that if they had a hope in hell of getting her to stay that they couldn't keep shutting her out. He shrugged his acceptance.

Mace cleared his throat. "He couldn't adopt. We all had living kin."

Her hazel eyes darkened. "Your...kin...never wanted..."

"No," Johnny said tersely. "We took Sam's name after we each hit eighteen. Outta respect. And because he was more of a father to us then we ever had."

"I'm sorry about that," she said softly.

"I'm not," he bit out. "Sam's a good man."

Her chin shot up. Her eyes glittered with challenge. "I meant, I'm sorry your families weren't ideal."

"Was yours?" Killian asked, deftly diverting her.

Her mouth relaxed into a small smile. "It was. My mother's still living. In Dallas near my sister."

"How'd you end up here?"

She lifted a shoulder. "Dallas is big. Fast-paced. I didn't go to college, so it wasn't like I was going to have a career. I packed up one day. Headed to the Hill Country. I worked in a German restaurant in Fredericksburg for a while then decided to move on."

"Why?" Jason blurted.

Her head dipped, and she twisted her fork around an egg noodle. "Because I broke up with my boyfriend. It wasn't pleasant staying there. Everyone knew him and sided with him."

"They had to take sides? He cheat on you?" Jason asked.

Johnny could see how uncomfortable she was and gave his brother a quelling glance.

Ellie set aside her fork. "Yes. As a matter of fact, he did."

"We'd never do that," Mace said, sitting forward, his expression earnest.

A brow arched. "That supposed to be a selling point?"

"Just sayin'—we'd never do that to a woman."

Ellie shook her head, her gaze locked with Mace's like he'd mesmerized her. "Never say never," she murmured. "You might fall in love."

Jason choked on his iced tea.

Killian rolled his eyes. "Those two don't believe in love."

Jason set down his glass. "Bein' friends, enjoyin' sex—why does it have to be about love? It's just hormones."

She straightened her shoulders. "I guess I understand what you mean. I've never felt that connection some women talk about when the subject of love comes up. Maybe you have a point."

Johnny didn't like her agreeing with that sentiment. He'd want her happy. Satisfied with her life. If she fancied herself in love, she might stick around longer. Not that he believed in a roses and promises kind of love either. Love of family, now that he believed in. He had that now.

Killian gave her a smile. "So how'd you end up here?"

Ellie grinned, looking a little sheepish. "I ran out of gas."

"Seriously?"

"Yeah, right on Main Street. I wandered into Katie's Diner and asked for the nearest station. Katie sent Ole Win with a gas can to get me fixed up, served me a meal, and by the time I was done, offered me a job. Katie had been desperate to find someone to take over for her. The hours were long and she wasn't up to it, not fighting morning sickness and swollen feet. And her husband, Cutter, hovered over her. 'Bout drove her crazy. It was sweet, but he was driving her nuts."

"So it all worked out," Killian said.

She nodded. "Yes. I like Two Mule. It's small. You get to know people. I've never really had that."

"Bein' on a ranch is smaller," Johnny said.

Killian gave him a frown then gave Ellie an easy smile. "We have hands and they come and go, but it's the same guys, seasonal work. No women around."

The way they all homed in on her had her twitching in her chair. Now she knew for sure she'd be the lone woman among a pack of lonely men.

"A woman might get lonely for girl talk," Johnny said, ignoring Killian's warning glances. Ellie had a right to know, up front, what it would be like.

"I'm not much for girl talk," she said.

Did that mean she was thinking about it? A foot connected with his shin.

Johnny eyed Killian who sat opposite him. He didn't need to be reminded he hadn't said a positive word. He turned to Ellie. "You'd be too busy to be lonely."

The twins frowned.

Killian snorted. "Bro, we're trying to woo her not scare her away."

"That's okay," Ellie said. "I'm not scared of hard work, but I haven't said I'll stay." She set down her fork. "I'm not doing dishes. Who's taking me home?"

"You're not goin' anywhere," Johnny grumbled, then cursed to himself for being so blunt.

Her hands folded tightly in front of her. "You mean you're going to keep up this farce? We've had our date. I made you dinner. Now I'd like to go home. I have work in the morning. A diner to run."

"Stay closed," he said, afraid he sounded like a cranky bear because he was growling. "Call Cindy and say you're sick. She can put up a sign."

"I'm not sick."

"You're also not goin'." Johnny stood slowly, until once again, he dwarfed her.

Her gaze rose and rose. Her jaw lost its stubborn edge. Again, her tongue darted out to wet her lips.

Was she hoping for another kiss?

"We thought we might have some fun," Jason said as though he hadn't a clue about the tension between him and Ellie. "Show you what it'd be like."

She blinked and glanced sideways toward him. "We?"

"Wouldn't you like to know who you like best before you decide?"

"Who I like best?" Bright red spots stained her cheeks again. "What are you planning on, takin' turns so I can judge?"

The way her voice rose with each slowly enunciated word said more about her agitation than the spark of anger in her eyes.

"Choose two," Johnny blurted.

"Choose two for now," Killian amended.

"Which of us do you want?" Mace asked.

"Or we could draw straws," Jason said, then nodded to his brother.

"Draw straws?" Her hands hit the table and she shot up from her chair. "Why do you need my input at all? You choose and just let me know what you decide." She turned sharply and walked toward the kitchen door, the one leading to the living room.

"Where ya goin'?" Jason called after her.

"Home. Walkin' if I have to." And then she slammed the door behind her.

Johnny started after her.

Killian caught his arm. "Really, bro? You think you can talk her into stayin'?"

"I was gonna drive her. If she wants to go, we have no right to make her stay. It ends now."

"Let me talk to her first. She's a lady and this has to be more than a little shocking. You're lookin' too mean to do anything but make her run faster."

Johnny balled his fists, but nodded. "I'll take her home if that's what she wants—after."

Killian nodded then hurried out the kitchen door.

"I'm headin' out to see Zach," Johnny said, mentioning one of their hands' names to make it seem less like a lie. "I'll make sure he doesn't need a hand in the barn. You two—dishes."

With that, he stalked out the opposite way, through the mudroom. In the distance he could see Ellie walking with her head high, her arms swinging, Killian walking backwards beside her. He couldn't hear what was being said, but it sure didn't look like Killian was making any inroads into changing her mind.

Damn, could things have gone any worse? He turned toward the barn and things he understood a whole lot better than the female mind.

Ellie stalked all the way to the big iron gate at the entrance of the property. She was out of breath, sweating, and Killian still hadn't shut up. "Does it look like I'm listenin' to a word you have to say?"

"Sweetheart—"

She gave him her dirtiest glare.

"What has you maddest? The fact they were rude or the fact Johnny or me didn't lay claim right away?"

She halted in the middle of the gravel road. "I'm not like that. I'm not some desperate, *horny* woman...some slut who's gonna hop from bed to bed to decide who's the best lover."

"They're all overeager," he agreed, letting her vent.

"Maybe the twins, but your other brother doesn't look as though he wants me here. Maybe he's the only one with a lick o' sense."

"Oh, he wants you here. He just doesn't have much experience with women. He doesn't know how to ask."

She rolled her eyes. "What are you, his pimp?"

"No, but we're close. I know him better than anyone. He came here at the same time as me. From the same day at court. Sam sat in the back as the judge sentenced us..."

"What for?"

"Stealing food."

She swallowed hard and looked away. The thought of these two strong, proud men being hungry enough to steal cut deep.

Killian stepped closer, but didn't touch her. "Johnny doesn't know how to ask for what he wants." His voice lowered. "He waits to see what's offered because he doesn't think he deserves more. If you expected him to ask you to stay, you'd be waitin' all your life. That doesn't mean he doesn't want it."

Ellie wrapped her arms across her belly. A hug only she could give herself. Johnny seemed like an impossible dream. "What about you?" she asked, softening her glance, because she didn't want to fight. She wanted the truth. "What do you want?"

"I want him happy."

"Nothing for yourself?"

Killian's lips twitched. "I wouldn't mind bein' there to make sure things work between you two. That you two find a way to communicate."

"You mean, be there in bed with us."

"I think if he has trouble talkin' to you now, that he'll be a damn mute when he's got you under him. I know him. I've had years readin' him. Judgin' his moods. There's not much expression to read, but I can see what pleases him, what scares him, what drives him. Level with me, Ellie. Do you want him?"

Her eyes filled, and she glanced away. "I'm not sure what I want. But I've never felt so uncomfortable. So..."

"Hot?"

She ducked her head to stare at her feet before continuing. "Yes...hot just about says it all...when he looks at me."

"He needs you, Ellie. If there's any hope of him finding happiness, he needs your spirit, your smart mouth to goad him. If you think he could be the one for you..."

Truth was, she was scared. Johnny was more intense, more *everything* than any man she'd ever met. They'd only exchanged a few dozen words over the months, but those few were ones she remembered. Could she handle that kind of intensity on a permanent basis?

"This is crazy. It's too fast."

A roughened fingertip lifted her chin. "It may be fast, but does if feel wrong?"

She slowly shook her head.

Killian's smile was soft and approving. "We'll take it slow. Promise. Let you set the pace."

She tilted her head and wrinkled her nose. "And if I don't want it slow? Maybe I don't want to be in control."

Killian chuckled and caught her hand to reel her in close to his chest. "I knew you'd be the one."

She burrowed deep, pulling courage from him. "I've never done anything like this."

"Me neither. But we can't let this go too smoothly. We have to keep Johnny on less than solid ground. He's got to think he's got competition for your affection to draw him out. You shy about gettin' naked around a bunch of men?"

Her body vibrated at the thought. "The twins too?" she squeaked.

Killian's head nodded, bumping against her head. "Johnny gets the most irritated when they're playin' around. He'll be more apt to break if they're in the mix."

"Will I have to...go all the way with them?"

His chest shook with soft chuckles. "I'll talk to them on the sly. They'll only go so far. They got themselves in a heap of trouble tonight. But that's how they roll. If ever one of them sets his mind on a girl, the other has to follow. Not gettin' to have you will be punishment enough."

She snorted. "I'm not some great prize."

A finger lifted her chin. "Don't sell yourself short," Killian said, staring into her eyes. "There's plenty here for a man to enjoy besides your talent in the kitchen."

Her whole body warmed to the sudden tension in his face and body. A shiver worked its way down her spine. "I don't know. It feels...dangerous."

"And that's a bad thing?" he asked, his eyes crinkling at the corners.

"It's like I'm stepping off a cliff. And I don't know how I'll handle the aftermath if things don't work out."

"There's no guarantees in this life, Ellie. Sometimes you have to step off the edge."

She searched his steady gaze, but didn't find any answers there. Only time would tell his true intentions. Slowly, she slid her arms around his back and relaxed inside his embrace.

When his head bent close, she whispered, "Is he watching us?"

"Yup." His lips twitched again. "Looks dark as a thundercloud. You ready for this?"

"You'll be there?"

"Every step of the way." And then he kissed her, taking her mouth with a confidence that made her knees buckle.

His mouth rubbed against her lips until she opened, accepting the thrust of his tongue.

She was oddly reassured by his masterful kiss as much as by what he'd said. She hadn't a clue how this would work, what was expected, but for once, she'd just let go. What was the worst that could happen?

She'd have a night she'd never forget with four handsome cowboys. A sensual adventure she'd never imagined embarking on.

Groaning, Ellie rose on her toes and pressed her body into his, loving the way his arms tightened around her and the evidence of his desire grinding gently against her belly.

Chapter Four

Johnny stood with his back against the wall, legs braced apart as he listened to the sound of running water. He wondered if she hoped they'd fall asleep before she finished. "That's a long damn shower," he muttered.

"Give her a chance to relax," Killian said from the bed, where he sat, leaning against the headboard. "We've pushed hard to get her this far. Let the idea of it sink in."

A tap sounded at Johnny's bedroom door. He reached to the side and opened it a crack, keeping his hand on the knob.

The twins stood in the hallway. Jason raised the bottle of fragrant oil Killian had told them to find under his bathroom sink—a chore to get them out of the room for a minute, Killian had said, because Johnny looked ready for a fight the minute Ellie had escaped into the bathroom.

Johnny wanted nothing more than to slam the door in his brothers' grinning faces, but he opened it wider, admitting them. Killian had said she wanted this. To be the object of their combined attentions. A favorite fantasy of hers.

He'd never have guessed she'd want that. Not in a million years. In fact, he'd thought up until the moment she'd called Cindy Luckadoo, saying she wouldn't be in the next day, that she'd insist on going home.

The twins strode inside, barefoot and shirtless like Killian.

Johnny had yet to shed even his boots, unsure whether he could be in the same room when things went down. The thought of all the others swarming her made him feel ill at ease. Not because he really thought it was sordid, but because he was unsure he'd have what it took to enter the play. He'd never done anything like this, never even watched a porno movie to see what a ménage scene looked like. Not that he didn't understand how it could work.

He leaned against the wall again and eased his legs a little wider. His cock was hard, but crammed against his leg. His balls felt heavy. From the glint of humor in Killian's eyes, he knew exactly what was bothering him.

Johnny schooled his face into an implacable mask, determined not to give way beneath his brother's amusement.

The water stopped.

All the Logan brothers' gazes swung to the door.

Several long moments later, the door opened, releasing fragrant, steamy air.

Johnny inhaled the sweet, apple scent of her as Ellie stepped into the room, a towel tucked under her armpits.

Her gaze went to the three near the bed, then swung, searching the room until she glanced slightly behind her and found him. He stared back, catching a look of panic in her wide eyes, but before he could react, she broke with his glance and turned toward the bed.

Her chest rose; a deep breath blew between her pursed lips. "Well, boys," she said, her voice slightly husky, "you're the experts. Someone gonna show me how this works?"

That her thoughts were so close to his own almost made him smile. She wasn't as self-possessed as she'd like to pretend. The hand clenched at the closure of the towel betrayed her nervousness.

Johnny pushed away from the wall and walked up behind her, settling his hands gently on her shoulders.

She gave a little jerk then a short gusting laugh. "Guess I'm nervous," she whispered.

He leaned toward her ear. "Me too."

"I'm gonna make an ass of myself with an audience watching."

"Not possible," he muttered. Nuzzling through wet strands of hair, he kissed the side of her neck.

A delicate shiver slid over her warm, damp skin. "Killian promised to keep things from getting too out of hand," she said, her breaths shallow.

His fingers tightened their hold, and he swallowed hard. "You have any bad moments, all you have to do is say uncle and we stop."

"You're all right with this?"

He didn't answer. He wasn't. Not really. But this wasn't about him. He let his hands slide over her breasts, gently pushing away the fingers clutching the towel. Then he pulled the edges, opening it, exposing her to his brothers' avid stares.

His glance left the view of her pretty pink nipples to give a warning to his brothers. But not a one offered a dirty comment.

The twins' gazes raked her frame, their bodies tensing. For once, all humor erased from their expressions.

Killian's eyes narrowed as he looked. He turned on the bed, dropping his legs over the edge, and stood. He strode toward her, his hands lifting when he was right in front of her to cup her face. He bent toward her and gave her a soft kiss then raised his head to look at Johnny. "This is about her."

Johnny gave a sharp nod then stepped back, taking the towel.

The others had seen more of her than he had, but this view of her backside was just about perfect. Her frame was small, her waist deeply indented over pretty, flaring hips. Her buttocks were lush and round—heart-shaped, he thought, struggling to find words to catalog her attributes. Her legs weren't all that long, but were firm and smooth—they'd be strong enough to ride a man's hips when he went wild.

Killian lifted her hand and pulled her toward the bed.

Her buttocks jiggled a little with her stiff-legged gate, but she followed him, letting him lead her to the twins. When he dropped her hand, he stepped back, returning to take up a position next to Johnny as the twins moved in, sandwiching her between their naked chests.

She faced Mace. "Which one are you?"

The corners of Mace's mouth kicked up.

Johnny cussed softly. She was about to have sex with the twins but couldn't even tell them apart.

Jason's hands slipped around her belly and moved up to cup her breasts. "Mace is the biggest idiot. Me not as much."

"That's true," Killian murmured.

Johnny grunted, watching the way her nipples beaded as Jason toggled them with his thumbs.

Mace grabbed her hand and led it to the waistband of his jeans. "It's all yours if you've got the guts."

Ellie lifted her chin with a soft, feminine snort. She opened his pants then spread the sides open to reveal the tip of his cock. But then her hands smoothed around his body and sank beneath the waist to cup his buttocks.

Mace rose on his tiptoes and chuckled as she did whatever she was doing—caressing his butt? Her gaze never left his brother's as she withdrew. Then she gripped the waistband and shoved the jeans down to his thighs.

Johnny tried to avoid staring at his brother's dick, but her fingers wrapped right around it, gliding up and down his shaft.

Color seeped into her cheeks. Her mouth parted around a shaky breath.

"Any complaints?" Mace's voice was silky and low.

Johnny's own breath caught at her expression. This was the moment, he knew it, when she'd embrace the challenge or back away.

Her eyelids fluttered down then blinked rapidly. She tilted her chin and gave Mace's cock another slow stroke. "No complaints," she said, her tone smoky.

Jason chuckled behind her and dropped his hands. He shoved down his jeans and stepped on them as he freed his feet. Then he spun her to face him while his brother ditched his pants too.

Jason gripped her ass and raised her off her feet. Her legs dangled for a moment, then rose to hug his waist.

Johnny felt his whole body tighten at the intimacy of the embrace, jealous as never before because he hadn't been the first to feel that grip.

Jason turned to the bed and climbed onto the mattress, carrying her with him to the center of the bed. When she released him, lowering her legs to rest on the mattress, her sex was open. Jason's gaze dropped.

Johnny wished it was him looking there. He'd do a sight more than just stare.

"Jason," she whispered, a knee rising and turning inward, but halted by his thigh.

"That's right," Jason said, combing his fingertips through the pale hair covering her mound. "But do you really want to be able to tell us apart?"

"Shouldn't I?" White teeth bit into her bottom lip.

"Isn't it more fun to guess?"

Mace snagged the bottle of oil and climbed onto the mattress beside his brother. "Don't get too far ahead. We promised a massage."

"Jesus," she breathed. "I'm not sure I'll survive it."

"Why's that, sweetheart?"

"Because I'm already..."

"Wet?" Jason trailed a fingertip down her folds.

"That too. Was gonna say shaking." Her arms landed on the mattress, fingers sinking into the bedding as her back arched slightly in response to the slow, intimate caress.

Johnny glanced at Killian. "We just gonna watch? If so, I'm not stayin'."

Killian caught his arm. "Then let's join them. Bed's big enough for us all."

Killian stripped off his jeans and sauntered naked to the bed, sitting beside her, blocking Johnny's view of whatever it was he did to Ellie as Mace lifted the bottle and trickled oil over her belly. Her sharp gasp pierced the air, followed by a throaty moan.

Johnny cursed to himself and toed off his boots, in a hurry now to make sure Ellie was all right with what was happening, and because he didn't want to miss a thing.

Ellie writhed like a wild thing. It was all too much. She said so.

But the twins chuckled. She'd already forgotten who was where, but one was swirling a finger in her pussy and another was stroking a flat palm over her oily lower belly and mound.

Killian shushed her, his fingers pinching her nipple harder until she cupped his hand over it and tried to drag it away.

It was painful, yes, but the sensation pushed her faster toward full-blown arousal than she could handle. She'd thought she could keep her cool, keep control of her body if they'd just give her a little room, a little time to adjust to all the sensations bombarding her. But lord, it was like being in bed with an octopus, too many hands and swirling, pinching fingers.

And where the hell was Johnny? Had he slammed out of the room in disgust? She gave a jagged sob then felt the mattress dip one more time. Johnny came into view on the side opposite Killian. But he didn't stop. He pulled her up, then slid behind her, leaning back and taking her against his chest, stretching his long legs to either side of hers as he settled against a mound of pillows.

A finger tipped her chin, lifting her gaze to his. "You get scared, tell me."

A man of few words, as always. She nodded, strangely reassured by that fact and by the dark, terrible glitter in his eyes. Christ, would he kiss her again? She wanted the assurance he still wanted her, but he stroked a thumb over her mouth and turned her face again, forcing her to watch as one of the twins came down on his elbows between her legs.

She squeezed shut her eyes. But the image was already seared in her mind. Men surrounding her, touching her, gliding over her hot skin. She peeked at the man parting her folds, her breath hitching when he pulled upward to expose her clit, then gusting sharply when his tongue darted out and caressed it.

"Too much?" Killian asked beside her, giving her other nipple a hard tweak followed by a sexy, rasping glide.

She nodded, incapable of answering. Her whole body was so tense she felt brittle.

Killian reached between her legs and pulled up one thigh, the twin beside her pulled up the other. They opened her, urging her to bend her knees then pushing them toward her chest where Johnny's darker hands reached out to slip inside the bend to hold her up and open.

Her sex was exposed for them all to see, her labia parting, cool air sifting over her slick flesh.

The twin hovering over her sex stroked his finger over her outer folds, then ran the tip along the furled pink edges of the inner set. When it paused, she mewled.

His crystal blue gaze rose to find hers staring back. The finger sank inside her and her breath left in a whoosh as he tunneled deep, twisting the digit as he stroked her inner walls. When he glanced across the nerve-rich spot of spongy tissue, he stroked it again. "Found it, didn't I?" he asked, his voice a low, sexy rumble.

The scent of her arousal grew richer, stronger as he stroked her intimately, drawing down moisture to coat his fingers, to cause wet, succulent sounds to fill the room.

Behind her, Johnny's chest hardened, his heart beat stronger. She rubbed against him like a cat, trying to escape, trying to free her legs—but did she want to close them or widen them farther? She wasn't sure. She couldn't think.

Johnny pulled gently on her thighs, widening them. Killian stuck a finger in his mouth then used the wet tip to swirl atop her clit. This time, her hiss of breath wasn't because the sensation jarred her, but because it felt so damn good.

"Too much?" Killian asked again.

She shook her head, closing her eyes, surrendering to the feeling building inside as one brother thrust two fingers inside her and the other teased the knot swelling painfully hard. Ellie whimpered.

Johnny's cheek rubbed against her head, and she turned, desperately seeking his kiss.

His mouth glided along her cheek, then found hers, trapping her moans, taking her breath. His tongue met hers to play, the tip pushing hers, then withdrawing, then stroking deeper and deeper.

When she came, it was sudden. As though the band constricting around her womb had snapped. She gave a garbled cry and jerked back her head, rolling it on Johnny's shoulder as wave after wave of heat flushed through her.

Many hands stroked her body as the tiny internal contractions expanded then diminished.

When she calmed, she opened her eyes to find three brothers watching intently. Johnny's hands clutched possessively around her belly. Her feet were on the mattress, knees still bent and splayed. The twin between her legs eased up to kneel.

She marveled over how strange it was to find herself here. Three men she barely knew hovered around her, their bodies taut with arousal, cocks jutting against their bellies—aroused by the sight of her.

She was thankful Johnny was behind her or she'd have been completely unnerved. However, his solid body was a comfort, a rock to cling to in the storm. She liked the feel of his embrace, the jut of his hard cock against her back. Her breaths deepened as she slowly came down.

The twin in front of her licked his mouth.

"Smack your lips," she said, her voice sounding a little rusty, "and I swear I'll open a can of whoop-ass."

The men around her chuckled.

The twin beside her snatched her hand from the coverlet and raised it to his cock.

She wrapped her fingers around him, excited to discover that they didn't quite meet. He was thick, long, perfectly straight. Her mouth watered.

Johnny's hands dug into her sides, holding her against him, but then eased away. She took that as a sign that she was free to choose what came next, and pushed up with her free hand, still gripping the twin's cock, and knelt in front of him, bending, not caring that Johnny and Killian both had a view of her ass and pussy. She hoped they'd take advantage, because even though she'd come, she hadn't felt the stretch of a cock inside her. Lord, not yet. And right now, she didn't care whose pushed inside.

Johnny's legs retracted. Both he and Killian moved while she glided her hand up and down the twin's shaft then stuck out her tongue to swab the broad, round head. The taste of him, of the pearly bead of pre-ejaculate squeezing from the eyelet slit, made her groan.

A hand landed on one buttock, gliding over her skin. Another cupped her pussy, pressing against it firmly. She pulsed backward, giving whichever brother permission to continue, rubbing on the rough palm and opened her mouth to suck the head of the cock right in front of her.

Her lips closed around it, latching around the edge, and she swirled the flat of her tongue over the soft head while firming her grip to ride the shaft.

Fingers teased her entrance, circling the opening then thrusting inside, and again she moaned, coming off the cock to lick the sides, wetting it with her spit, pushing her lips up and down the sides while she tasted him with slick glides of her tongue.

Fingers dug into her scalp, pulling her up, centering her over the cap again, and then he pulsed forward, spearing into her mouth.

She suckled him, her cheeks drawing then billowing as she pulled him deeper and deeper, surging forward then back, fucking the fingers thrusting inside from behind. She cupped his balls, gently kneading the hard orbs, rolling them in her palm, then grasping them to tug more firmly, gauging his comfort by the deepening of his breaths and the tremors of his thighs.

"That's it baby. *Dayum,*" the twin said, pumping faster, deeper, gliding over her tongue, pushing against the back of her throat.

She gagged.

Johnny cussed to the side of her. Which meant Killian was playing with her pussy. That was fine with her. Let Johnny watch. She'd give him a show he'd never forget.

She opened her jaws, fighting the reflexive gag, and let the cock pumping in her mouth sink deeper.

Ellie resettled her knees, widening her stance, tilting up her bottom in invitation, knowing her breasts were swaying beneath her, her nipples hard and taut.

A hand slid under her belly from her right—the other twin. Fingers dragged through her curls, tugging them hard enough to sting.

She gasped around the cock, her teeth scraping his shaft.

"Jason, fuck! It's my dick she's chewing up."

Jason chuckled. His fingers stroked her belly then dove toward her pussy again, fingers tunneling into the top of her folds while Killian sank another finger inside her.

Her pussy burned with the stretch. Tension built, sharpening when Jason found her clit and tapped it.

Again, she gasped, but kept her lips wrapped around the edges of her teeth. She looked up at Mace, whose face was a tense mask, red spots of color staining his cheeks.

His hands cupped the sides of her face. "You swallow?"

Like he expected her to answer with her mouth crammed full of cock? She gave him a wink.

A tight smile stretched across his face. "Not gonna last much longer."

She released more moisture in her mouth, not worrying about the mess or the slurping sounds.

His hands held her face, controlling the tilt to ease his quickening strokes.

She concentrated hard, breathing through her nose to keep from strangling as he pumped faster and faster.

At the first scalding spurt, she gave a muffled shout, nearly as excited by his explosion as he was. With his head tossed back, his expression screwed up in exquisite agony, she felt a measure of pride that she was responsible.

The fingers teasing inside her from behind withdrew. But she didn't mind. She knew three more men were waiting their turn. Lord, when had she embraced her inner wanton?

When Mace's cock slowly pulled free, she sat back on her haunches, wiping the back of her hand across her mouth, flicking her gaze from one man to the next, at last arriving at Johnny, whose face was anything but stony.

His eyes blazed with heat. The skin cloaking his cheeks was taut, revealing the sharp, high blades.

They held like that for several moments, chests billowing, but then Killian slipped his hands beneath her armpits and dragged her backward. Jason straightened her legs.

When her head was dropped over the edge of the mattress and her thighs were parting, she had an inkling what would come next.

Killian gave her a rakish look. "Seeing as how you like givin' head so well..."

She gave a husky chuckle and reached with her hands, clutching his buttocks to pull his hips toward her. Bracing his hands on the mattress, he leaned over her, standing at an angle to lower his cock toward her mouth. She opened eagerly, digging in her nails as he sank inside.

They wasted no time on teasing preliminaries. He stroked deep, his thick, long cock filling her mouth, his balls tapping her nose and between her eyes, which she found funny. She chuckled around him.

But her laughter dried up when her legs were pushed upward together until her thighs pressed against her chest. She didn't understand what Jason intended until cool gel was rubbed around her tiny back hole.

She pushed her tongue against Killian's cock, her hands against his hips to dislodge him, but he stubbornly pushed forward and held still inside her mouth. "It's all right, you know. They won't fuck you there. Not with their dicks, sweetheart. This is for you."

This was for her? She murmured loudly around his cock, alarmed as the finger swirled and swirled and the tension already riding her hard tightened. When the finger pushed against the opening, tucking a tip just inside, she thought she'd die. She wasn't a virgin there, not by a long shot, but her last boyfriend had cajoled her for months until she'd given in. It wasn't something she'd really enjoyed.

And now they were all looking at her asshole, watching one of their own do the nasty while she was completely at their mercy. She continued to give muffled complaints.

Killian sighed and withdrew, and then knelt beside her head while she dragged in deep breaths to fill her starved lungs.

"Does it hurt?"

She shivered with tension and embarrassment, knowing her face was beet red.

"Does it?"

"Some..." She wrinkled her nose. "Not really."

"You're embarrassed?"

"You wouldn't be?"

"It's different. We're guys. *Hetero* guys," he said, giving her a pointed look. "We like to do it, not receive it."

"That's not fair," she said, giving a sniff of irritation.

He arched a brow. "You want to fuck my ass?" he murmured.

"I don't want any *ass*-fucking going on at all," she said scathingly.

"You sure?"

Jason's finger swirled again on her hole, and she strained to lift her head and deliver a searing glare.

Jason's eyebrows waggled. "You have a pretty pink hole and I'd love nothin' better than to see it stretched around me. But you're jumpin' ahead. I was only plannin' to get you good and worried, maybe a little excited. Then I was gonna slip my dick between your thighs."

"And do what?"

His shoulders lifted. His glance darted to Johnny then back to her. "Rub?"

"You're not going to...come inside me?"

Killian and Mace chuckled.

"Ellie, someone else gets that privilege first."

Chapter Five

Ellie swung her head to look at Johnny, who leaned against the headboard with his arms crossed over his chest. From the tension riding his square jaw, she knew without having it spelled out that he would be the first, maybe the only one to claim her pussy this night.

She swallowed hard, then groaned, the muscles of her neck burning from the effort of holding up her head. She dropped it over the edge of the mattress again, as much to relieve the strain as to hide her own expression. They'd see in an instant just how much she wanted him. "Dammit."

All her blood rushed to her head. Maybe she'd die of embarrassment before they finished with her, but now she hoped she lasted long enough to know the pleasure of being claimed by Johnny.

Soft chuckles sounded all around her. Killian rose again, staring down at her. "Understand now?"

"Not really," she said, her voice thick.

"Let us make the decisions tonight, okay? We'll take care of you."

And then he bent over her, and once again, guided himself into her mouth. This time when Jason's fingers played with her ass, she was thankful her face was obscured even if she had to close her eyes to keep from being blinded by Killian's swinging balls.

His cock was thick and pulsing, filling her mouth, her throat. She'd never considered herself a deep-throat expert, but a body'd never know it by the deep moans he gave up as he thrust into her mouth.

She sucked hard, letting her own arousal build as she proved to them all she was in this to the end. A slick finger plunged into her ass and she bucked her thighs, more of a knee-jerk reaction than an effort to escape the intrusion, but Jason kept her thighs jammed against her chest.

She could barely breathe, barely move—her body restrained, her excitement controlled. The finger fucking into her was joined by another thick digit, which stretched her, causing a burning sensation that only heightened her arousal. When the finger stopped swirling inside her and pulled away, and Jason moved to fit her legs around his waist, she was desperate for release.

He stroked his length between her drenched folds, making long firm glides that raked over her clit. She was grateful for the friction and quickly came unraveled. She sucked harder and harder on Killian's cock while Jason thrust powerfully against her, dry-humping her faster and faster, until she shot over the edge, giving a muffled scream.

Killian jerked in her mouth, come jetted, and she swallowed around him, milking him until he pulled free and bent to lift her head to watch as Jason ground against her, his broad chest coated with a thin sheen of sweat, his lips peeled back over his teeth in a primal grimace. When he came, she clutched him with her thighs, holding him until he slumped against her breasts.

Her gaze met Killian's upside down one. They shared a smile. Jason scooted back and pulled her under him. She didn't know how much her neck ached until her head rested on the mattress again.

"Ouch," she grumbled.

Jason's chest rocked against her as he laughed. When he raised his head, he bent to kiss her. "Johnny's luckier than he knows," he whispered against her mouth.

She grinned lazily, gliding her hands over his damp back. "You gonna tell him?"

"Only if you think it will make him even madder."

She glanced at Johnny, whose stony expression was back in place. However, there was a darkness lurking in his eyes that spiked her blood with renewed heat.

"Let's give her some space," Killian said, easing away from the bed. "Why don't we head to the living room? We can turn up the air and put logs on the fireplace."

Jason groaned, but rolled off her.

Cool air brushed over her sweaty body. *A fire?* She shook her head. "That makes no sense at all."

Killian shook her head like she was mentally deficient. "We'll stretch out on the rug in front of the fire. It's romantic."

"It's eighty degrees outside."

"Which is why we'll up the AC." He winked, then held out his hand.

She was reluctant to leave Johnny. But he didn't ask her to stay.

Killian's glance flicked from her to Johnny, as though he too waited for his brother to say something, do something. When his brother didn't, he cupped his fingers. "Come on." He tugged her up. "No clothes. That's the rule."

"You got many rules?"

"Just that you call the shots."

She shook her head, smiling slightly. Trying to find something to laugh about because Johnny's lack of reaction disappointed her. "As if," she scoffed. "If you didn't notice, I could barely speak."

"A trait you and Johnny share."

She snorted and laughed, glancing back to see Johnny easing off the bed. For the first time, she saw his whole body straighten, and she stumbled.

Killian's arm caught her waist to keep her from going to her knees. He pulled her against his chest, his erection prodding her belly—this time without the protection of layers of clothing.

She marveled over how disturbing it was to feel the press of one naked man while watching another stride toward her.

Johnny was tall, rangy, broad. A smattering of hair around his groin but none on his chest. His dark cock was long and pointing upward—thick. The Logan boys were all blessed in that department.

She swallowed hard. When she looked up, his usual hard glare drilled her.

Killian squeezed her. "Like what you see?"

Ignoring Johnny's lethal stare, she leaned back her head to meet Killian's gaze. "And what I feel," she whispered.

His hand snagged hers and he stepped back, letting her look her fill, until every part of her body blushed. His chest was cloaked in dark brown hair that narrowed over his belly then fanned out again at his groin. His cock was thick, reddish, and slightly curved toward the ceiling.

"Built for a woman's pleasure," he said, fisting his cock to stroke it while she stared.

Johnny growled.

Ellie shook her head and turned on her heel, walking away as quickly as she could on wobbly legs, Killian's soft laughter following her into the living room.

She'd seen it all. Every glorious inch of every Logan brother. And it looked as though she'd be a very lucky girl indeed.

Keeping Killian's advice about Johnny close to her heart, she decided she was done being shy. Done with waiting for them to decide how this was going down. It was her body they planned to enjoy. They could take their pleasure, they were more than welcome to it, but she'd take hers as well.

If Johnny Logan wasn't happy about it, it was too damn bad. She'd felt just how much he hated his brothers' bringing her to orgasm, but he hadn't intervened. In fact, he'd held her while they'd plundered her.

Maybe Killian was only partly right. She was beginning to think Johnny liked sharing his woman more than he would ever admit. It gave him a chance to break free of his quietude, a reason to assert a possessiveness he hadn't ever allowed himself to feel.

The thought sent a blissfully cool shiver down her back. Belonging to him. Being shared among the rest.

Maybe being a wife among the Logans wasn't the sort of relationship she'd always dreamed she'd have, but she wasn't going to scoff at it any longer. It could work out to be her wildest fantasy come true.

Johnny didn't like the sassy sway of Ellie's backside as she walked away. It was a slow, seductive wag that had his cock tensing even harder. Impossibly harder.

The woman didn't need to tease. If she knew what was going through his head right now, she'd run screaming. She brought out the primitive in him. His basest desires. He didn't know how much he could take before he threw her down and mounted her.

Holding her while she'd moaned and shivered through an orgasm had been pure hell. He'd wanted to be the one with his mouth pleasuring her, the one tasting her. And yet, he'd also wanted to be the one who held her while she shook. He'd been the one she kissed there at the end when she could have sought any of four mouths, but bent back to seek his.

However, watching her take on Killian and Mace hadn't been as pleasurable for him. Was it because he hadn't been touching her? He'd felt like a voyeur, watching the woman he wanted being used. She'd done it with throaty groans that had teased him to the edge of violence. Had she been goading him? Was he a fool to think she'd even given him a thought?

He raked a hand through his hair, striding with heavy stomps down the hallway. He knew Killian wanted her, but he'd made it seem at the start like he was setting this up for him.

Johnny felt surly and mean, and so goddamn hard he didn't trust himself around her, not without his brothers there to protect her. Was this why Killian had engineered this night? He didn't trust him to be gentle when the moment came?

He hesitated in the hallway, gripping his shaft and wondering if it would be wiser for him to jerk off before he went near her again, but then he heard laughter coming from the living room. Hers.

He sped up, entering the room, then slowed as he took in the sight.

His younger brothers had been quick to clear the furniture from in front of the fire. The large flokati rug had been pulled up to the ledge of the fireplace.

The twins sat cross-legged on the carpet while Ellie stood over them, staring down, her lips pressed together to suppress another laugh.

When he cleared his throat, she glanced his way, pointing at his brothers. "They have no sense of modesty."

Mace grinned. "She thinks our ball-sacs must itch."

Her arms folded over her chest. "I did not call them that."

Mace's head tilted back. "You didn't call 'em anything. You just pointed and laughed. Took some of the starch right out of little Mace."

"Mace isn't little," she said, another giggle erupting.

Johnny felt his eyes narrow, irritated that the twins had her attention, and that they'd managed to make her forget for a moment that she was every bit as naked as they were. He couldn't. Her breasts were lovely, round globes, topped with cotton-candy pink nipples. Her belly was slightly rounded, womanly. Her mound was cloaked in fine, pale curls. Everywhere he looked was soft and feminine, and since he'd held her, he knew the scent of her was just as sweet.

Mace patted the white wool carpet. "Come on down. Enjoy the fire."

"I'm not cold," Ellie shot back.

"Sure about that?" he asked, his eyebrows waggling while his gaze zeroed on her nipples.

Ellie's pretty breasts lifted, and she looked down as well. "That's not because they're cold," she said, her tone tart.

Killian pushed through the swinging door leading into the kitchen, bottles dangling from his fingers. "Beer, anyone?"

Now, Johnny had never been particularly shy about nudity around his brothers. And there had been occasions, usually when they skinny-dipped in the creek, when a hard-on had become the butt of some raunchy jokes, but he found it damned uncomfortable joining the rest of them as they lounged casually on the floor, dicks tapping their bellies while they all stared at the same woman.

A woman who seemed to have just as little of the modesty she'd complained his brothers didn't possess.

She sat between the twins, her legs straight and drawn together, toes pointing toward the fire. "It does so itch," she groused.

"You could sit on something a little less furry," Jason said, waggling his eyebrows.

"Guess I could," she said, rolling her eyes. "But then, I wouldn't exactly be resting, would I?"

"Think you couldn't relax? Drink a beer, sitting right on my lap?"

Her jaw dropped, but then so did her eyelids as she not-so-subtly studied his brother's impressive erection. "On your...lap?"

"I didn't stutter."

Johnny growled and prowled into the room.

Killian dangled a beer from his fingers. The wicked gleam in his eyes spelled mischief. "Wanna make a bet who moves first?"

Johnny's cock jerked, bobbing to the beat of his heart. Something he couldn't attempt to hide without his brothers laughing their asses off.

He strode toward Ellie, looming over her, willing her to keep her gaze locked with his, rather than stroking over his cock as she had his brother. If she did, he couldn't be sure he'd hold it together.

"Maybe she'd be safer with Johnny," Killian said, crimping his lips together.

Mace grimaced. "Just when I thought I'd get to be the first."

Johnny felt his breaths coming faster, steam rising off his hot skin.

"I get choices, right?" she said, her expression every bit as mischievous as Killian's at the moment.

Johnny knew he'd been maneuvered. That everyone in the room had made sure he couldn't back down from the challenge. He reached to the side, felt the cold bottle slap against his palm. He waited as Mace scooted away, then he knelt beside her and stretched out his legs. He took a slow sip of his beer.

Her expression lost its sass, color washing over her cheeks, down her neck to her breasts. A hand lifted to press against her belly.

Killian stepped beside her. "Go ahead and take your seat, sweetheart. I have your bottle right here."

"Oh hell." She blew out a deep breath, her lips pursing.

Killian took her hand and urged her toward Johnny.

She gulped, but tossed back her hair. Then she came up on her knees and leaned toward Johnny, not meeting his steady stare as she gripped his shoulders and climbed over him. Her knees snuggled close to his hips. Her pussy poised over his sex.

He could feel her heat against the tip of his cock. He held himself rigid, waiting for her to take him inside her.

Her hand was cold when it wrapped around him and pointed it toward her entrance. Her whole body shivered. Her eyes closed, and she sank over the tip, taking him into her body.

She was so wet, so hot inside, he nearly groaned aloud. But he forced his face into a mask, watching her every expression, every movement as she worked her way down his cock.

Her pussy was tight, and gripped his shaft as she settled in three slow pulses, downward. When their groins met, they sat face to face. She was unable to hide her strained expression or the blushes that deepened on her cheeks.

Another beer was dangled. She reached for it, wrapping her shaking fingers around it, then laid the side of the bottle against her cheek. "Fuck, I'm hot."

He growled his agreement, sweeping a glance around the room. The twins wore grins that stretched wide across their faces. Killian gave a waggle of his eyebrows, then sat right beside Johnny and clinked his bottle against Johnny's. "To women."

"So not funny," she said, putting the bottle to her lips and tilting it back.

"Tell me. Is she squeezing you?" Killian asked in overloud whisper.

"Shut the fuck up," Johnny said, beginning to sweat.

Moisture oozed around him, and her eyes widened even more. She shrugged. "Not something I can help," she squeaked.

"Drink your damn beer," he muttered.

The twins crept closer on their knees.

"Back off," he snapped.

"Whatcha gonna do about it?" Mace asked, grinning like a monkey. "This is way too much fun."

"Besides, you can't exactly make us move at the moment, can you?" Jason said.

Ellie glanced at Killian. Something seemed to pass between them. Since when had those two bonded enough to read each other's minds?

She drank from her bottle again then leaned toward his face.

Johnny began to get worried when she pursed her mouth. Did she expect him to kiss her? As it was, he was holding on by thread.

She pressed her lips to his, waiting, her eyes wide open.

When he opened beneath the press of her lips, she squirted beer into his mouth. He gulped it down, felt it dribble down his chin, but she was quick, sticking out her tongue to capture it before it hit his chest.

"How'd that taste?" she whispered.

"Good." He grunted. "Again."

The corners of her mouth lifted and she drank again, giving him the beer pooled in her mouth. This time he drank it then sucked on her lower lip, preventing her from pulling away.

His dick twitched inside her, and she groaned into his mouth, her eyelids fluttering downward. Her thighs quivered.

"Think I'm gonna win that hundred," Mace murmured.

Killian laughed. "I'd leave them alone to finish their beer, but they might forget about us."

Johnny broke the kiss. The sight of her blurred lips and gaze filled him with a sense of possession. He'd put that look there. He nodded to Jason. "Come around behind her."

Jason moved quickly, coming between Johnny's spread legs.

"This is about her," he said, echoing Killian's sentiment, believing it now. She was lovely and coming unraveled, and he hadn't moved an inch.

"Give me another drink," he whispered.

She transferred another gulp of beer, but this time he didn't swallow it down. Instead, he kissed his way down her neck, keeping the beer in his mouth. When he reached her collarbone, Jason got the idea and raised her, pulling her up on his cock, just far enough so that she could offer him her breast.

With the cool beer in his mouth, he nuzzled the hard tip of her breast, then carefully drew it inside, sucking harder to pull the whole areola and wash it with the slowly warming liquid in his mouth.

When he swallowed, she sighed. Jason lowered her back down Johnny's cock. She rested her head against his shoulder.

Johnny felt the subtle squeeze of her pussy, clasping and releasing, around him.

"Kil—"

"Yeah, Johnny?"

"Grab our beers."

Killian laughed but quickly plucked the beers from their hands. Jason climbed over his leg to move away.

Johnny sank his fingers in her soft, blond hair and cupped her lush ass. Then he rolled, tucking her beneath him.

Her legs whipped around his waist, holding him deep.

"This what you wanted?" he asked, his mouth an inch from hers.

"Yesssss," she hissed, pumping her hips.

"I can't be gentle."

"I'm countin' on that, cowboy."

Johnny rested his elbows on the ground and began to move inside her, shallow strokes because she refused to ease her grip. "Baby," he said, dipping down to kiss her mouth, "gimme some room to move."

"Can't." She mewled. "It's too much."

"Let go. It'll be all right."

Her eyes filled, her head lifted to kiss his chin, his cheek, then rub quickly against his mouth. But she eased her legs from around his hips, opening her thighs to give him greater access.

Johnny closed his eyes, prayed for control, but it was already too late. Her moist heat surrounded every inch of him, subtle contractions rippling all along his shaft. He reared back, nearly pulling free, then slammed forward, grunting hard, unable to control his breaths any more that he could the quickening in his groin that fed his urgent motions.

He hammered her pussy, thrusting deep again and again, building friction, tension tightening his balls, his thighs, until he closed in, his strokes shortening, sharpening.

Her head tilted back, her chest rose. Her face screwed into a mask of ecstasy, reddening until she cried out and clawed at his back. "Faster, dammit, faster!"

He gave her what she needed, bringing his knees closer in, sliding a hand under her ass to keep her close, then pounding harder. She keened loudly and her body stiffened. He couldn't hold back a moment longer, shoving his face against her shoulder to muffle his shout as he came, cum jetting deep inside her. "Fuck! Fuck!"

"Yes!" she cried.

"No, *fuck*. I forgot a rubber," he ground out, still pulsing against her.

Killian laughed. The twins joined in. A hand patted his shoulder, and Johnny aimed a glare at his closest sibling. "Not a fucking word."

"We had a whole box sitting next to the fireplace. Funny neither of you thought of it."

"You could have said something."

"I figure Ellie here's a good woman. Not much to worry about. And you haven't been with anyone in a while, have you?"

"I'm clean," Johnny said, finding it strange he could look at Killian but not meet Ellie's eyes, and he was still fucking her.

"I'm clean, but I don't know about timing," she said softly.

Reluctantly, he turned to meet her gaze. "Anything happens, I'll do right by you."

Her hands shoved against his chest. "I don't need any man doing right by me. Not out of obligation."

Johnny blew a breath, exasperated because he'd managed to get her back up again. "Can't think," he growled. "Not what I meant."

Her lips pulled into a mulish pout. "You through?"

He saw the hint of moisture in her eyes, and wondered how he'd managed to spoil everything so quickly. "Sorry." He withdrew slowly, reluctant to leave her slick heat. When his cock slid free, it scraped along the coarse wool of the carpet.

"Damn stuff itches." His brothers moved back and he raised up, kneeling in front of her. He raked back his hair. "Ellie…"

"I'm all right. Just…just give me some space. And I need a towel or you'll have to wash this rug."

Killian dropped a cloth between them.

Ellie's eyes bulged, silently admonishing them all.

Johnny backed away from her to give her privacy then aimed glares at the rest of the guys.

His brothers left the room silently. Johnny turned his back, but stayed where he was beside her. "I'm sorry," he repeated.

"It's all right. I'm fine."

"It was good."

She snorted. "Maybe you shouldn't try to talk to me right now."

His lips twisted. "This wasn't how I wanted our first time to be."

"It wasn't how I imagined it either…but I was okay with it. Until you poured cold water all over me."

"Give me another chance?"

He heard a sigh. Felt warmth close to his back.

"I already called in sick," she said, leaning her head against the back of his shoulder. "We've got plenty of time to figure out other ways to piss each other off. I'm not goin' anywhere."

"I wasn't lettin' you."

He glanced over his shoulder to find her grinning at him. His own mouth stretched into a smile.

Her expression softened. "I think that's another first. A genuine smile. You're a handsome man, Johnny Logan."

Johnny leaned back and waited. She leaned around him. The kiss she gave him was sweet. The nip she gave his bottom lip was sharp.

"Just so you don't go thinkin' I'm gonna be easy from here on out."

"Baby, I'm not takin' a thing for granted."

They sat on the itchy carpet, staring at each other until Ellie's eyelids dipped. "I'm not through playin'. You all right with that?"

Johnny grunted but nodded, happy she was enjoying herself. He nodded toward the kitchen door. "Those three probably have their ears to the door."

"Well, they're in the kitchen—they're headed the right direction. Think they can rustle up something for us to eat? I'm starved. And since it looks like I'm the one who's gonna be burnin' the most calories, they can feed me."

Chapter Six

Ellie felt a tug on her hair, and reached back to swat away the fingers as they pulled again. She muttered and snuggled deeper into the warmth surrounding her.

"Ellie." The whisper was quiet but insistent.

She cracked open an eye to find Killian hovering over the bed.

He curled his fingers. "Come with me."

She stretched, but arms enfolded her from behind. She was sandwiched between the sleeping twins. Johnny had left her with them sometime during the night to rest while he'd showered.

Killian offered his hand and pulled her up. The twins muttered and rolled to their backs. She spared a glance for each of them. They were beautiful, after all, and she'd had the pleasure of exploring their taut, toned bodies, one lick at a time. Even with their cocks softened, a lazy curl of heat stirred inside her.

A soft chuckle sounded. "We've created a monster."

She gave him a baleful glance, noting for the first time that he was dressed. Had he come to take her home? She felt her face fall.

"Sweetheart, it's not over. Come with me. Johnny and I have a surprise for you."

Eager now, she slipped from the bed.

"Five minutes, then meet us on the porch."

She hurried through a shower and dressed in her jeans and diner T-shirt. When she wandered through the living room toward the door, she heard a whinny.

Bemused, she slipped out the front door to find Killian and Johnny astride horses. Killian's was red with a long flowing mane. Johnny's was a pretty, splotched gray.

"You're going riding?"

"*We're* going riding," Killian said.

Johnny pulled on his reins, guiding his horse beside the steps, then he kicked free of his stirrup and held out his hand. "Step into the stirrup. I'll pull you up behind me."

She bit her lip and gave him a dubious look. "I've never been on a horse."

The men shared a glance. Both smiled.

Johnny curled his fingers twice, a gesture she was tempted to tell the men might work better on a dog, but she kept her tart comment to herself, not wanting to spoil their surprise.

Taking a deep breath, she climbed down to the first step, then accepted his roughened hand while stepping into the stirrup. He pulled her up so fast, she gasped, swinging her leg instinctively over the back of the saddle and scooting closer so all of her ass was over the lip.

"It's high up here," she squeaked.

Johnny gave her a look over his shoulder that was at once reassuring but also managed to make her hot all over.

"I won't let anything happen to you," he said, his voice a rusty grumble.

She slid her hands around his waist and pressed herself close to his back. "I'll hold you to that. So we're goin' for a ride?"

Killian trotted his horse up beside Johnny's. "We're gonna check the herd. Thought you might like to get some fresh air and maybe see what it is we do."

The ride to where the herd was gathered in a far pasture took long enough the gray dawn burned away by the sun rising swiftly over the horizon. Everywhere she looked filled her with a sense of awe. Tall green grass rustled to the slight breeze. Birds twittered from the branches of mesquite and lone oaks. Before they topped a hill, she could smell the herd. The odor wasn't overwhelming, but put her to mind of the faint scent the boys brought into the restaurant. A scent she'd never minded, because it reminded her of what they were.

The herd was large and stretched across the shallow valley they entered. "It's beautiful."

Johnny snorted.

"You don't think so?"

His shoulder shrugged. "Didn't think a woman would appreciate it."

She pinched his belly. "Don't go makin' assumptions about what I like, Johnny Logan."

"I told you. I'm not takin' a thing for granted."

They pulled to a halt atop a grassy knoll overlooking the valley. Killian dismounted then came around to Johnny's horse and held up his arms. Clumsily, she let him drag her down to the ground.

She winced when she straightened.

"Sore?" he asked, a hint of a smile in his eyes.

She wrinkled her nose. "A little. You must think I'm a wuss."

"Not even. I've seen you in action."

Ellie blushed and ducked her head, aware of every movement behind her as Johnny dismounted and led the horses to a tree to tie them off.

Killian pulled a thin blanket from a saddlebag and spread it on the ground. Johnny brought a lumpy paper sack and a thermos and knelt on the blanket. He pulled out three apples and a chunk of cheese. "Just a snack. We'll go back for a proper breakfast."

"This is fine. Just enough," she reassured him, happy that they'd planned to spend some time alone with her. "No one else around?"

Killian grinned. "No one but us. We sent the hands off elsewhere checkin' fences. Come have a seat. Let us feed you."

She knelt gingerly then sat on her bottom, hiding a grimace for the slight ache, watching as Johnny pulled a pocketknife from his jeans and carved a slice of apple. He held it out for her.

"I could get used to this," she said. She took a bite of sweet apple and moaned. She hadn't realized how hungry she was.

Johnny's smile was soft, but his gaze was sharp, watching her so closely she wondered if she had a smudge on her face. "Stop it."

"Stop lookin' at you? Can't."

She turned away, feeling shy and knowing it was completely ridiculous given all things he'd observed her do, all the things he'd done to her. Another sliver of apple was shoved in front of her and she took it. Then a slice of cheddar.

When he handed her the thermos cap filled with steaming coffee, she sighed and closed her eyes. "The perfect breakfast."

"Because you didn't cook it?"

She laughed and shook her head. "No. Because of where we are and who I'm with."

Killian stretched out on the blanket next to her, leaning on an elbow. "It's not a bad life."

"So are you back to the sales pitch? Are we gonna talk about pie again?"

The wrinkles beside his eyes deepened as he smiled. "No, sandwiches maybe."

Heat flared deep inside her belly. Her eyebrows rose. "Here?"

"We fed you."

Johnny's lips twitched. That hint of humor was sexier than anything else she could think of at the moment. And since he didn't seem opposed to the idea Killian proposed, she leaned back on her arms. "What do you have in mind?" she asked lazily.

Killian laughed. "Reach into the bottom of the bag."

She eyed him with suspicion and picked up the bag, rooting into the bottom until her fingers curled around a tube. "Oh hell, no," she muttered, pulling out the lube.

"We want to share you, Ellie. The two of us."

Her breath caught and she eyed them both. Both so handsome. Both their bodies tense, as though waiting for her consent before springing into action. The thought of it was a delicious tease that sifted through her mind.

Sunlight, crisp grass—two well-made men, their darker skin blanketing her front and back. She fanned her face and glanced away. "Why bother asking?"

"Because this isn't a game. It's not for fun. Not something done in the heat of the moment. Give yourself to us now, and we won't ever let you go."

"The two of you...?"

Killian reached for her hand and drew it to his mouth. He kissed her knuckles then opened her fingers and threaded his own between them. "I know you love Johnny. But I think there's room in your heart for me too. We've talked about it. For now, he's your number one. But if you think we might give it a try, I'd like to be a part of this too."

She ignored the part about loving Johnny since it was so shocking, and she didn't want to think it through with both men watching her. "You'll let him be number one for now?"

He shrugged. "I like you. I'm attracted. I don't know if I can shut it off if you choose only him. I'm willin' to wait for you to know me better." One brow arched. "I like to think I'll grow on you."

The thought was tantalizing. Sure, they'd mentioned it before, sharing her in the long-term, but she'd thought they were only teasing. However, the calm air of expectancy surrounding Killian said just how serious he really was. "What about Jason and Mace?"

"They were only playin'. They have plenty of playmates and never take a one seriously. They won't have their noses out of joint if we keep you to ourselves."

She could have Johnny. And Killian. "Sounds selfish. Like I'm getting more out of this than you."

"Well, you'll certainly never want for a thing in the bed department."

"Relationships are about more than sex."

"They can start with sex and liking each other."

She opened her mouth, then shut it again, afraid to admit too much. Afraid to lay her heart out for the man who sat so silently beside them both. "What if I never feel as much for you as I do him?" she whispered, not looking up.

Johnny scooted closer and lifted his hand to cup her cheek, turning her toward him. His dark eyes burned with an intense heat. "You've got a big heart, Ellie. Even if you hide it behind a sharp tongue."

"Open up to the idea of it," Killian said. "It's new, I know. A girl expects to love one man. I'm willin' to wait."

"Why would you?"

He turned to look out over the valley. "I want family. It's like Sam told us, ranchin's a family business. But I don't want a wife. Not one I have sole responsibility over. I'd share it, though. My mom and dad were married a long time, but hated each other. I have a tainted view of marriage."

"What if you find someone you'd be willing to risk your heart for?"

He turned and winked at her, but his smile was sad. "I did. But she's in love with my brother, my best friend."

Her mouth dried, and tears filled her eyes. "It was the pie, wasn't it?" she said gruffly.

"And the spice." He tugged her down, framing her face, then lifted his head to kiss her.

"You don't think this is ridiculously fast?" she asked when he let her up for air.

"Sam said we had the house to ourselves for four days."

Ellie shook her head. "Your father told you to get yourselves wives?"

"He did. And since it only took him a weekend to woo his Gracie, he figured he'd give us a couple extra days because we're a little slow."

The glint of humor was back in his eyes, and she felt her mouth stretch slowly into an answering grin. "If that was what you consider slow..." She whistled.

"Let us love you, sassy."

Without another word spoken, they knelt in front of each other and began stripping each other's clothes away while Johnny sat beside them.

"Does he need an engraved invitation?" she muttered.

"I think he likes to get worked up before he wades in."

"Sounds wet."

"It will be." He pushed her on her back and wrestled off her boots, socks and jeans, then quickly finished removing his own clothing. When they were both naked, he cloaked his cock in a condom and came over her.

He filled her vision and nestled close enough that not a part of her body wasn't covered. She welcomed his weight and breathed in his fresh male scent. With his elbows planted, he cupped her head and kissed her, rubbing his lips against hers in a slow circle until she melted, sighing. His tongue slid between her lips and played with hers.

Her breaths shortened as her excitement escalated. Everywhere they touched, she warmed. Her breasts grew heavy, her nipples beading tightly and tangling in the light fur on his chest. Where his cock dug into her belly, her skin trembled. Her pussy grew moist, softening with lust. When he pulled away and centered himself between her legs, she opened willingly, crying out when he drove inside her.

He pushed through her moist tissue, tunneling relentlessly until he was fully gloved. "Nothing's ever felt this good, Ellie," he said, a rasp in his voice.

She combed her fingers through his thick hair, then dug in her nails to rake his scalp. "I know," she whispered. "Lord, you fill me up."

"You sore?"

"Guess I should be, but I'm so damn wet..."

He pumped his hips, pushing, withdrawing, pushing deep again. "I'm gettin' ahead of you. Should have played with your pussy for a while first."

Clutching his shoulders now, she shook her head, breathing harder, because the heat flared swiftly, flames licking at her core. "Just move, damn you."

He chuckled and came up on his arms, glancing down between their bodies. She followed his gaze, watching as he stroked into her over and over.

"It's a pretty sight."

"Pretty's not the right word," she bit out. "Hot, it's so damn hot."

He hooked his hips, rubbing the tip of his slightly curved cock against her happy spot as he continued to drive into her. "Gettin' it now?"

"You're killin' me." But she held on to his hips, bent her knees and slammed up to meet each stroke.

When the spiral of her orgasm began, he suddenly halted.

She opened her eyes and glared. "I was right there."

"You two, roll onto your sides."

Startled by the rough growl, she rolled her head. Johnny had moved beside them. And he was naked.

Her mouth opened, taking in the sight of all his burnished skin, the firmness of his large cock. His mouth was a thin, tight line. "Do it now," he said.

Killian snorted then cupped her buttocks to keep them connected, and rolled to his side, taking her with him. "Slide a leg over my hip."

His arm slipped beneath her head to pillow it, and she did as he asked, sliding her leg over him, opening herself.

Behind her, Johnny scooted in close. His mouth skimmed her shoulder then pressed against her neck. "You know what I'm gonna do."

"Taking first dibs?" she quipped, even though she was nervous. Johnny wasn't small.

A gel-slick finger slid between her cheeks and rubbed against her anus. "My brother wasn't wrong about a man wantin' this. A woman has to trust. When she gives it, he feels like he's a king."

When he slid the finger slowly inside her, she hissed air between her teeth. "That's just one of your thick fingers."

"You're tight," he admitted. "But you'll take me."

Her pussy and asshole tightened right up at the sound of his graveled tone.

Killian cupped her breast and played with the tip, twisting it hard, then plucking it over and over until it stung. But the pain distracted her, allowed her to ease around the intrusion of the *two* fingers that Johnny thrust inside her now. She undulated, just a shallow undulation because she burned, but it still felt too good to ignore.

The fingers pulled free, and she slumped against Killian.

"Don't get too comfortable," he whispered against her hair.

She huffed a breath. "As if." Behind her, she heard the snap of latex, and groaned even before Johnny's hands sought her ass again.

He parted her. The thick round head pushed between her cheeks.

The pressure was too much. He was too damn big. "Oh-oh-oh..."

"Shhh," Killian said, kissing her forehead.

She tilted up to brush her mouth over his. "Ever had a pipe rammed up your butt?"

His teeth gleamed. "And he's gonna expect you to bounce all the way home on a hard saddle too."

She gave a short, strained laugh, but concentrated on easing her muscles.

Johnny pushed again, and this time he sank inside an inch or two. His deep groan was worth the burn.

His hand clutched the notch of her hip. "I'm gonna start moving. You ready?"

"If I say no, will it matter?" she asked in a small voice.

Both men chuckled.

"Baby, if it truly hurts, I'll stop right now."

It hurt all right. However, she was pinned front and back to the two men she'd wanted for the longest time. And Johnny's breaths, gusting in her ear, spoke of how excited he was. She couldn't deny him a thing.

"Just do it." she whispered, then buried her face against Killian's solid shoulder.

Johnny's groan rattled in his throat, and he pushed deeper and deeper, his strokes slow and controlled. Killian growled between gritted teeth, but began to move his hips as well, matching Johnny's rhythm.

Ellie held on to Killian, buffeted front and back, so overwhelmed by the sensations rocking her that her entire body shuddered. Smooth thrusts into her pussy. Johnny's hard steel plowing into her from behind. She burned and ached, and was so damn wet, so hot, she felt on the edge of a huge explosion.

"Killian. Johnny," she moaned.

"What, baby?" Killian said, kissing her cheek.

She cracked open her eyes to meet his brown gaze. His face was red, sweat breaking on his forehead and upper lip.

His mouth trailed across her forehead. "It's crazy, isn't it?"

"Crazy good," she groaned. "I'm so..." She bit her lip as Johnny thrust harder. "Full. I'm tight. Hot. When I come..."

"Just let go."

"It's gonna be loud."

"You won't scare the cows."

"Oh. *Oh.*" And then she jerked back her head and screamed.

Which must have been taken as a signal by the men to up the fireworks. They pounded her, working now in opposition, Johnny thrusting, Killian withdrawing, rocking her forward and back.

She was limp between them, moaning, colors exploding behind her closed eyes, sounds diminishing as everything darkened.

When she awoke, she found herself tucked against Johnny's chest, her thigh raised over his to open her as Killian wiped her clean from behind.

"I'd be embarrassed, but I think I'm dead," she muttered.

Johnny's chest shook against her.

"All done here," Killian said cheerfully.

Maybe he thought she'd want to close her legs for modesty's sake, but the cool air brushing between her legs was a relief. "Glad to hear it."

A hand patted her behind. A kiss landed on her hip. "I'll leave you two alone to talk."

Johnny's arms tightened around her.

She let him have his little moment of concern as Killian moved away. Sooner or later they had to learn to communicate. The paper bag crackled, and she had a fleeting thought that she hoped like hell the used condom was inside it.

"We should head back," Johnny said, nuzzling her hair.

"I s'pose." But she nestled closer.

"You gonna sleep?"

"You'll have to help me dress. My whole body feels as limp as cooked noodle."

He did help her, clumsily. When she was finally dressed, she eyed the horse he led toward her.

"I'll need a long soak when we get home."

One corner of his firm mouth kicked up. "You too sore to ride?"

"Yeah, but I don't see another way to get there."

"I'll hold you in front of me."

The idea appealed, but wasn't as easy as she'd imagined. After she'd kicked his shin and butted him with her elbow, at last she was settled sideways in front of him, the saddle horn between her legs.

"Lean against me, I won't let you fall."

She gave herself over to him, leaning against his broad chest as he turned his horse back the way they'd come.

The sun was midway up the blue sky.

"It's beautiful here," she said, trying to fill the long silence.

The wind shifted, bringing the smell of the cattle. She wrinkled her nose.

"Most days, this is what I smell like," he said.

Was he trying to talk her out of wanting him? Or warning her again, like he had at dinner—just to make sure she knew what she was in for? She'd lived in Two Mule long enough to know what the stockyard smelled like when the wind changed direction. This wasn't near as bad. "Do you bathe before you come to bed?"

He nodded.

"Then why are you tellin' me this?"

"You already know why."

The way he said it, with conviction, and then held his breath, made her heart trip. Still, it wasn't in her DNA to make this easy. "Uh-huh. That's right. One of you wants a wife—who can bake a pie."

"Stop with the pie," he growled. "I don't want you just for your pie."

She ignored the *just*. "Then what?"

"I want you for the way you make me feel."

"Hot?"

"That too."

He was going to drive her stark-raving crazy. Fully demented. Most times she could take his "man of few words" way of getting to the point, but she was a woman and wanted just a little more drama. "Don't you think you should wait to find out if you like me before you tell me you're going to marry me?"

"I like you fine."

Her eyes bugged and she reached up to catch hold of his collar. "I've teased and insulted you just about every time we've met," she said, giving him a scowl.

"It's your way of flirting."

"You think you know me so well?"

His mouth pulled into a bland smile. "You're like me. Tougher on the outside than the inside."

"Is that so?"

"Yes."

She dropped her hand and settled against his chest again, exasperated and grumpy.

"Do you want me to get down on one knee?"

"Hell no. Besides it's too soon for us to even talk about getting married."

"I'll give you 'til next week to organize a dress and reception."

That sucked the wind out of her. It was so concrete. So visual. Her in a white dress. Him waiting at the end of the church aisle. All his brothers lined up beside him to welcome her to the family.

"No more arguments?"

She shook her head. The arm supporting her back tightened and she didn't mind one bit that he stayed quiet the whole way home.

Once he got there, he helped her from the saddle, setting her on her feet only long enough to throw the reins over the porch rail. Then he picked her up in his arms and strode up the steps.

Without being told, because for once, she was completely in tune with his desires, she reached out to open the door and he swept her inside.

The trip down the hallway to the bedroom took only three short breaths. Their clothes a dozen. When they both lay naked, facing each other on the bed, it felt like a first time.

His eyes glittered with stark emotion. Hers filled as his fingers closed around her breast. When he took the tip into his mouth, at last, she threaded her fingers through his thick, silky hair to anchor him there.

Johnny pushed her onto her back then licked and suckled at her breasts until her whimpers turned to curses.

His laughter was low and dirty as he worked his way down her belly, nipping her skin, pausing to sink his tongue into her navel, before gliding straight down to her pussy.

There, he surprised her, kneeling, then lifting her thighs over his shoulder and straightening, so that only her shoulders lay on the bed. Suspended, unable to move, she delighted in the wicked stroke of his tongue and the gentle nibbles that had her clit so hard and throbbing she was seconds from release.

"I'm there," she whispered harshly, blood rushing to her head.

Johnny kissed her mound then lowered her to the mattress. "Get on your knees."

And even though her whole body was trembling, she scurried to comply. On all fours, she let her middle sink to raise her ass.

His large hands roughed over her bottom, caressing her, parting her. The swat shocked her, but thrilled her so much, she said, "More," and tilted her ass higher. "Was that because I've been bad?"

He grunted. "Just wanted to leave a mark or two."

"A brand?"

"You'll wear that on your finger. I want your ass hot every time you sit."

"How sweet," she teased. "You want me thinking about you."

His hands gripped her bottom, fingers digging into her soft flesh. His cock prodded her pussy, found her entrance, then plunged inside.

Ellie reached for the headboard and wrapped her hands around it, sinking deep, spreading her knees a little farther so that she could take him deeper.

Lord, he pounded so hard the top rail battered the wall, and her entire body jerked with the power of his forceful thrusts. Behind her, his breaths grew choppy, rasping loudly, and she knew he was close.

She was closer. Friction burned through her channel. Liquid fire seeped from her, coating him, the wet sound of his churning cock so crude, it heightened her arousal.

Johnny was relentless, hammering hard and fast. And though she fought it, wanting to savor the rise just a moment longer, she peaked. Ellie threw back her head and keened as her vagina convulsed, the pulses rippling up and down inside her, caressing the thick cock stroking her still.

He lowered his torso, blanketing her back. His lips glided along her shoulder, to her neck. There he bit her, holding her still.

The sharp pain caused another flare of heat to erupt. "Now!" she shouted.

His hips pounded twice more, then jerked against her.

Hot streams of semen spurted inside her.

"Ah. Ah," he gasped against her skin, then snuggled closer to her back.

Tremors racked his body, matching hers, as his hips slowed their motion.

She let go of the headboard, and he wrapped his arms around her middle and brought them both to the bed, spooning her close to his body. His hands smoothed over her belly, trapped her breasts and squeezed.

Ellie moaned and snuggled closer. As she drifted off in a happy haze, she spared a thought for Killian, the one who'd engineered this and who seemed happy enough to let Johnny take the lead in this odd relationship. Somehow, she'd figure out a way to show him how she felt about him. Maybe it wasn't love. Not yet, anyway. But it was strong.

What she felt for Johnny had been brewing a long time but she couldn't imagine a future without the other brother standing beside her too. The simple fact was, Johnny had needed reassurance first. Behind the stoic mask, his heart had been open and ready for love. Killian teased and cajoled, but his easy ways hid a past just as painful. It would take time to earn his love and trust.

Johnny stirred behind her. "What are you thinkin' about?"

"Us. All three of us."

His hands tightened on her belly.

She placed hers over his and gave them a squeeze. "Tell me straight," she whispered. "Are you sure you want to share?"

He sighed then placed a tender kiss behind her ear. "Only if you want it too."

The *too* reassured her. She turned inside his arms, studying his expression, which, for once, wasn't a neutral mask. Fierce emotion smoldered in his dark eyes.

She swallowed down the lump at the back of her throat and leaned toward him to press a kiss against his mouth. "I will come to love him," she promised.

He nodded then gathered her closer. "I love you."

For once, she wasn't even tempted to offer a smart quip. Happiness had softened every edge. "I love you too."

"We'll provide you a good life," he said, his voice turning raspy with emotion. "You won't want for a thing."

She gave him a tender smile. "I'll make you pie."

Sam Logan entered the house quietly, sneaking inside because he knew something was up. The two trucks parked at crazy angles in the driveway were warning enough that something was happening.

He heard the soft laughter coming from the kitchen, and peeked through the door to see three of his boys sitting at the kitchen table, looking rumpled but happy.

Backing away quietly, he sauntered down the hallway. Outside Johnny's door, he heard soft whispers. Heard his first boy's declaration of love, then a woman echoing the sentiment with enough emotion thickening her voice he had no doubts the couple were well on their way to fulfilling his dream.

He'd come home early, wanting to catch the boys unaware, see if they'd followed his advice. They might have been surprised to know his money had been riding on Johnny.

The boy whose alcoholic mother had kicked him to the curb was the one who most needed to learn what it was like to be loved by a good woman. That his brothers looked as though they too had been through the wringer, didn't bear too much reflection. Who was he to judge how it had come to pass? One son had bitten the bullet. The rest would soon follow. They'd only needed to see a happy outcome to be tempted.

Satisfied, for now, he slipped back down the hallway and onto the porch. Taking a seat on the top step, he looked around at what he and Gracie had built. "Wish you were here to see it, darlin'. All your dreams are comin' true."

A soft breeze touched his face like the light stroke of her fingers. Maybe she did know after all. He closed his eyes and gave himself over to the image of her face, alight with joy, while the wind caressed his skin. "Won't be long, sweetheart. We've got a little more work to do."

Two Wild for Teacher

Dedication

To my fans, again—because you have made all my dreams come true!

Chapter One

Sam Logan couldn't sleep. He had one last chore to take care of. One he'd been putting off. *No time like now to get 'er done.*

He walked softly on bare feet down the long hallway, past the master bedroom he'd given up when Johnny married Ellie and moved both his new wife and his brother Killian into the large room to share it. He shook his head, a glimmer of a smile tugging at his mouth. Sounds that hadn't been heard in this old house in over three long years echoed up and down the hallway.

Sexy sounds—happy sighs and laughter, slick slaps, an occasional yelp from Ellie. He could only imagine what his two oldest boys were doing to the girl. But they all seemed happy with the arrangement and both men were gaga for Mean Ellie Harker. Who would have thought one simple pronouncement would produce such lightning-fast results?

It's time you boys found yerselves a wife.

That's all it had taken. Sam had disappeared for a long weekend to attend a cattle auction and give them time to think about what he'd said, what was missing from all their lives, only to return and find all four men looking as though they'd been wrung through a wringer and put up wet.

His sons hadn't told him everything, but he'd heard the rumors—from Ole Win at the diner who'd witnessed how the oldest two had swarmed Ellie like bees around a hive, and then from Wade Luckadoo whose daughter had witnessed Ellie's kidnapping by the twins, but for some inexplicable reason hadn't called the sheriff.

So they hadn't wooed Ellie in a traditional way. Didn't much matter to Sam. A pretty woman stood in the kitchen every morning, a happy smile on her face, and all the boys had perked up, falling over themselves to please her.

These days, meals were an event. Ellie had been running the town's only diner and knew how to cook a mean chili, sear steaks to perfection and bake glorious pies.

The pies had become a bit of a joke in the house over the last month.

Ellie had figured out right off that Johnny loved apple pie. However, Killian wouldn't commit, sampling the varieties she lined up on the counter every Sunday and sighing, but never telling her which one was his favorite.

Sam thought he knew why.

Killian wasn't sure about his place in Ellie's heart. She'd melted first for Johnny, but had accepted Killian in her bed too, and even told him often that she loved him. Killian only half believed her, and given his upbringing, living in a house with two people who'd hated each other's guts and whose anger had spilled over onto him, Sam understood why Killian had doubts anyone could love him.

Ellie's unending search for the perfect pie to please Killian was her way of proving she loved him. From the way his second adopted son beamed each time Ellie introduced a new set to sample, Sam didn't think Killian would ever tell her which pie he loved most.

Pie was taking on mystical properties, a true elixir of love in every bite. And pie was what the twins, the youngest of his brood, huddled over now.

A single light shining from the stove was all that lit the kitchen. The boys sat, bleary-eyed, blond heads in need of a good haircut and a comb, with elbows propping up their chins while they shoveled sweet pie into their mouths.

Sam crept in silently, opened a cabinet door and gave it a good slam.

Both boys jumped, startled stares swinging his way.

Mace gave Sam a tired grin. "Hey, Pa."

Sam never tired of hearing that. The two older boys still called him Sam. The twins had been eager to accept him and Gracie as their parents when they'd first arrived for fostering. Something Gracie had loved as well. She'd always wanted to be someone's mama. He felt a pinch in his chest at how happy she'd been—all the way to the end—surrounded by her boys. "Why aren't you two in bed?" he snapped, his voice gruff. "You'll be fallin' off your horses tomorrow."

"Couldn't sleep," Mace grumbled, rolling his eyes.

"Why's that?" Sam asked, although he had a pretty good idea why.

Mace grunted. "Too much damn noise. People gettin' happy. Wish't I was that damn happy." He lifted his fork and turned to take another bite.

Sam came closer and peered over Mace's shoulder. "That the cherry pie?"

"Mmm-hmm," the younger twin groaned. "S'good."

Sam arched a brow. "Think we should tell Ellie that Killian's not a pie man?"

Both boys' heads jerked up, eyes rounding.

"Hell no!" Jason said around a mouthful of peach pie. "She might stop bakin'."

"We'd still get lots of apple," Sam said with a dry chuckle. "Girl wears herself out tryin' to please y'all."

"That ain't what has her all wore out," Jason muttered, then grimaced from the audible whack his brother gave his leg.

"You know," Sam said, "there's a simple solution to your problem..."

"Earplugs?" Mace quipped.

Sam shook his head. "Seems all y'all need is a little somethin' to keep your minds off what you've got no business hearin'."

Jason's eyes narrowed. "I know what you're gonna say. We need to find ourselves a wife."

"*A* wife?" Mace quipped, his mouth stretching into a wide grin.

Both boys shared a glance then dipped their heads to continue milling into their pie. In that one glance, they seemed to share the same thought. And maybe they did. No two boys could be closer.

Men, Sam amended in his mind. They weren't scrawny teenagers anymore. A woman, a good woman, would have herself a fine husband—if they could ever decide which would marry her.

"Strange times we live in," Sam murmured, thinking about how the town was changing. Multiple men taking up with a single woman. He'd never have imagined it, but then, for him, there had only been Gracie. And she'd had eyes only for him.

On that melancholy note, he turned. Pie wasn't going to satisfy his yearning. Sleep, a chance to dream about a golden-haired girl with freckles on her nose—that's what he needed. "I'll say good night. My job's done. 'Night, boys."

Jason turned his head to watch Sam leave the room, not liking the hint of sadness he'd seen in Sam's eyes before he'd turned away. They all missed Gracie Logan, but none more than Sam. "Think he's really okay with how things worked out for Johnny and Killian?"

"He hasn't said a word about them holing up in the same damn bedroom. Don't think he cares so long as everyone's happy. Why you ask?"

"Don't know. Sometimes, he gets a look."

Mace nodded. "Know the one you're talkin' about, but I think it's 'cause he's missin' Mom."

Jason pushed away his empty plate and sighed. "Only thing's gonna make him happy again is when we all start makin' babies."

Mace grimaced. "Think we don't get any sleep now..." He shrugged. "It's not like Johnny and Killian aren't doin' their best on that end. Still, Pa's not gonna rest easy 'til we find a woman too."

"*A* woman?" Jason said, reminding his brother how Mace's sly joke had started the ball rolling with Ellie. They'd been teasing Sam and had irked the hell out of Johnny, who'd taken Sam's pronouncement as marching orders and didn't like them making light of it. Jason felt responsible for how things had worked out. Johnny might never have considered sharing a woman with Killian if Mace hadn't first planted that seed. Not that both Johnny and Killian didn't appear satisfied with the arrangement. Still, it was his job to curb Mace's wildness. He was the oldest. Little brother needed to get serious about this business of finding *a* wife.

Mace shrugged. "Be easier havin' just one woman. Less yap. And we've got lots of practice sharin'." He picked up his glass of milk and downed it in a couple of big gulps.

Jason knew Mace would prefer to drop the subject of the marrying part. The thought of taking a wife and starting a family made both of them feel itchy. Until they'd come to the Doubletree Ranch, they'd never known what a loving family could be like. Who knew whether they would follow their birth parents' sorry footsteps rather than Sam and Gracie Logan's? But Sam expected them to man up and give it a try. "How the hell we gonna find ourselves *a* woman?" he said aloud, although he didn't really expect Mace to have the answer. He wasn't the thinker. "We can't settle on one for a whole weekend—how we gonna settle on one for the rest of our lives?"

Mace nodded. Then his blue eyes glinted, narrowed. He sat forward in his chair. "There's only been one woman we ever wanted for longer than a day."

Jason had an instant image of soft brown hair pulled back into a messy bun, dark-rimmed glasses perched on a pretty, slender nose, green eyes peering over the tops. He and his brother had fantasized about her for years. "She's a pretty thing, but doesn't even know it."

"I like the way her eyes bug when she's mad. She doesn't like losin' it." Mace's grin said he couldn't wait to push her to the edge.

A smile twitched the corners of Jason's mouth. Wouldn't she be appalled to see them again? The thought didn't dampen his enthusiasm one bit. On the contrary, just the idea of pursuing pretty Molly Pritchet caused heat to fill his loins. "We ain't jailbait anymore," he drawled.

"No, we ain't."

Both men shared wicked grins as they let the thought of what it might be like to seduce Miss Pritchet blossom.

"School's out tomorrow," Mace murmured.

Jason gave a firm nod. "She's gonna have time on her hands. A whole summer's worth."

Both men scooted closer to the table, pie forgotten, and made their plan.

As she adjusted her burden in her arms again, Molly Pritchet wished she'd driven. She was hot, starting to sweat, and the muscles in her arms were beginning to burn with the weight of her box of personal items she'd emptied from her desk. Earlier, traces of roses and honeysuckle scenting the warm air had drawn her from her house, enticing her to get ready to embrace the last day of school and the start of her plans for a summer of blessed solitude, free of responsibility. That morning, she hadn't wanted to think about anything but the pretty day, the flowers she had purchased to set into their beds and the small, decorative pond she wanted to install in her backyard.

Besides, walking to and from the little high school was the only real exercise she ever got.

With every passing year, she fought a little harder to keep padding from settling on her rear and upper thighs. So she walked, getting more of a workout than she'd planned, but enjoying the sounds of lawnmowers growling, birds chirping and children playing.

Lord, she loved the sounds of children. Not something that had changed over the eight years she'd been teaching. And it was a true joy to meet up with graduates who remembered her and stopped by to tell her about their lives, and how she'd touched them.

She might never have her own, but there were plenty of children she'd helped raise in her own limited capacity.

The sound of footsteps on the sidewalk—heavy tread, a little hollow—men's booted heels, came from behind her, and she edged to the side to let whomever was approaching pass.

However, the steps slowed, and before she knew it, she had a man at each elbow.

Her breath caught when she recognized them. "Mason, Jason," she said, hoping they'd take her reddening cheeks for exertion, not delight. She'd always had the most inappropriate thoughts where these two were concerned.

Some things never changed. They both looked so handsome and tall—shaggy blond hair curling beneath the brims of their straw cowboy hats, matching blue work shirts—nicely ironed— and dark Wranglers that molded to powerful thighs. The only notable difference in their appearance was their boots. Mace Logan's boots were saddle-brown leather while Jason's were black. She didn't need visual clues to keep the two of them straight. Unlike most folks in Two Mule, she'd always been able to tell them apart. Mace had a lazy smile that invited a woman to linger. Jason was a tad sharper, with a keen glance that had burned right through more than one woman's defenses, or so she'd heard.

Good Lord, she'd just checked them out, and from Mace's slow grin and Jason's razor gaze, they both knew it.

Two sets of blue eyes glinted with humor.

"Howdy, Miz Pritchet," Jason said, his smile wide, perfect white teeth gleaming.

Mace cleared his throat, drawing her attention. Before she had a chance to sink into his brilliant blues, he reached out his arms. "Let me take that box for you."

"No need," she said, wheezing a bit because she couldn't manage a deep breath with both of them towering over her. "I need the exercise. Home's not far." She knew her voice was a little shrill, but she couldn't help it. She needed them gone before her cheeks heated until they were as purple as sugar beets and she really started to sweat.

The Logan boys, these particular two, were trouble with a capital *T.* Any sensible woman would steer well clear of them. A teacher with a pesky morals clause in her contract had even more to worry about.

"I swear I can manage this box on my own. Always have."

Mace gave her a crooked smile. "Didn't say you couldn't manage it on your own, ma'am. But why deprive us of a chance to do a good deed?"

Stiffening her spine, she gave him her best "teachery" steel-eyed glance. "You're here to do a good deed? Why do I suddenly feel like an old lady a Boy Scout's about to help cross the road?"

"Oh, you're not old, Miz Pritchet, and we're not Boy Scouts," Jason piped in, probably to get her flustered because she had to look left and right to hold this conversation. Her foot stumbled on a rock and she fell forward.

Hands reached to grab the box, another slipped around her back.

Breathless and embarrassed, she let go and tried to straighten away from a hot palm that branded her lower back.

Jason bent toward her while Mace juggled the box. "I know you're a little flustered, but if you'd quit fightin' us, this'd be over so much quicker," Jason whispered then gave her a wink.

Molly gulped, cheeks aflame, but gave a terse nod and lifted her chin. "Your hand is no longer needed," she said, her voice clipped.

"Fair enough," he said with a wicked waggle of his eyebrows, slowly sliding his hot palm away.

Pushing her dark-rimmed glasses up her nose, she backed up one pace, then whirled on her heel and stepped out again, leaving both men to follow in her wake. "Well, seeing as how you were both so insistent..." she threw over her shoulder, "...don't dawdle!" She picked up her pace, arms swinging, angry with both of them, angry with herself for letting them get under her skin.

It was just like her first year teaching. She'd been fresh out of college, eager to take command of her first classroom and both Logan boys had landed in hers. They hadn't lingered in the back like most of the football players—no, they'd taken seats at the front. Their handsome faces had greeted her with smiles and compliments every morning. She'd begun every day gritting her teeth because she couldn't suppress the heat in her cheeks or the breathless hitch in her voice that their attentions brought. Back then, they'd been beautiful young men, horny and popular with the girls—not so much with the girls' parents because they could tempt an angel into parting with her wings. They'd turned their considerable charms on Molly, making the ninety minutes they'd shared a constant trial on her nerves.

No doubt, they'd done it on purpose, to test the new teacher. She had never been so glad to have a semester end.

Still, until they'd graduated, she'd had to endure seeing them in the hall, knowing their interested stares followed her. She'd dressed as frumpily as she could bear, foresworn makeup, all to discourage them.

They were just too handsome, too cheeky. And she'd been all too aware there weren't that many years between them. Just five. Something the boys teased her about.

The last few months they'd been in school, they'd begun to drop hints that they'd like to see her—after they weren't jailbait anymore, but she'd had better sense. Even though they likely had more experience than she did in the sex department, she was starkly aware of how a relationship with two former students would look. Despite their sly and charming efforts at tempting her, she'd remained firm.

Unfortunately, it seemed time hadn't changed them a bit. They may have left boyhood firmly behind, but they still liked to tease her to the point of exasperation.

And Lord, she wished she hadn't noticed they weren't boys anymore. Both were tall and their rangy frames had filled out nicely. Any woman they passed couldn't help but pause and watch, be she ten or a hundred. They knew their attraction and took full advantage of it. She'd heard the rumors of their sexual exploits. Apart, together—they only had to give a girl a sly wink to have her sidling their way. Then it didn't take more than a sexy smile to have her panties around her ankles—an image which shocked Molly because it came so readily to mind.

No, she was not imagining it was her. How ridiculous would that be? Her, standing in broad daylight with lacy pink panties pooled around her feet.

And yet, what made it so real, so tempting, was that she knew if she wanted it, all she had to do was signal them with a crook of her finger. One lazy summer afternoon spent between the sheets with the Logans might just get the yearning out of her system.

The thought lodged tightly inside her head. But then another, of her getting naked with two perfect specimens of manhood, splashed cold water all over the dream.

She could never stand to be just another one of their conquests—even if they only intended to tease. They couldn't be seriously thinking about doing anything more. They had their pick among the female population. She wasn't the prettiest or the shapeliest. Sure, she was smart, but men like the Logan twins didn't prize a high IQ. What they wanted was a woman with a single-word vocabulary.

So, why did the word *yes* feel as though it sat perched on the tip of her tongue, ready to take flight? Was it because she didn't have a boyfriend or plans for a romantic summer? Until that moment, she'd been happy about that fact.

Molly's house loomed in the distance and she sped up again, trying not to think about what they might be looking at. Her butt might be a little soft, but there was muscle underneath. She lifted her arms and power-walked the rest of the way home.

Chapter Two

Jason couldn't get enough of watching the flex of Miz Prichet's ass. It was delectable. Not a word he often thought, but then, Miz Pritchet had been his and Mace's English teacher, and he'd learned a whole new vocabulary in his quest to please her. She still inspired him, so it seemed.

Mace turned his head toward him. "Do you think she knows we're checkin' out her ass?"

Jason flashed a grin. "Why do you think she's walkin' so fast?"

"This might be harder than we thought," Mace muttered. "She didn't seem happy to see us."

"Told you just because she was single didn't mean she was desperate. A woman like her has a lot to offer a man. Why the hell would she want us? We have to convince her we're serious. That we have plenty to offer a woman like her."

Mace grinned. "Maybe we should kidnap her."

Jason gave his twin a scowl. "Just 'cause it worked with Ellie doesn't mean it would with her. She's a lady."

Mace's eyes narrowed. "And Ellie's not?"

"Ellie's...earthier."

"Earthier?" Mace chuckled. "You're just brushin' up to talk to Miz Pritchet."

"So what if I am?" Jason said, tucking his thumbs into his front pockets. "It's gonna take more to impress her than givin' her a wink."

Mace's grin dimmed. "Man, maybe we should've asked Killian for some pointers."

"Let's just stick to the plan." And they were running out of time to put it into motion. The schoolmarm's house was just ahead. A quaint little clapboard house, painted a pale blue, a shallow garden of flowers flanking both sides of the front porch and rose bushes climbing a privacy fence. The grassy lawn, however, looked in need of a good mowing.

The woman they both watched so intently bounded up her front steps and fished in her purse for her keys. She looked in a hurry to get the door open and to get them out of her hair.

"One good thing," Jason said, eyeing her flushed face.

"What's that?"

"We bother her. Has to mean somethin'."

Mace snorted. "Might just mean she wants us gone."

"Might mean she's more attracted than she wants to be."

They shared a glance, both starting to smile again.

Mace pursed his lips and began to whistle.

Jason ran up the steps and reached out to take the keys she'd pulled from her purse. Her mouth dropped open, no doubt to deliver a set-down, but he tugged on the keys. She held firm. So did the set of her pretty, lush lips. He pulled again and she let go, but her chin rose higher, two spots of red blooming on her cheeks.

He unlocked the door, pushed it open, and then held it for her to enter first. "You just tell us where you want us to put the box."

She shook her head. "I'll take it. It's going in my office."

"Which way's that?"

"Upstairs, but—"

Before she'd finished the thought, Mace brushed past her and headed straight up the stairs.

Jason followed on his heels.

"Boys! I said I can manage."

Her shout sounded more like a wail, and he nearly laughed. But he hid a smile and turned to find her right behind him. "But why should you have to?" he asked. "It's no bother."

"Well it shouldn't take two of you," she huffed.

He arched an eyebrow. "Sometimes, ma'am, it does."

A scowl furrowed her forehead, and she raced up the stairs then pushed past both of them to quickly close her bedroom door, but not before they'd gotten an eyeful.

Miz Pritchet's bedroom was a sultry surprise—rich red bedspread, the covers mussed and turned back, a slinky pink nightgown tossed over an arm chair. Fresh flowers on the dresser, a vanity covered in perfume bottles and feminine items Jason couldn't wait to sniff and explore.

"My office is down here," she said, glaring at them through glasses that made her eyes look larger.

Still smiling, the men trailed down the soft, pale beige carpet toward the door she held open.

Mace settled the box atop the cherry-wood desk and stepped back. Both men stared around the room. The walls were covered with pictures of smiling young faces, her students.

This woman needs to be a mother, Jason thought, and knew by his brother's satisfied expression that he was thinking the same exact thing.

"Thank you for your help," Miz Pritchet said, slightly out of breath, her hands folding over her middle. "I appreciate it very much."

She was dismissing them. Her intent was clear.

Mace tipped his hat. "It was my pleasure, ma'am." His words caused her blush to intensify.

Jason gave her a wide smile. "Be seein' you, ma'am." *And sooner than you think.*

Turning on his heel, he whistled all the way down the hall and stairs, all the way out the front door, which he closed softly behind him.

"Yeah, we made the right choice, bro," Mace said, meeting his gaze.

Jason was pleased by the stubborn set of his brother's jaw. Mace was every bit as sure Miz Pritchet needed them in her life.

"No doubt about it," Jason murmured. "Never saw a woman who needed a man more. Two of us'll be more than she can refuse."

Mace nodded, then blew out a deep breath. "But how we gonna convince her?"

Jason took a look around her spotless front porch and raggedy yard. "I have an idea. We're about to become indispensible."

Mace's gaze followed his, glancing at the thick Bermuda, the flowers, then locking gazes again. His eyes gleamed with humor. "We'll have her so flustered she won't know which end's up."

Jason chuckled. "Oh, she'll know. The trick'll be gettin' her so she won't give a damn."

Molly felt more herself as she took a long, cool shower. She stood under the showerhead and let the water beat her head, long enough her toes were wrinkled and her mind was blank.

However, her traitorous body was slow to let go of the arousal both men had stoked. As she slicked rose-scented soap over her skin, she massaged her heavy breasts, pinching the tips now and then to keep them throbbing. She slid a hand between her parted legs and glided fingers between her folds, felt the ripened nub at the top and swirled around and around it until her breath caught and held.

She rubbed a moment longer, but fingers weren't enough. Hers were too soft, too slender. She craved something substantial pushing up inside her. *Damn them.*

Breathing hard, she turned the tap to add a distinct chill to the water, then pressed both hands against the tiled wall. At last her heart slowed to its usual, unnoticeably steady beat. She switched off the cool water and reached for the fluffy towel hanging from a peg beside the door. She held it to her face, drying her eyes and cheeks, and inhaling the reassuring fragrance of the springlike conditioner she used in her wash.

Nothing teased her senses. Not a whiff of male cologne or musk.

Now, she was ready to start her summer. And she had plans. This year, she'd put in more flowers, maybe dig a bit in the backyard and put in the koi pond, something she'd dreamed about doing and had already begun to assemble the things she'd need to complete the project. On her salary, it was a splurge, but it wasn't like she didn't have the money in the bank to handle it.

Fact was, she was a frugal woman with modest needs. She didn't spend a lot on clothes, did her own nails, and other than a trim a couple of times a year, didn't spend it at the beauty shop. Her house was finished to her liking. However, her yard, especially the backyard, was in need of a little TLC to make it a perfect haven from the world.

She opened the towel and swung it behind her, rubbing her back and bottom then brought it forward to dry her breasts. The terrycloth abraded her nipples, just enough she was aware but not enough to excite. She'd had enough excitement for one day.

The twins had had their fun. Her mind almost got away from her when she thought about how they'd looked, standing in her bedroom doorway to peek inside.

Something no man had ever done. Not since she'd had her satellite dish and receivers installed had a man even traipsed up her stairs, and that had been shortly after she'd bought the house her second year in Two Mule. Not that she was a prude, but, at first, she'd been busy trying to be the best teacher she could, spending evenings over lesson plans, tutoring after school, lending her supervision to several school-related clubs.

When she'd finally grown comfortable in her job and her role, she'd felt awkward stepping outside it. Sure, she attended functions at church, but there again, parents sought her out to talk about their children. She'd begun to feel as though her life was predetermined, that maybe, this was all she was supposed to be. A child's teacher. Never his or her mother. And the thought of the actual baby-making... She no longer felt comfortable in her own skin. When she looked into a mirror, she saw a pale moon of a face, a figure more suited to plain shirts and dowdy skirts than one that might entice a healthy, horny male.

The sexual side of her was dormant, unawakened, except for brief moments like today, whenever she spied the twins in town or at the diner. Always, the two of them reminded her of her first days here, about her unexpected and unwanted attraction to them both.

Molly rubbed the soft terry over her nipples again. The tips were fully engorged, so sensitive each back and forth pass shot darts of hunger straight toward her womb.

Not that she was ashamed about how easily they affected her. Intellectually, she understood her reactions were natural. They were beautiful specimens of manhood who exuded sexual confidence. Something she, as a relative novice, responded to on a very primal level...

Primal. A word she loved. One that made her think of sweaty, naked bodies. A word she could roll around her tongue...

And good Lord, she was thinking about them again! Her skin felt warmer, her breasts heavier, her nipples tingly and tight.

In the moment she stood inventorying her physical reactions, she was right back at square one—intensely aroused and overheated. Her brain short-circuiting, letting her hunger grow.

She wondered where she'd stashed the vibrator she'd bought the last time she'd visited her family in Houston. She'd been shopping with her sister Sarah who had nagged her about all the elusive details regarding her private life until she'd discovered Molly didn't have a sex life to gossip about. Sarah had made it her mission to find her a vibrator sure to awaken her dormant hormones.

The unopened box was probably somewhere deep in her closet. Top shelf, behind her Snuggie. And if that wasn't the definition of a spinster, she didn't know what was. Short of the prerequisite dozen cats, she was well on her way.

She finished with the towel, hung it over the rail to dry, slipped her glasses on and reached for her robe for the walk to her bedroom, but then decided she could walk naked through her own damn house. Feeling daring, and knowing it was daylight so her silhouette passing any windows wouldn't be seen from the road, she strode into her bedroom, picked up the stool in front of her vanity and carried it to the closet.

When she was on her tiptoes atop the cushioned seat, reaching to the farthest corner, she heard a sound coming from her backyard. A metallic *chink*, then a soft masculine curse.

Curious, she leaned back and tugged her lace curtains to open them just a couple inches and peered down through the branches of the mimosa tree, into her yard. The sight that greeted her caused her breath to hitch.

The twins stood in her backyard, in the center of the area she'd neatly staked and tied with twine to define the place she intended to put her koi pond. And they'd made a mess. Clumps of turf lay beside the big hole they'd dug. Water ran freely from a hose into the middle of a muddy pit. The black pool liner she'd bought and left leaning against the garage had been dragged beside the hole.

Anger flushed another kind of heat through her veins, and she climbed off the stool, hurried to the bathroom for her robe, and then she was stomping down her stairs to the sliding glass door, which she slammed open with all her righteous anger.

Two begrimed faces turned her way. Before she let herself think better of her plan, she was standing in front of them with her sheer bathrobe flapping in a breeze and staring at two broad, naked *muddy* chests. "What the hell do you think you're doing?" she asked, trying to temper her voice, because she didn't want neighbors hearing her screeching like a banshee.

Mace's gaze raked over her body. "Wishin' I had x-ray vision," he drawled.

Molly scowled and clutched the lapels of her robe in one hand. "I'm talking about this!" she said, waving her other hand at the rapidly filling hole.

Mace shrugged. "Dirt was too hard. And since we couldn't find a pick or a backhoe in your garage—"

"You think I'd have a backhoe?"

"Or a pick..."

"You were rummaging through my garage?" she said, her voice raising.

"It wasn't locked."

She rolled her eyes. "Why are you digging up my yard?"

"We saw the stakes, found the pool that fits the space you marked off..." He shrugged again, a little smile tilting up the corners of his mouth as he gave her body another sly once-over.

She hoped like hell the bright sunshine wasn't giving him that x-ray vision. "I don't need your help. And now I have a huge mess—"

Jason cleared his throat, pulling her attention to a sharp, crystal gaze alight with amusement. "It only looks like a mess 'cause of the mud. But actually, we have more dug here than you can see."

Molly gaped at both men, covered in sweat and dirt, but somehow still looking more attractive than she could stand. She felt moisture pool beneath her feet and glanced down at the hose still gurgling water into the pit they'd dug. Before she could suppress the urge, she bent and picked it up, pressed her thumb over the end to increase the pressure and aimed it at Jason, spraying him with water.

His eyes closed and he stood in the stream, water running off his face to his chest and soaking his jeans.

Mace erupted in laughter, but quickly shut up the moment she turned the hose on him. When he lifted a foot to climb out of the hole, he slipped and landed on his butt in the middle of the muddy pool.

Elation filled her and she laughed, still spraying. But Jason climbed on his hands and knees, over the edge, toward her. She dropped the hose and turned to make a run for it, but he caught the hem of her bathrobe, and jerked it toward him.

Her feet slipped beneath her and she began to fall backward...into a pair of strong arms which wrapped around her and carried her down to one side of the muddy pit, to soft, gooey ground—with those same arms buffeting the fall.

When she caught her breath, she was covered head to toe by one very wet, very amused man. Mud oozed between her toes and beneath the back of her robe, and both lapels had pulled apart. Although his body shielded her from view, nothing stood between their naked chests.

Jason leaned to one side and lifted one finger.

Her eyes nearly crossed watching it descend toward her face.

He pushed up her glasses. "Seems we got ourselves a situation here," he drawled, settling on his elbows to take a little of his weight off her.

She opened her mouth to demand he move, but then Mace sauntered into view to take up a position leaning against her back porch to watch the couple in the muddy hole. If Jason did move, both men would have an unencumbered view of her torso.

Molly became aware of every sensation: the heavy chest pressing against her stiff nipples, the jut of his jeans-enclosed sex against her mound. She swallowed hard. "Seems we do. I...apologize for acting like a crazy woman."

Jason grunted and his chest jerked against hers. "You're not sorry."

Knowing she was at a distinct disadvantage, she nevertheless lifted her chin. "It's just plain rude to disagree with me. I'm trying to handle this delicately."

"Only handlin' to be done will be done by me—and Mace here, if you ask real pretty."

Her mouth dropped open. Shock vibrated through her. "You did not just say that to me."

His eyes narrowed. His jaw tightened just a fraction. "I said it. I'd like to do a whole lot more. Fact is, I like the way you feel, Miz Pritchet, all stretched out underneath me."

She drew in a sharp breath. "This was a mistake."

"Moved up our timetable a bit, but this is no mistake."

"Your timetable?" she parroted dumbly, her mind and tongue seeming to freeze as he moved against her, snuggling the bulge in the front of his jeans between her legs.

"We planned to woo you gently, like you deserve," he said, his tone silky, "by spendin' time with you, helpin' you sink that pond, then maybe enjoyin' a meal before we sweet-talked you into that pretty bed you've got upstairs."

"That would never happen. I was your teacher."

"See there? That's a piss-poor excuse, ma'am. Pardon my French, but that was eight years ago. We aren't kids anymore."

"I'm still older than you. Old enough not to want to play games."

"Only by five years. Not enough to cause anyone any problems. Unless you don't think we're good enough for you. You should know, we ain't exactly without prospects."

Molly held still, resisting the need to squirm beneath him even though the urge was strong. His jeans-covered cock was right there, and the thought of the friction... "You keep saying *we*. Do you seriously expect me to...be with both of you?" She sniffed. "It's sinful to even suggest it."

He gave her a quick, wicked smile, then did the thing she craved most—flexed his hips and ground the hard ridge right between her folds. "You've thought about it, haven't you?" he whispered. "Even before today. As many times as you've caught us lookin' at you, we've caught your stare."

She closed her mouth. To deny it would be ridiculous. He'd know she was lying. "If you'll both close your eyes, and you'll lift up, I could close my robe."

Blue eyes burned. "Molly..."

It was the first time either of them had called her by her given name. And the sound of it, coming from his lips, was her undoing. Suddenly, she wasn't *teacher* and he wasn't *student*. They were a man and a woman, gazing into each other's eyes, and she was beginning to melt beneath the heat of his very aroused body. "Jason..."

He must have known her resolution was wilting. His smile was softer. More satisfied. "I never gave it much thought, how you always knew, from day one, which one I was. Says something, don't you think?"

She shook her head.

"Says you've been aware of us. Thought about us. *Know* us."

"I don't know anything."

"And that's okay. Because we know a lot. We'll make this easy for you."

"Easy? I have a reputation to protect."

"You think we want anyone lookin' at you, decidin' you're a whore 'cause you chose us? We'll keep this our secret. For a while. Long enough for you to decide whether you're strong enough to call us your own."

Molly nearly wept. Eight years of denial, of subduing every natural instinct, crumbled beneath the weight of his body and steady stare. "I must be out of my mind."

"Makes three of us, sweetheart. Crazy in lust."

Not love, she noted, but then she knew something about the two of them. Knew their history, at least what she'd gleaned from Gracie Logan, who'd met often with the school counselor because both Mace and Jason couldn't seem to keep out of trouble. Never anything really bad, just the sort of trouble two rambunctious young men inevitably found.

They'd been the product of a broken home. Raised by an unmarried mother and a no-account dad until the mother had let life and a substance abuse problem kill her.

No, neither young man would ever be easy about falling in love. That way led to pain, and they'd taken great care to let the world know they were only interested in short-term pleasure.

Perhaps, therein lay the answer. For her. A chance to let loose. To explore a part of her life she'd let go fallow. She cleared her throat. "No one has to know?"

His gaze bored into hers. "Not until you're ready."

She'd never be ready for that. But a chance to have a little fun—without having to find the vibrator at the back of the closet...?

"She's thinkin' about it, Mace," Jason said without looking away from her.

"You should let me up. The neighbors..."

"Mace'll be our lookout."

She licked her lips. "But it's broad daylight."

His hips ground again, this time swaying side to side, opening her. "Better to see you, sweetheart."

"I'm...not much to look at," she whispered.

"Beg to differ. There's plenty I'd love to see."

She wrinkled her nose. "A girl doesn't like to be reminded she has a little too much padding."

"You're perfect. Healthy."

"Good teeth too. Shall I show you?" she said, then grimaced to expose her pearly whites.

"Come on," he growled. "We're already half naked."

Her nipples spiked, poking into his slick chest. Not something he could miss. "We'll make noise."

"God, I hope so. But Mace'll let us know if anyone comes home. Right, Mace?"

Mace's sigh was overloud.

Strangely thrilled about the fact she and Jason would be observed, she smiled. She'd never done anything like this, never thought she'd be into it.

But it was summertime, and the warmth of the wet ground at her back, of the hard body blanketing her, filled her with a lazy, languid heat. She could do this. She just hoped she didn't make too much of a fool out of herself before she was done.

She bent back her head as far as she could to see Mace, still leaning against the porch, hands in his front pockets, but a dark, searing stare all for her. Somehow, that look filled her with courage. She could be shameless. This once.

Looking at Jason again, Molly drew in a deep breath and said, "All right, boys. Let's do this."

Chapter Three

Jason nearly groaned aloud, but then he wouldn't sound like the man of the world she expected. She knew their reps, but didn't understand that the women they'd had, other than Ellie, had been equal hell-raisers. Whatever nasty thing he and his brother had wanted to try, the women had been more than willing to go right along.

With Molly, they had to tread lightly so as not to scare her off. He wanted this to be perfect for her. For him and his brother to steal her heart by not only overwhelming her one sexy act at a time, but by proving to her that the life she led now was an empty shell without them.

A tall order for two men who didn't know a thing about real love, except for what they'd seen between Sam and Gracie, and now Ellie and their two brothers. But Ellie had plenty of game, had taken them all on with hardly a flutter of fear.

Molly's large, solemn eyes, blinking behind her demure glasses, told him they'd need to have a little finesse. He sure as hell wished he'd read a romance novel or two for clues how to do that.

"Might start by gettin' her naked," his brother said, a smile twisting his mouth.

Most times Jason took for granted the connection he and his brother had, but today, he was all too aware. Both of them were committed to this. Despite the fact only one of them held her at the moment, this was a mutual seduction.

"Can we not talk about this?" Molly said, a hitch in her voice.

Apparently, she wanted no reminders that this dance they were ready to begin wasn't a warm and cozy twosome. "Yeah, you're right. Put a sock in it, Mace."

Jason rose up to straddle her hips—so swiftly, she gasped and cupped her hands over her breasts so that he only had a glimpse of pretty pink nipples before she hid them away.

"No, no," he said, cupping his hands over hers still clutching her breasts, but not moving them. He wanted her to make the choice. "No hidin'."

"But you're dressed," she said with a firm tilt of her head. "I'm at a disadvantage."

He grunted, amused by the annoyance evident in her straight mouth. "Want me naked first? Guess that's fair. I'm gonna raise up slow-like, so if there's somethin' else you're achin' to cover..."

Her eyes narrowed, but as soon as he began to rise, she whipped over the edges of her robe to cover herself.

Standing in his socks, because he hadn't wanted to ruin his boots in the mudhole, he scraped off the soggy stockings and then unbuckled, unzipped and pushed his pants and underwear off his hips, all the while keeping his gaze fixed on her face.

Her cheeks were pink, her eyelids dipping as she scanned his mud-streaked belly and sex. Her hands tightened around the fabric she held, but there was a telltale shifting of her legs and hips, a deepening of the curve of her hips that indicated she liked what she saw and her body was ripening.

When he stepped out of his jeans, he went to his knees beside her, aware his cock jutted from his groin and that her gaze kept dipping between his face and his manhood, so quickly he wondered if she was even aware.

"Your turn," he growled.

"I don't know..." She shook her head. "This is embarrassing."

He shook his head, then cupped his fingers and wiggled them. "Come here. Sit up."

She eased up slowly to sit, then scooted over the edge of the pit and onto the grass. He wondered if she was even aware that her back was coated with mud.

He glanced at Mace, just a quick look, but their connection ensured his brother's cooperation.

"What's not fair is that Mace isn't gettin' to touch your pretty soft skin. I'm gonna turn you. Face you toward him. He's not the one feelin' you up, but we shouldn't leave him out."

He grabbed her shoulders and urged her around. She was slow to move, but didn't fight the suggestion. When she faced Mace, her legs drawn up to one side, Jason slid in behind her.

With a single glance of warning to his brother to keep quiet, he slid his hands over her shoulders and down to her breasts. When he cupped them through the thin, silky fabric, her breath held. He squeezed gently, molding the firm, lush globes, felt the scrape of her aroused nipples and paused to give them a light tweak.

She jerked against him, still tense and uneasy, but he wasn't worried. Her back leaned against his chest, rubbing him like a kitten, so he continued the massage, liking the way her soft mounds filled his large hands.

He bent toward her ear. "I used to sit in class, so hard I couldn't think, waitin' for you to bend over and let me see some cleavage."

She gave a soft, feminine grunt. "I know. It's why I started wearing buttoned blouses. I couldn't concentrate with you both ogling me."

His brother's lips twitched, but he remained silent, his eyelids dipping as though gaining lazy pleasure from watching Jason mold and pleasure her breasts.

Jason smoothed a hand between her breasts, to cover the one small fist holding her robe closed. "Time to let go of it, baby."

She mewled. "Not sure I can. He'll see everything."

"He wants that. So much. There's not anything you have to be embarrassed about."

"I need to lose a little weight."

He nuzzled into her hair. "You really don't know, do you?"

"What?" she asked, angling her head to let him kiss the tender spot behind her ear.

"That we like your curves. Every one of 'em. When we see all that softness and it makes us hard."

"Really?"

"God, yeah. Please let him see. Let me ride my hands over those sweet curves. I promise you're beautiful. Perfect. For us."

"Sweet Jesus," she whispered, then eased her hand from beneath his and let him part the sides of her robe to bare her flesh. She sat so stiff, he knew she waited for a comment, a gesture to reassure her.

Mace gave her a rude affirmation, cupping the growing bulge at the front of his jeans and growling. "Damn, girl."

Molly gave a small, strangled laugh, and turned her head to hide her face against Jason's shoulder. He let her hide. Let her feel safe cuddling closer while he glided down, rubbing her soft belly then sinking his fingers between her closed legs. Roughened fingertips touched the tops of her folds. Steamy moisture greeted him, and he bit back a moan of his own.

Glancing over her shoulder to see what he touched, he frowned at the dirt smeared on the back of his hand. "Where's that hose? We're covered in dirt."

"Doesn't matter," she breathed.

But it did, because neither he nor his brother wanted an impeded view of her sweet body or to leave a trace of their dirt on her skin.

Mace stepped forward, snagged the hose from the ground and held it out to Jason who stood and let the water trail first down his body. He scooped it against his skin, enjoying the coolness, splashing his chest and letting it trickle down his belly to his cock.

When he began to rub away the dirt, she turned on her knees to watch then reached out, tentatively. "You missed a spot," she said, cupping water in her hands and using it to clean a smudge on his shaft before wrapping her fingers around him and rubbing up and down to remove it.

Shock held him still. Pleasure kept him silent.

"Turn around," she said, her cheeks pink but determination glinting in her gaze. He handed her the hose, then turned away, waiting patiently as she sent the water washing down his shoulders, a hand following to smooth away the grime. Each graze of her hand became more sure until she cupped water against his buttocks and gave him a squeeze.

When the water fell away, he glanced back to find her standing in front of Mace. "Your turn. Both you boys need a good washing up."

Mace's smile was wide with delight. He stripped off his clothes, hopping from one leg to the other, his cock bouncing against his belly in his eagerness to comply.

Molly surprised them both, taking charge, telling Mace to turn this way and that, to lift your arms, then boldly handling his cock as she cleaned him.

When she was done, she gave them both a look, warning in her narrowed lids to keep back, and then turned the hose on herself.

Both men watched, entranced, as water spilled against her pale, smooth skin, and she used her free hand to touch herself and rub every bit of dirt away. It was like every teenaged fantasy he'd had of her coming to life as her small, soft hands scooped water against her skin.

But he wasn't a teenager anymore. And this was oh so real. When her hand slid between her legs, Jason's body clenched, fists balling. It was that or stride toward her and lift her up to put his aching cock inside her.

Molly lay down the hose, walked to the spigot and turned it off. Then she slowly turned to face them both, her gaze raking one then the other, her cheeks as rosy as her chest, her pink nipples reddened and distended, her thighs pressing together as though trying to contain her own lust.

Jason lifted his chin to Mace, ceding control because he was feeling savage, and watched as his brother strode toward her, his hand reaching out, palm up. "Miz Pritchet, let's take this inside."

Mace's hand shook just a little as it closed around her chilled fingers. He couldn't believe he was here. That she'd touched him willingly. His body still burned everywhere she'd laid her hand. His cock felt ready to burst after the way she'd calmly, methodically, stroked away the dirt.

It had felt almost like a baptism. All sins washed away. He felt lighter of heart and intent. Happy in way that he hadn't been in a long time.

Molly Pritchet had always been a goddess on a pedestal. A sweet-faced woman with sharp eyes and a sharp tongue. He'd felt the sting often enough, he'd known she didn't think of him as more than an ornery boy, and yet moments ago, she'd handled him like she might a man she admired.

Something inside him melted. He wanted to be worthy. Standing naked as a jaybird beside her, he wanted her to never question her decision, to never regret she was about to lie down with him.

Unable to resist, he tugged her close and folded her against his chest. Their first intimate touch was a hug. Skin to skin. Heartbeats mating, matching rhythms, slowing to a steady, heavy thrum. "Ma'am, I'd really like to lay you down in that pretty bed of yours," he said softly.

With droplets of water shining like diamonds on her skin, she leaned back her head to smile up at him. "I have no objections, sir."

Her eyes blinked dreamily at him, and his chest expanded. He tugged her hand again and pulled her toward the glass doors. Once inside, with the AC prickling their damp skin, he headed straight for the staircase, halting at the bottom step because she'd lagged, her head turning to Jason.

"You're going to watch my ass all the way up those steps, aren't you?"

Jason grinned. "Sure am."

Molly's brows furrowed.

Mace grunted, bent quickly, and swept her into his arms. Problem solved.

Her fingers dug into his shoulders. "You aren't going to carry me up. Your back!"

"Don't you worry about either of our backs. We're strong, Molly. We can handle you."

Her eyes widened.

"I'm not sayin' we have to be strong, just that you don't have to worry. You feel just right," he said, giving her a bounce to prove to her she was safe in his arms.

She relaxed, sighing. "I've never been carried by a man."

"There's gonna be lots of firsts, sugar. Just you wait."

The trip up the stairs took seconds and didn't strain his body a bit. He carried her to her bedroom and set her on her feet beside the bed with its pretty red covers. Reaching out a hand, he pulled away the comforter, tossing it to the floor at the end. "Sorry, we don't want to mess that up."

He lifted both hands toward her face. Molly pulled back. "Let me set these aside," he said, gently easing her glasses down her nose, then setting them on the bedside table.

Her blush was strawberry red, and he smiled then made a gesture toward the mattress. "You first." He waited while she backed onto the mattress and swung her legs over the side. "All the way to the middle. Have to make room for us both."

Her head shook, like she was arguing with herself, but she scooted deeper, toward the center, then lay down, her head resting on a pillow, an arm folded over her middle as she stared, her green eyes wide and showing her uncertainty.

"We've loved lots of women, Molly. Gave 'em pleasure. We know how to do this. Don't you worry."

"I don't really want to hear about all your other women."

"Don't be jealous. We were just practicin' for you."

She scoffed. "Sure you were."

"It's true. Didn't know it until just now." He knelt on the edge of the mattress then lay down beside her, turning her toward him before moving closer to snuggle his body against hers. "Any time you get scared—"

She glared. "I've had sex before."

"How long ago?"

Her lips tightened. "I don't see how that's your concern."

"We're gonna be your concern. From this day on. No lies between us. How long?"

Moisture filled her eyes, but she blinked it away. "Not since college. Since before I came to this town."

He gave her a nod. "I'm glad. But that means we'll need to have some care." He glanced up at Jason who had made his way around the bed, and who was slowly easing onto the mattress behind her. His brother's gaze locked with his. They shared a silent message. They'd be gentle. Not spook her. Not go crazy on her just because they finally had her in a bed and at their mercy.

Mace rose on an elbow and leaned closer. "You're a pretty woman, Molly Pritchet. But it's not why we chose you."

With her expression softening, growing dreamier by the moment, she lifted her gaze to his. "You chose me? That sounds...like you've been thinking about this for a while. Like you might want more than just this time."

"Then it sounded just about right." He ducked his head and pressed a kiss against her mouth, stifling a moan because her lips were soft and pliant, and opening beneath his. With a gentle tease of his tongue along the bottom lip, he entered her, tasting her fresh breath, enjoying her moist heat while their breaths comingled and grew deeper, charged with lust.

He stroked her tongue, tangling with it, teasing her with short, gliding thrusts, reminding her what the outcome of this would be. When he pulled back, she followed, whimpering at the loss of contact, but settling again, because Jason was petting her belly and nuzzling into the corner of her shoulder.

She reached up a hand to cup Jason's chin, then pulled his face toward hers to share a deep kiss. Mace's already tight body hardened like steel. She was a natural—a sweet, giving woman who would never leave one of the brothers wanting. He knew it instinctively.

Hunger riding high, his gaze swept her body as his brother lingered in the kiss. Her breasts were flushed, her reddening nipples taut and dimpled, the tips tight little buds. Her belly had begun to undulate on gentle waves of arousal, lust evident in the sweet, hot fragrance wafting in the air.

He scooted down the bed, palmed a generous mound and latched onto it with his mouth, burrowing deeper as her thighs moved restlessly together.

The kiss ended, and Jason raised his head. His mouth was blurred and red, his eyes a little glazed. The hard edge of his jaw denoted the fact he wasn't going to be long on patience.

Mace had himself under better control. He pushed Molly to her back, aimed a glare at Jason and urged her legs apart with gentle nudges of his knees. "I know it's been a while, baby. I'll go slow."

She gave a nod, then cupped his shoulders and raised her knees. Her pussy was as lovely as the rest of her, thicker outer lips pink and swollen, a light dusting of dark hair on her mound. The pink petals of her inner folds were a delicious fringe that protruded slightly. He couldn't wait to suck on them, but that would have to be later, because she was waiting to be filled. Eager for it by the way her belly and thighs quivered.

Planting one hand on the mattress, he gripped his cock, centered it at her opening, then held her lips apart to watch as he slowly sank inside. He bared his teeth, hissing softly between his gritted teeth. "Baby, you have no idea how good this feels."

The blunt head of his cock stretched her opening, and he gave a little shove, gently breaching it, then plunging inside an inch or two. Slick heat surrounded him. Her pussy clamped down. To hold him? To eject him? He glanced at her face to find her avidly watching his cock sink inside her. Tightening his abdomen, he flexed, giving her another gentle shove, tunneling deeper. "You're tight," he growled. "It's damn near killin' me. Jason, you're gonna die."

Her gaze swept up, caught him staring, and she gave him a tentative smile. "It stings a bit. You're bigger than anyone I've had before."

Elation filled him as well as a jealous pride. They'd give her something she'd never had. Something that couldn't be replaced. Settling on his elbows, he dipped his head to give her a hard kiss. "Hold tight, baby."

She murmured something he didn't understand, couldn't hear. Blood was whooshing through his veins. Sweat sprouted on his chest, his face, as he powered into her, pushing deeper and deeper, loving the feel of the gentle clasps her deep channel gave his cock as he entered and withdrew. She was liquid fire and gripping muscle, clenching around his cock so tightly he knew he wouldn't last a minute longer. He rolled to his side, bringing her with him, then withdrew. "Your turn, bro."

Her eyes rounded.

"That sounded crass, I know. But I don't wanna blow. Not yet. You're not nearly ready."

She groaned, hiding her face against his chest as Jason lifted her upper thigh and draped it over Mace's, then came closer, his cock glancing against Mace's skin before he found her entrance and sank inside.

Mace slid a hand between his and Molly's body. He spread her folds at the top, forking his fingers to expose her clit, then applied circular pressure to the knot as Jason stroked her from behind, moving in strong, but gentle pulses, then powering harder.

Her body vibrated, jerked. Her breaths grew jagged, held, then blew hard with each deep, powerful lunge of Jason's hips.

Mace exerted pressure against her lower belly to hold her still, and continued to ply her slippery clit with tender caresses until she shook between them, eyes closed tight, mewling like a kitten.

Her orgasm, when it hit her, was a lovely thing to watch. She came unraveled in an instant, her lush mouth rounding around a silent scream. Her back arched, breasts pushing toward him, her head thrashing on his shoulder then Jason's as she rocked herself between them.

When her movements and breathing slowed, Jason pulled free and wrapped his arms around her from behind. Mace jutted his hips against her, letting his still-rock-hard cock dig into her belly.

Her eyes opened slowly, blinking sleepily until they focused and her gaze landed on him. Tears filled her eyes. "That was incredible."

"Glad you approve. But, baby, we're not done."

Jason tightened his arms to give her a squeeze. "Not by a long shot."

"Neither of you...?" Her voice held a tinge of dismay.

"Not because we weren't into it, promise. We wanted to be perfect. To be the best you've ever had."

"Good Lord, you're both gonna kill me."

"Rest a little while," he whispered. "We've got all the time in the world."

While her eyelids drifted down, both men stroked her skin, soothing her to sleep. When she began to snore softly, they both grinned.

"Think she knows she snores?" Jason asked, an eyebrow arching.

"No, and you're never gonna tell her."

"What are we gonna do while she sleeps?"

For once, Mace thought beyond his aching cock. Molly was prideful and little reluctant to believe they were serious about wanting her for longer than a day or night. She needed a gesture. Something that proved this wasn't just about fun and games—although he hoped there'd still be plenty of that to come. "I've got an idea," Mace said, pressing a kiss against her forehead before rolling away and onto his feet.

"You with ideas? Should I be scared?"

Mace shrugged. "You're not the only one she inspires to be a better man."

Chapter Four

Molly awoke alone with a sheet pulled over her body. She lay for a long moment, wrapped in dreamy memories of her encounter with the twins. They'd been surprisingly selfless. Had seen to her pleasure without pressing for their own.

Thinking of her own bold actions made her blush. Had she really washed them and herself? Stood naked in her backyard in the middle of the day while two men watched, jaws dropping, well-muscled bodies tensing, as she'd teased them with sensuous glides of her hands over her own less than perfect frame?

And good Lord, she'd lain with both flanking her body—sandwiched between two mirror-image Greek gods—and hadn't died from the pleasure of it...

Speaking of which, she lifted her head and strained to hear where the men were.

However, the house was silent. No footsteps in the hallway. No water running in the bathroom. Not a single muffled voice coming from the yard outside her window.

No. Molly lay perfectly still while her mind whirled. They'd left her. Mace and Jason had snuck out of her bed and left her behind. Job done. Conquest made.

She rolled to her stomach and pulled a pillow over her head to scream into the mattress. The bastards! Everything they'd said, everything their eyes had intimated had been a big fat lie. They didn't want her for their own. They'd wanted another notch to carve into their bedpost.

As disappointed as she was, she wasn't really surprised. Hadn't she known all along she wasn't in their league? That she was a momentary thrill? The teacher they'd finally seduced to check off the list of their favorite fantasies?

However, she also wasn't truly angry. They'd given her more than they'd gotten. She'd fallen asleep before either man had had a chance to come.

She grunted. Almost smiled at that thought. What did she need with a man anyway? Having two was just ridiculous. She'd had her fling. Gotten her mojo back. Now she could move on to more important things, like enjoying her blessed solitude for the rest of the damn summer.

So why did she suddenly feel like crying?

No matter her internal arguments, Molly grieved. For one afternoon, she'd dreamed of having a different life, a different future. One where she was adored as more than a teacher. The way the men had treated her, like she was special, beautiful—*incredibly desirable*—had made her feel exactly that.

Worse, as she'd drifted off to sleep, she'd remembered the fact that no one had bothered with a condom, and she'd been glad—deep inside, syrupy happy about the oversight. She'd been sure in her little dreamy bubble that she was pregnant. That a child rested inside her. One she could call her own and on whom she'd shower all the love and affection she'd been storing inside herself for years.

"I'm so stupid," she whispered aloud. But there was no use crying over something she'd never really had. Pushing back the sheet, she decided to shower and get to work before dusk fixing the mess the men had created in her backyard

She'd do something practical, something to keep her mind off the delicious pleasures she'd enjoyed. If she worked really hard, then maybe she'd sleep so well she wouldn't dream about two blue-eyed liars who'd made her feel more like a woman than she had in years.

The shower was quick. She didn't allow herself to linger over or touch any of the parts they'd left tender from their touches and thrusts. She dressed in comfortable slacks, a loose

T-shirt, slid her glasses on and wrapped a rubber band around her hair to keep it off her neck, because it was still hot outside.

When she stepped through the glass doors and onto her back porch, she drew in a deep, harsh breath. The muddy hole was gone—filled in and dirt tamped down—and so was the black pool liner.

Anger rattled through her, making her shake. They couldn't have left the hole, making it a bit easier for her to finish the job? And why had they felt the need to move the heavy liner?

She walked around the side of the yard, to the spot where she'd left the liner originally, leaning against the garage—but it wasn't there either. And it wasn't inside the garage or in any other part of her yard.

Sweating and getting angrier by the moment, she charged into her house, grabbed her purse and keys and slammed out again, determined to read them both the riot act about poaching other people's property. "I ought to call the sheriff. Wouldn't the Logan brothers like that?" But she wouldn't, all too aware the family had had their share of courtrooms and trouble.

No, she'd seek out Sam Logan, the patient and kind father who'd taken in *a brood of hellions!*

Stomping on the gas, and wishing her little Scion had a little more oomph so she could leave a trail of rubber as she left her driveway, she pointed her car down the highway toward the Doubletree Ranch.

The little blue Scion's engine sounded like an overheated lawnmower as it bumped along the gravel drive to halt beside the house. Jason winced as the little car ground to a halt.

"Think she drove in second gear the whole way here?" Sam Logan drawled from the porch where he'd taken a seat on the top step to watch the twins at work.

"Looks like she's so mad she forgot to change 'em," Mace said, his voice even. He leaned on the shovel and tilted back his cowboy hat to get a better look.

Jason threw down the bandanna he'd used to wipe sweat from his face and sauntered toward the little car. However, before he could reach for the handle to help her out, she shoved it open hard, hitting the side of his thigh. He grimaced, but forced a smile. "Hey, sugarplum. You get a nice nap?"

It was the wrong thing to say.

Molly's face screwed up into a fearsome scowl as she flounced out of the vehicle. "You have something of mine."

Jason clapped a hand over his heart. "It's beating only for you."

"Cut the crap, Romeo. You two stole my pond."

He suppressed a grin because her little hissy-fit was adorable. "Beg to differ. We simply relocated it."

"What?"

He stepped aside. Her gaze went to Mace who tamped down another shovel of dirt, filling in the sides around the pond they'd sunk in the front yard, just off the porch.

Mace swiped his forearm over his sweaty face. "Had to use picks, all right. And a backhoe. But she's ready for water."

Molly stomped over to the pond liner, now set firmly in the ground. "Well, you can just dig it right up again. That's mine!" she said, pointing a finger toward it. Then she raised her hand and stubbed her finger against Mace's chest. "The nerve! Did you romance me for my pond?"

Mace laughed and grabbed her finger, using it to pull her closer.

Her heels dug into the grass, and she resisted, her face getting redder by the second.

Jason walked up behind her, set his hands on her hips and snugged his body close to hers. "Easy, now," he said softly next to her ear. "We'll stop teasing. Give us a second to explain."

She stood rigid between them, her chest heaving with her angry breaths. "There's nothing you have to say that I want to hear."

"Yes, there is... Baby, it's gonna be okay."

Her head turned, brows still scowling, but something dark and hurt glittered in her eyes. "No more games. No more playing with me. It ends."

Jason shook his head. "We're only startin', baby. But we didn't do this right. We didn't expect to be away this long. We would never have deliberately hurt you."

Mace flung his cowboy hat aside and stepped closer too, trapping her between the two of them. Her hands came up to shove him away, but Mace bent toward her and kissed her.

Leave it to Mace to go straight for her heart.

Jason felt the moment when the anger drained away. Her body swayed, her head tilted back, resting on his shoulder while Mace gave her the kiss she needed. Jason slipped his hands around her belly and hugged her, then began to murmur softly in her ear. "We wanted the pond sunk before you woke. We planned to have you over. Meet the family. Show you the house and the plans we have to make it right for you."

She whimpered and drew back from Mace's kiss. Her head turned toward Jason, confusion clouding her sage-colored eyes. "What are you saying?"

"That we didn't lie, Molly. We want you. Not just for today. Not just for a week. We want forever."

"But..."

Mace kissed her cheek. "We love you. We've decided you're the one for us."

"You've decided...?" She shook her head. "That's ridiculous. I can't have you both."

"Why not?" Jason asked, feathering the side of her neck with light kisses. "You want us. We're good together—*fuck, better than good.* And we'll spend our lives makin' you happy."

"But you don't know me. This is too quick."

"We know you want a family. Kids of your own. So do we."

Her body stiffened again. "Kids who won't know who their daddy is?"

Jason glided his hands up to cup her breasts, not to arouse, but to soothe, then slid them again, one curving around her shoulder, the other on her hip. "Does it matter? We'll both be their father. We shared a womb. We damn near share the same mind, and we both want you."

Molly stayed silent and so still that Jason worried they'd gone about this whole thing the wrong way. That they'd blown their chances with her by rushing her.

"I wouldn't be able to teach anymore..." she said weakly.

Not an emphatic *no* to his suggestion. He breathed a little easier and gave his brother a stare to tell him to let him handle this.

Mace's lips tightened, but he nodded.

Jason sighed. "What we want isn't wrong, Molly. But one of us will marry you. If you want to keep teachin', we can keep secret the fact you're sharin' a bed with both of us."

Her head shook side to side, but her body was relaxing, leaning into his caresses. "But that wouldn't be fair. Not to one of you. And I couldn't keep a secret that big. Not when I kiss one of you, then the next day kiss the other where people can see."

"Folks can't keep us straight anyway. How'd they know?"

"They'd know," she said, her voice softening to a whisper, "because when the two of you are together, I can't help myself..."

"Can't help what, sweetheart?" he said just as quietly.

Her head dipped. "I can't help what you make me want. I can't help touching you. Kissing you. Melting like goo if you give me a wink."

Mace's expression changed, love gleaming in his eyes, concern etching the edge of his jaw.

Jason kissed her cheek again and hugged her. "Do you love us?" he asked softly.

"I shouldn't. It's too soon."

A silly excuse, given how long this moment had been in the making. "It's not. We've known each other for years. Think, Molly. You haven't taken a lover in all that time. You waited for us."

Her head shook again. "I was busy."

Mace leaned in, rubbing his forehead against hers. "Busy waitin' for us to grow up?"

Jason tucked a finger under her jaw to turn her face so he could see her expression. All her uncertainty, her confusion shone in her glossy green eyes, only magnified by the lenses. "We had a plan. A good one. We'd have wooed you slowly. Made ourselves indispensible in your life. But you surprised us. Baby, you're ready for us. Ready to be ours. Now, if you want time to think, to be sure, we'll back off. But why waste time? We're here. We're sure. You don't have to wait to make that family you need. You have one. Ours."

"Might need to give that girl some room to breathe," Sam called from the porch.

All three turned startled glances his way. Jason had forgotten he was there.

Molly jerked as though she expected him and Mace to move away, but they stood firm, waiting as their father rose from the top step and dusted off his jeans before ambling toward them.

His expression was neutral, but his smoky gray eyes were alert, searching when he looked down into Molly's eyes. "Ma'am, these boys may have gone about this all wrong, but they have good hearts. They won't ever cheat. They won't ever raise their hands or voices to a woman—'cept when they're bein' ornery. They told me they'd found themselves a wife. If you're wonderin' whether you'll find acceptance, you might not find all folks happy about your arrangement, but you won't have any trouble here." Sam glanced at both of his sons, gave them a grave nod, then walked away. Whistling.

Mace's eyes wrinkled at the corners with silent laughter. "Think maybe we should take this *discussion* inside?"

Jason remembered the last time the two of them had brought a woman home. Ellie Harker had been livid, a writhing bundle they'd hoisted between the two of them before they'd decided they'd have to tie her to a chair while they talked sense to her.

Mace's eyebrow arched. "Look how that turned out."

Jason grinned over Molly's head, turned her with a quick twist of his hands on her shoulders and bent to pick her up. With the woman they both loved folded over his shoulder and just beginning to wiggle, he bounded up the porch stairs.

Mace followed close on Jason's heels, eager for the coming confrontation. Molly still had doubts, not about whether she wanted them, but about whether she was doing the right thing. Not that he blamed her a bit. Some folks weren't too kind about the alternate living arrangements that seemed to be popping up all around the county. Ellie had had her share of snide remarks and he knew she smarted over the intolerance.

Speaking of which, Ellie poked her head out of the kitchen just as Jason slammed through the front door. Her mouth dropped open then clamped closed, but not before he saw the twinkle in her eyes as she ducked back inside.

Yep, she'd have a sister-in-law in no time to commiserate over all the stubborn men who lived in the house. Her complaints about the place stinking up with testosterone would quiet as she and Molly got to know each other and shared the burdens of being ranch wives.

Molly's concerns over whether she'd be allowed to teach didn't amount to a hill of beans. He and Jason would have to fill her belly quick to make sure she never stepped foot in a classroom again, unless she decided to home school all the kids the Logan boys were going to make.

"What do you think you're doing?" Molly grumbled loudly as Jason turned down the hallway toward his bedroom.

"Don't know why you always ask that?" Mace said cheerfully. "You know the damn answer. We're gonna get you nekkid, get you between us, and remind you that you matter."

"I don't have to be *nekkid* to be reminded. All you have to do is tell me."

"Wouldn't be near as much fun, sweetheart."

Jason chuckled, opened his bedroom door and carried her to the bed, where he flung her down in the center then crawled over her squirming body until she grew still.

"That's effective," Mace said, making a mental note that all future arguments should end just like that. He reached to grab the glasses Jason swiped from her face.

Jason rose up to straddle her waist and rucked up her T-shirt, forcing her arms over her head to remove it. Then he went to work on the front clasp of her bra.

Her hands covered her tits the moment he had them freed. "I haven't finished talking," she muttered.

"Doesn't matter if you keep yappin', woman. Won't change a damn thing."

"I'm still angry. We shouldn't do this when we're angry."

Jason scooted down her body, fingers slipping into her waistband to pull down her pants. "Who says? Seems the perfect time to let you work out a bit of that aggression."

"But I'll never win an argument!"

Both men laughed.

Mace folded her glasses and placed them carefully on the table. Then he sat on the side of the mattress and chucked off his boots as Jason finished stripping her nude and tossing away her clothing. "Fact is, you'll win every damn time," he said, smiling. "If you're smart. All you have to do is put your hands on our privates—"

Her eyes bugged. "Mace!"

Jason turned his head. "Love the way she says that. Used to get me hard when she said my name like that and tapped the side of my desk to get me to look at my tests."

"I loved it when she'd erase the whiteboard. Her butt would get to jiggling…"

"Boys!"

"We're not boys!" both men said, humor draining from their faces.

Chapter Five

Mace ripped his shirt over his head, opened his belt and shoved down his pants. Wrapping his fingers around his cock, he jiggled it. "Maybe we should make sure she doesn't forget again, Jason."

Jason gave a waggle of his eyebrows. "Seems you're farther along than I am. How about you keep her busy while I finish strippin'." He rolled off Molly.

Molly pushed up, legs nearly clearing the side of the bed, but Mace pressed his hand against the center of her chest and forced her to lie back. Then he thrust his arms beneath her knees, pulled her ass to the edge of the bed, and leaned over her. With a single nudge, his cock found her center.

Her mouth opened on a sharp, indrawn breath.

"Say you don't want it and I'll stop," he said, knowing by the instant glazing of her eyes, she couldn't refuse.

"This is crazy. What the hell's your father going to think?"

"That we took our goddamn sweet time. He met and married his wife inside a weekend."

"But I can't marry you both."

"That what's got you worried? That we'd make you choose?"

"That's just one thing that's problematic about this...relationship."

"*Problematic?*" Mace shook his head. "Don't know how you can even think big words when I'm about to come inside you. My brain's about to shut down."

A dark brow arched. "It's the difference between boys and girls."

"Molly, Molly..." he replied silkily. "There's a helluva lot more differences. Want me to show you one?"

Her mouth thinned into a crimped, straight line, then stretched slowly as the grin she fought won the battle. A peal of laughter followed. "I don't know how you do that," she said. "Make me smile when I should be screaming down the house."

"You'll have to wait for that part, sweetheart," Jason said as he joined them on the bed. He lay on his side, nude, his head supported on an elbow as he gave Mace the signal to begin.

With the amount of moisture slicking the head of his dick, Mace didn't worry whether she was ready. He flexed, impaling her with a single, forceful thrust.

Her back arched. Her hand reached over her head.

Jason grabbed it and held it tightly inside his as Mace began to move, hammering her pussy.

Her body writhed, legs straining in his grasp, straightening, widening to allow him closer, deeper. Mace gave her what she wanted, quickening the motions of his hips while he watched her movements and her expression grow more frantic the closer she came to exploding.

"Finish it," Jason said, his gaze glued to Molly.

Mace gave silent thanks that, this one time, he didn't have to consider his brother. He knew there'd be plenty other times when he'd get some one-on-one, and when Jason would whisk her away for his own pleasure too. Right now, he could barely think for the pressure building in his thighs and balls. Sweat rolled off his face and chest. He gave in to the rapture, powering harder, deeper. Then just when the pressure grew painful, so tight inside his balls and chest he thought he'd explode, he came.

Come splashed inside her, hot, scalding, easing his pistoning thrusts as they gradually slowed. When he finished, he opened his eyes.

Jason kissed the back of the hand he held. Molly's free hand cupped one of her breasts, something she probably didn't even realize. The gesture caused an ache inside his chest. She'd felt the need to comfort herself.

"Was it too much?" he asked gruffly.

Her eyelids drifted open. Green eyes glittered. "You overwhelm me. You both do. I lose any sense of self."

"Is that a bad thing?"

One corner of her mouth rose in a tired smile. "Oh, hell no."

He pulled free, set down her legs and turned her with gentle shoves until she lay lengthwise on the bed between both brothers. "No more talk about this not workin'. About what's not right. You know, don't you? That we're serious. That this is real."

Molly rubbed a hand across his chest, not meeting his gaze. "Give me a little time to get used to the idea of it. Please."

He tightened his jaw, but nodded. "Do you want to go home?"

She sucked her bottom lip between her teeth, then peeked up from beneath the fringe of her dark lashes. "My pond's here."

His heart beat faster.

"And I can't really get to know you unless I'm here, can I?"

He gave her a soft smile then leaned in to kiss her. "Wouldn't make a lick o' sense, a long-distance courtship like that." Never mind town was just minutes away. He liked the way the conversation was going.

Jason gave him a nod, telling him he'd done well. Then he snaked an arm around her middle and nuzzled her shoulder. "You too tired to help a cowboy out?"

She angled her head toward Jason. "Since it appears I'm responsible for your condition, I suppose it's only fair I lend a hand."

"Or a mouth?" Jason asked hopefully.

Hers opened. Then she bit her lower lip and sucked it between her teeth. "I'll see what I can do," she whispered.

Molly had never given a man a blow job. But she didn't worry about whether she was doing it right. Whenever her touch wasn't firm enough, Jason wrapped his hand around hers and squeezed to show her how he liked it. When she'd been worried about whether to suck or if her teeth would scrape, Jason had pulled her hair, showing her which touch and how much suction and scrape he wanted.

Mace had given her a pillow to kneel on, and had sat in the armchair beside the bed, watching and offering his advice—although he'd fallen silent in the last few minutes. Likely because his cock was hardening again.

Worries and insecurities forgotten, Molly relaxed. She followed an instinct she'd never tapped into, let her inner wild child out to play. Both small hands encircled Jason's thick staff, stroking up and down. She bobbed to meet each upward pull, sinking deeper and deeper as she gained confidence she wouldn't gag.

There was surprising pleasure to be had in giving such an intimate service to her man.

She pulled off, licking her lips and staring at the thick, blunt crown, so soft, and yet so powerful. Ejaculate sat like a precious pearl atop the slender eyelet slit. She licked it, liked the musky, salty flavor of it, then proceeded to lick him like an ice cream cone.

His cock was a glorious instrument of pleasure, as strong and vulnerable as the man himself. Cupping his balls in one hand, she ran her tongue up one side of his thick stalk and down the other, humming with excitement.

"*Dayum*," Mace muttered from the chair.

Her glance cut to the side to find him stroking his own cock with his large hand.

She pulled back. "Uh-uh. None of that, now."

He grunted and let his hand fall away. Sitting back with his cock standing straight out from his groin, he should have looked lewd, but instead, she didn't think he'd ever been more beautiful.

"You have two hands," he growled.

"I do," she said, pausing before another up-and-down lick. "But I can reach only so far."

When her gaze rose to meet Jason's narrow-eyed stare, she sank deep on his cock, sucking hard as she rose again. She came off him and smiled. "Guess I shouldn't talk with my mouth full."

His lips quirked. "Mace, get your ass over here."

Molly went down and up again, watching from the corner of her eye as Mace approached, then sidled up beside Jason.

With barely a pause, she let go of Jason, scooted herself and her pillow between them, then gripped both cocks and pulled until both men angled their bodies so she could move easily from one to the other.

Then she stroked Jason's wet cock with one hand while she leaned toward Mace and took his sex into her mouth. The same fat, blunt head glided over her tongue and to the back of her throat, but when she tried to pull back, he caught her ears and pinched the lobes. "Swallow when I bump your throat."

She didn't know if it was possible, but sank again, letting him butt the back of her throat. She took a tentative swallow and found she enjoyed the feel of her throat pushing against him as it closed, then opening again. From his groan and the curl of his fingers, she knew she'd done it just right.

Molly moved back to Jason, gripped Mace's cock and pleasured them both until her jaws grew tired and her hand ached.

Their musky scents surrounded her, similar, but she thought she might be able to tell the difference between them even in the dark. Mace's was a touch lighter, fresher—like warm breezes on a summer day. Jason's held a masculine mixture of sage and sawdust.

With all that masculine strength in her mouth and her hands, her mind wandered, imagining many more magical days and nights spent exploring their bodies.

She liked the way they felt, liked the heat emanating from their bodies, the way their thighs tensed, hard as steel, and yet quivered the longer she played.

Both men rocked on the balls of their feet. Both men watched, cheeks flushed, stares so intense they made her shiver. But she was done. Her pussy was swollen, so juicy she could feel it wet the ball of her heel, which she'd been sitting on to try to alleviate a little of the ache that had grown exponentially as time passed.

Maybe something of her dilemma showed on her face, because Mace crimped her ear and drew her back. "Sweetheart, let go."

She pulled away, wiggling on her heel and waited.

"Havin' a little trouble there?" Mace asked, gaze dropping to where she squirmed.

She nodded quickly, heat flushing her cheeks.

"There's a way we can all find our pleasure. All at the same time."

"Tell me," she blurted, eager to ease her own discomfort.

Mace crooked a finger and walked backward toward the bed, a wicked smile stretching his mouth.

Jason snagged her hand and pulled her up. Molly's heart raced as they followed Mace. He lay on the bed, feet against the headboard, then bent his knees and moved up so that he lay over the top three quarters of the mattress.

Gripping his cock, he held it perpendicular to his washboard belly and gave her a challenging glare. "Climb over me and put your mouth here."

With Jason's help, she climbed over Mace, her breasts brushing his face. When her mouth hovered over his cock, he pulled her by her hair, taking her the rest of the way down.

"Let Jason position you," Mace said, his voice muffled.

The end of the bed dipped behind her, hands settled on her ass. Jason nudged apart her knees and pushed her down until her pussy rested on Mace's mouth.

The first dart of his tongue against her sensitive folds caused her to jerk, then to quiver, because his lips latched on to her clit and pulled.

Sparks ignited; her clit swelled as he suctioned against the tiny nub.

The strong hands on her rump began to massage her, manipulating her buttocks together then apart, up then down.

Molly opened her mouth and sank onto Mace's cock, eager to give him the same extraordinary pleasure, but also needing to muffle the sounds she made. She mewled and whimpered, gasped and moaned.

Fingers slid into her pussy. Two she guessed, thick, clever. They touched the spot inside her, the one she'd read about but never believed existed. They swirled and swirled while Mace's head circled beneath her and his mouth gathered her folds and sucked them whole.

The fingers withdrew. Mace's mouth fell away. She sank deeper, laving the sides of his cock with her tongue, desperate to please and to be pleasured again. When firm hands lifted her bottom and the solid, substantial column of Jason's cock drove inside her, she gave a squeal and shuddered, sure she'd faint from the powerful swells of hot pleasure washing over her skin. Her vagina clamped around him, faint ripples feathering along her inner walls, clasping, releasing, tightening harder as his strokes quickened and grew in strength.

With her hands fisting in the bedding, and Mace's hands bracing her hips above him, Jason's hard thrusts shook the bed, slapping her buttocks and thighs, churning in the liquid spilling from inside her, which Mace leaned up to lick from the top of her folds.

The glance of his tongue against her distended clit pushed her past the precipice. Her back arched, ass held high; her body grew rigid, then liquid, and swayed with the push and pull of Jason's hips.

Her mouth sank deeper, swallowing Mace down, urgently sucking, drawing comfort and at last his seed, which she swallowed without hesitation, each loud gulp accompanied by his own pained groans.

Jason's fingers dug into her ass, and he gave a shout that echoed against the walls. Come filled her. His cock continued moving, pushing fluid out in sticky streams down her inner thighs.

Molly flew. Freed by the intense pleasure and the comfort rough, calloused hands provided as they glided on her buttocks and back. Whispers of praise made her smile. "Someone catch me," she said, her arms collapsing beneath her. She rested, her butt in the air, her face pillowed on a hard thigh.

Again, she was moved. Her body arranged for her because she didn't have the strength. Lying stretched between them, on her side facing Jason, Mace cuddling close to her back, she fought to stay awake. To tell them how amazing it had been.

Jason kissed her forehead and set her cheek on Mace's forearm. "It's okay to sleep. We won't desert you."

The room was dark. Night had fallen, and she hadn't even noticed. "Best workout ever," she mumbled.

Warm chuckles shook her back and front.

"This can be yours forever," Jason said, then kissed her mouth.

It was a sweet kiss. Short. Just a smoothing of lips. When he drew back, he studied her expression.

"You're waiting for an answer?" she grumbled. "Really? Like I can think?"

Mace gave a sleepy moan behind her. "No thinkin' necessary. Just be with us. It's an easy decision."

"What about when I get old and fat?"

"What about it?" Jason said, one side of his mouth quirking up. "There'll be more of you to share."

"What about when you get bored with the same woman? Because I'll tell you now, I won't stand for either of you cheating. I know it's selfish, but I couldn't bear it."

"Be selfish all you want," Mace said. "There's only been one woman we've ever wanted longer than a night."

Her eyes filled. "Me?"

"You."

"You."

The men moved closer, pressing into her so tightly she couldn't breathe without moving them with the soft gusts.

"All right," she whispered. "But you have to promise me something."

"Anything, baby," Jason said. "Name it."

"Promise you'll be good fathers."

Jason swallowed, his jaw tightened. "I'll be the best I know how."

She studied his expression, the fear in his eyes. "You've had Sam Logan to show you how. That's good enough for me." Then she sighed sleepily. "I want lots and lots of children."

"Yes, ma'am."

Sam Logan tiptoed down the hallway toward the front porch, a smile on his lips and tears burning his eyes.

When he eased onto the top step he glanced toward the sky. "Looks like I'm done, Gracie."

"Like hell," came a quiet voice in the darkness.

He glanced to the side to find his oldest son, Johnny, leaning on the railing. He was shirtless, barefoot, his long, thick black hair sticking to sweat on his chest. "Why aren't you inside with your pretty wife?"

Johnny shrugged. "Ellie asked for some alone time with Killian. She thinks he doesn't believe she loves him. She said she's gonna prove otherwise."

Sam grunted. "You coulda headed to one of the spare rooms."

"Too damn noisy," Johnny said, a faint glint of humor flashing in his black eyes.

"Now, that's a fact."

"Ellie's pregnant, Sam."

Sam's chest expanded, his heart quickening with a happiness so raw he started to shake.

"Grandkids are gonna need you." Johnny pushed away from the rail and walked into the house.

Sam understood the message. Johnny was a man of few words, but the ones he chose got straight to the point.

Sam gazed heavenward again. Sad, but smiling. "Sweetheart, we're gonna have to build a bigger house."

About the Author

Until recently, award-winning erotica and romance author Delilah Devlin lived in South Texas at the intersection of two dry creeks, surrounded by sexy cowboys in Wranglers. These days, she's missing the wide-open skies and starry nights but loving her dark forest in Central Arkansas, with its eccentric characters and isolation—the better to feed her hungry muse! For Delilah, the greatest sin is driving between the lines, because it's comfortable and safe. Her personal journey has taken her through one war and many countries, cultures, jobs, and relationships to bring her to the place where she is now—writing sexy adventures that hold more than a kernel of autobiography and often share a common thread of self-discovery and transformation.

To learn more about Delilah Devlin, please visit www.delilahdevlin.com.

Send an email to delilah@delilahdevlin.com or join her Yahoo! group to enter in the fun with other readers as well as Delilah: DelilahsDiary@yahoogroups.com.

When temptation catches fire,
saddle up and hang on for the ride.

Lone Heart
© *2012 Delilah Devlin*
A *Red Hot Weekend* story

Lone Wyatt is a long way from his Colorado home. After his brother married the woman they both loved, he figured it'd be best if he was out of the way. He'd like to have his own one-and-only, but he's in no rush. Until he saunters into a small Oklahoma town and spots Charli Kudrow. One wary glance from her haunted eyes, and he knows there's hidden fire inside her just waiting to erupt. And he's ready to tear through every objection she can think up.

Charli intends to slip out of Shooters unnoticed as soon as she's done pinning a help wanted notice to the bulletin board. But there's a cowboy at the bar with a killer smile who seems hell-bent on seducing her. And she feels something she hasn't felt in five long years of widowhood—a spark of attraction. Thinking she'll never see him again, she succumbs to temptation, only to discover that little "spark" is more like a raging wildfire.

One weekend is all he asks. One weekend to prove there's more between them than just blazing hot sex...

Warning: Sometimes, love happens in an instant, but it takes a lot of sexin' up to make one stubborn woman a believer.

Available now in ebook and print from Samhain Publishing.

Enjoy the following excerpt from Lone Heart...

She dug into her pocket for her truck keys and didn't look back to see if the cowboy followed. She knew her place. It was back at the Lucky K. Not mooning over a younger man.

"Why are you in such a hurry? Did I scare you off?"

Her head whipped up, her gaze landing on the young cowboy.

He stood beside her truck, his gaze shadowed beneath his hat. "I'd like to buy you a drink. Get to know you."

"I can't stay," she blurted. "I've got someplace to be."

He nodded, then sighed. "Do I make you nervous?"

She forced a laugh—and told a lie. "No. But I'm late."

"Yeah. I can see that. Can I buy you a drink some other time?"

Why was he so insistent? "Look, it was just a dance. And it was nice."

"Nice? Huh." His lips twisted, then settled into a slight smile. "I made you nervous. Made you want something more than you were prepared to give. I apologize."

"I'm not nervous. I'm not anything other than late."

He stepped closer, and her heartbeat thudded. The parking lot was dark—not that she was frightened of him—but the closer he came, the more her body responded. She held up her hands. "What are you doing?"

"I think I'm gonna kiss you." His gaze dropped to her mouth.

"Why?"

His shrug was casual, but the set of his chin wasn't. "Why not? You want it. So do I."

"I don't want anything."

"Sure about that?"

"Yes, I am."

"Then why'd you just lick your lips?"

"Wha—" Good lord, she had.

"Just a kiss," he said, close enough now she had to lift her chin to meet his gaze.

Damn, she'd forgotten how to breathe. "If I give you that kiss, will you let me go?"

"Negotiating with me now?" He tipped back his hat and a grin stretched slowly across his mouth. "What if you don't want me to let you go when I'm done?"

Charli shook her head, a smile beginning to tug at the corners of her lips. She realized with a start she was flirting—something she hadn't done in years. "Are you always this stubborn when a girl turns you down?" she asked, letting a teasing note seep into her breathless whisper.

"Have you? Turned me down, that is?" His hands rose and gripped the corners of her hips. He pressed her back against the cooling metal of her truck. When his head lowered, his hat blocked the light from the moon and distant lamppost, shuttering them in darkness.

His mouth was firm and soft, sweet and spicy. His tongue prodded the seam where her lips pressed together. She wanted to remain strong, but the thought of this handsome younger man and all that firm muscle pressed up against her made her yearn for things she had no business wanting.

She opened, moaning as his tongue swept inside her mouth. *I can do this. Keep it light. Dammit, Charli, keep it light.*

Her hand slid across the top of his shoulder; her fingers snuck beneath his hat to pull his hair. And just that quickly, the sweet, sexy tenor of the kiss changed.

Lonny groaned into her mouth.

Her thighs opened, and he slid his between them, resuming the grinding pressure that had broken through her walls while they'd danced.

When his hand palmed her breast, she laughed against his mouth. She was as horny as a teenager, uncaring who saw them standing like this.

I should stop him now. I should. Oh God, I should...

His hand slid down her belly and slipped open her belt, unbuttoning her jeans, and then his fingers were gliding down the front of her panties. They cupped her mound.

Shocked, she grabbed his wrist to stop him and drew her head back. "That's...far enough."

He held still, his hand warming her sex. "Sorry, I pushed." But he didn't withdraw, just stood there, his breaths coming fast.

"Your hand..."

"Likes where it is."

A snort of laughter broke the tension inside her. "Seems we're at an impasse, cowboy."

"Let me pleasure you."

Her breath caught at the slight movement of one of his fingers as it delved into the top of her folds. Without consciously agreeing, she widened her thighs again, making room for him.

Her head fell back against warm metal. "Don't think I'll let you do more."

"I'm not asking for anything in return. Just relax."

With the stars blanketing the sky behind him, she relented, closing her mind to all her worries, to her embarrassment. His finger teased moisture from her folds and swirled atop her clit. The contrast between his calloused pad and soft, measured motions drew a sigh.

"You're prettier than you know," he whispered, leaning a shoulder against the truck to block the view of what he was doing should anyone exit the bar.

She had a hard time forming words to deny his claim. At this moment, she did indeed feel pretty, wholly feminine, as he plied her hardening knot with ever-firming caresses. "I'm older than you."

"I noticed."

"Not nice."

"I don't mind."

"Because you don't have to worry about me thinking there's more to this?"

He nipped her nose and then her bottom lip. "I like a smart woman, one with experience. I'm not always the smartest guy."

"You want some woman to take care of you?"

"Same as I'd take care of her. Aren't I takin' care of you now?"

She smiled, but his finger pressed hard. Her lips puckered around a sharper breath.

"That too much?"

She shook her head. "More," she whispered.

It's all about the story...

Romance

HORROR

www.samhainpublishing.com

CPSIA information can be obtained at www.ICGtesting.com
Printed in the USA
LVOW13s2227140114

369483LV00005B/346/P